INFERNAL
MAGIC

DEMONS OF FIRE AND NIGHT

BOOK 1

BY C. N. CRAWFORD

INFERNAL MAGIC

DEMONS OF FIRE AND NIGHT BOOK 1

Copyright © 2016 C. N. Crawford

ISBN-13: 978-1535014311
ISBN-10: 1535014318

Edited by Tammi Labrecque
Cover art by Rebecca Frank
Interior design by C.N. Crawford

www.cncrawford.com

Contact the Authors:
cn@cncrawford.com

Twitter: @CN_Crawford
Facebook: cncrawfordauthor

First Edition

Printed in the U.S.A

Also by

C. N. CRAWFORD

The Vampire's Mage Series
Book 1: *Magic Hunter*
Book 1.1: *Shadow Mage*
Book 2*: Witch Hunter*
(August 2016)

Demons of Fire and Night
Book 1: *Infernal Magic*
Book 2: *Nocturnal Magic*
(Fall 2016)

The Memento Mori Trilogy
Book 1: *The Witching Elm*
Book 2: *A Witch's Feast*
Book 2.1: *The Abysmal Sea*
Book 3: *Witches of the Deep*
(June 2016)

For Leslie and Geoff

Chapter 1

*I*f Ursula had been able to plan her eighteenth birthday, the evening would be going very differently. First, she wouldn't be working in a nightclub owned by her ex. Second, she wouldn't have this weird fever burning her cheeks, setting her nerves on edge—like she was blazing from the inside out. And third, she definitely wouldn't be pushing through an unruly crowd to break up a fight between two hammered university students.

In an ideal world, she'd have called in sick and taken the whole night off. Of course, in an ideal world, she wouldn't be worrying about the rent that was due in two days.

"Excuse me!" She said, squeezing between a gawking couple, arms raised. *That shows authority, right?*

Two young men squared off on the dance floor, bathed in District 5's pulsing orange and pink lights. A pounding bass rumbled through the room.

Part of her wanted to let these two knobs stab each other with broken bottles, but she had a mission tonight, fever or not. She was going to prove to the world that she had her life together, that she was a valuable asset to the club—or at least, she was going to prove it to her ex. Granted, Rufus was an idiot, but he was her boss and she was hanging on to this job by a thread.

A small crowd gathered around the potential brawlers, and she tried to suss out the bigger threat—possibly the red-faced giant who swayed in place. His platinum hair, bushy eyebrows, and full lips gave him the appearance of a Muppet—a murderous one who might crush someone with his giant, meaty hands.

"I told you to watch where you step. You scuffed my shoe!" The Muppet screamed, a vein popping in his forehead. "Arsehole!"

His opponent, a stocky guy with a bushy beard, jabbed a stubby finger. His voice boomed over the music. "Oh, is that what I am, you fat-faced donkey?"

Oh, good. A totally rational argument over a scuffed shoe. Sweat beaded on Ursula's skin, and she wiped the back of her hand over her forehead. God, it was hot in here. She couldn't be the only one who felt like the room was on fire. Maybe that was what was making these guys act like lunatics.

The two drunks circled each other, and Ursula squeezed between them, ignoring the heat burning through her. "Everyone take a step back," she said, trying to project as much authority as possible.

Muppet was definitely the real threat here. He sloshed the remnants of his beer from his pint glass, baring his teeth. "You know your girlfriend still wants me," he growled at Stubby.

Of course. It didn't matter if the argument was about shoes or football, every bar brawl came down to one thing: a fight over some girl. Whatever the case, no one was civilized after five pints of Bombardier.

Stubby grinned. "She said you only lasted for two—"

"Okay!" Ursula cut in, holding up her hands. "Seems like you've both—"

The tall one lunged past her, trying to smash his pint glass over Stubby's head. With a reflex so fast it shocked even her, Ursula's hand shot out, gripping the man's wrist. Warm beer splashed all over her white shirt. *Bollocks. Now I'm getting really annoyed.*

And, incidentally, so was the giant Muppet. He clawed at the shorter man. "I'll rip your hairy face off and shove it up your arse."

Ursula needed to get control—now. And despite her petite size, she had one thing on her side: a surprising amount of physical strength.

Still gripping Muppet's wrist, she twisted his arm behind his back, wrenching it up high and forcing him over.

"Get off me!" He shrieked. "Stupid bitch!"

Not the B-word. It was one of those insults that really burned her up, and she was already way too hot. In fact, her body felt like some kind of inferno, and she could think of nothing but white hot flames.

"She's burning me!" Muppet shrieked.

Her attention jolted to his shirt—which, incidentally, was on fire.

What the hell?

Panicking, she released him. The man threw himself to the ground, frantically rolling to put out the flames. Within moments, a girl doused him with a pitcher of water, and the air filled with the scent of burnt cotton.

Ursula stumbled back, staring at her hands. Was it just her mind, or were grey tendrils of smoke curling from her fingertips? *This fever must be rattling my brain.* She really needed to go home and lie on the sofa.

She clenched her fists, trying to ignore the rising panic. She stood in the middle of Rufus's club, her shirt soaked in beer, having lit a customer on fire. Her plans to prove her worth to her boss had backfired just a bit.

Muppet rose, his hands shaking, and pulled out his mobile phone. "I'm calling the police."

Her pulse raced. *Time for damage control, Ursula.* "I'm very sorry about the fire. It was a complete accident."

Just as Muppet put the cell phone to his ear, another man stepped forward—someone she hadn't even noticed before, though she had no idea how she'd missed him.

At the sight of him, a shiver crawled up her spine. If she'd thought Muppet looked aggressive, this guy screamed pure malice. It wasn't his appearance: rich chestnut hair, sharp cheekbones, and perfect lips that could charm the knickers off a nun. No, it was the feral way he moved, and his piercing green eyes that bored right into her soul when he slid a glance her way.

His gaze flicked to Muppet. "I don't really think that's necessary." He spoke in a commanding voice, his accent posh as hell. "Give me your phone, and take your friend to another bar."

Wordlessly, the Muppet handed over his phone, and the green-eyed stranger pocketed it. Muppet and Stubby grasped each other's arms, staggering toward the exit.

A small crowd still stood, gaping at the stranger as he closed his eyes, muttering. As he spoke, goose bumps rose on Ursula's flesh, and the hair on the back of her neck stood on end. *What the hell is he doing?*

Whatever it was, the crowd seemed to lose interest, and when he opened his eyes again, the onlookers had drifted back to their tables.

Ursula stared at him, stunned. In the past few months, there had been rumors about witches in London, but... *No, that's insane.*

Whatever this stranger's secret was, his stunning physique now drew her eyes. A bespoke suit accentuated an athletic body, and a gold watch flashed on his wrist. *Definitely rich.* The way he had spoken wasn't just confident; he was entitled, too. Probably a total knob.

Still, he'd helped her out, so it wasn't like she was going to complain.

He turned to her, green eyes lingering on her drenched T-shirt. "You work here?"

"Yes." Despite her fever, she shivered again. There really was something *lethal* in those eyes.

"I'll have two fingers of the Glenlivet 21. Neat. A glass of water on the side."

Irritation simmered. Apparently, no one had ever taught him to say please. But it was more than just annoyance that unnerved her. There was something *strange* about him. *Am I losing my mind, or do his movements seem… otherwordly?*

She was losing her mind. That was the only explanation. She had a fever, and she was rattled by… whatever the hell had just happened.

She cocked her hip. "Well, since you just bailed me out, I guess I won't insist that you say please."

He stared at her, his lips a thin line.

Heading back to the bar, she cringed. She shouldn't have said that, but something about him really irked her—probably the rich-boy attitude that reminded her of Rufus.

This club was just one of the ways her ex invested his father's money. He was studying business at University College London, planning to build himself some kind of financial empire—a testament to his genius, of course. Frankly, she was getting a little sick of rich people thinking they were better than everyone else just because they'd been born lucky.

Ursula slipped behind the bar, reaching up for the Glenlivet. When she turned to pour the drink, he'd taken a seat.

She filled the tumbler with two fingers of Scotch and slid it over, glancing at the fifty-pound note he'd left on the bar. She didn't often see fifty-pound notes, but this guy probably had plenty. In fact, she could imagine him lighting them on fire in front of a homeless person for a laugh.

Then again, maybe she wasn't in any position to accuse others of pyromania. The bar smelled of burnt Muppet, and her stomach was still turning flips from the whole debacle. *What in God's name happened? Hell of a birthday.*

"What's your name?" the stranger asked, his deep voice resonating.

His intent gaze made her pulse race, but she needed to get a grip and focus on trying to salvage her job. "Ursula."

He unnerved her, and she could feel her chest flushing.

She turned, catching a brief glance of herself in the mirror with a shiver of distaste. Even on a shoestring budget, Ursula normally prided herself on her sense of style. Tonight, she'd chosen a white shirt with tight maroon trousers that could *almost* pass for leather. She'd accessorized with her favorite boots and a chunky black bracelet. But the look wasn't working out so well right now. Her ginger hair was a mess, and her soaked shirt clung to her body, showing off the pink bra underneath. Only her black eyeliner remained in place.

With any luck, she'd get the chance to clean herself up before Rufus saw her again. Otherwise, it would only confirm every terrible thing he'd said about her when he'd dumped her.

From behind, the stranger said, "Miss?"

She spun around. "Yes?"

"Pour yourself a drink, on me. It is, after all, your first night at the legal drinking age."

Her blood went cold. *How the hell does he know that?*

Just as she was stammering out a response, she caught sight of Rufus striding up behind him, a stormy look on his face. Her ex leaned on the bar, immaculate in a pressed white shirt.

"Ursula," he said. "We need to talk about what just happened."

Chapter 2

"*I*n my office. Now." Rufus inclined his head toward an open door behind the bar, his face pink with rage.

Flinching at his demanding tone, Ursula followed him through the door. She shoved her hand into her pocket, gripping her good luck charm—a smooth, white stone. Right now, it was doing fuck-all in the luck department, but touching it had become a nervous habit.

She plopped down in a chair. It wasn't much of an office. Since it was a former storage closet, there was only room for the bare essentials: a dingy desk and two chairs. Rufus took a seat behind the desk.

The room was oppressive—either the lack of windows or the wanker behind the desk. *Probably both.*

Rufus pushed his blond hair back, appraising her with cool, blue eyes. Maybe his Nordic good looks had somehow fooled her into overlooking his serious personality problem.

"What the hell happened out there?" he snapped. "We could get sued. *I* could get sued."

"There was a fight, and I was just trying to calm them down. That's all."

"By lighting a man on fire?"

The fever blazed behind her temples. She *really* should have stayed at home tonight. "I don't know how..." She trailed off. She had no clue what had happened. "One second, I was trying to stop him from hitting some guy, and the next thing I knew, his shirt was on fire."

"Was he smoking a cigarette?" Rufus narrowed his eyes. "Were *you* smoking?"

"Neither of us were smoking, as far as I know. I just looked down at my hand, and it looked—hot." No idea why she'd said that last part. She realized it made her sound insane, and quickly corrected herself. "He probably *was* smoking, now that you mention it."

"Did you say your hand was *hot*?" He winced. "You do realize what you could be accused of?"

Witchcraft. He was talking about witchcraft.

It would have sounded completely crazy a few months ago, but the world had changed, ever since a group of mysterious men had been caught on American TV slaughtering people in a Boston park, before disappearing into thin air in a whirl of demonic activity. Now half of London was talking about witches and magic. For her part, Ursula had no idea how they'd disappeared, but she liked to believe *magic* wasn't the culprit. There was enough shit to worry about without adding in a supernatural threat.

She loosed a sigh. "Look, all I said was my hand was hot. I have a fever. You know, I think I should go home."

Rufus leaned back in his chair. "It's not as crazy as you might think. Madeleine knows all about witches. She's been doing a lot of research since the attacks. She works with a professor at UCL."

"I'm not a witch, for God's sake. I don't even believe in them. And who is Madeleine?" His new girlfriend, no doubt. Poor lamb had no idea what she was in for.

"Never mind that." He gave her his puppy-dog eyes. "Oh, Urse. Why is it so hard for you to get things right? Why do you always feel the need to mess everything up?"

Somehow when he was trying to be nice it was worse than when he was just an arsehole. "That's what you think of me? That I can never get anything right?"

For a moment, he pressed his lips into a thin line. "You always look so lovely, and that's an asset in my club, though tonight you haven't even managed that. You've achieved remarkably little with your life. You never managed to get into uni. You nearly got evicted last month. Again."

She gritted her teeth. "We talked about this when you dumped me, and I told you, those are both the kinds of things that happen when you've got no money."

He leaned over his desk. "It's just that you've got no plan for success. No goals. I've been building an empire, investing money—"

"Your *father's* money." *Shit.* She shouldn't have said that out loud. It would hit a nerve, and that wasn't good for her employment prospects.

"Whatever," he snapped, cheeks reddening again. "I'm building *something*. Just because you were famous once, you think you've made it." He stood, throwing his shoulders back. "Honestly, you're just a sad cow who won't make anything of your life."

It took all of Ursula's willpower not to slap his smug face. Rufus had brought up that tidbit up all the time when they were dating, as if her former celebrity status was some kind of personal affront to him.

"I never asked for my fifteen minutes of fame. The press showed up as soon as they found me. And besides, after that fourteen-year-old gave birth to sextuplets, I was pretty much forgotten." She was desperate to tell him to sod off and head home, but she needed this bloody job.

A knock on the door interrupted their conversation.

"Rufus, honey? Are you in there?" A neatly-coiffed blonde poked her head in, smiling for only an instant until her eyes landed on Ursula. "What are you two up to?"

Rufus blinked. "I... I didn't know you were coming by now, Madeleine."

"The lecturer let us out early." She eyed Ursula warily, running a hand over a pink silk blouse. A week's wages right there—and Ursula couldn't even imagine how much her fat diamond earrings cost.

Rufus cleared his throat. "Madeleine is my girlfriend, Ursula. She's studying mythological history and cryptozoology. She's very accomplished."

"That sounds really *interesting*," said Ursula, trying—and failing—to mask her irritation. "Looks like it's time for me to go."

Madeleine's eyes lingered over Ursula's soaked shirt. "Did something happen?"

"Beer accident," said Ursula. It was all the explanation she needed.

Madeleine's hand flew to her throat. "Oh. Well, I stopped by so you could escort me home, honey. You don't know what sort of creatures are lurking on London's streets these days. Professor Stoughton said the city's been *filled* with magical activity in the past few months. Witches, demons, all sorts of horrible things. He has a meter to measure it." Madeleine blocked the exit, her voice laced with jealousy. "What *were* you two talking about, anyway?"

"I was discussing Ursula's future here," said Rufus.

"Oh?" Madeleine plastered on a saccharine smile. "There's a future?"

"Well, that's just it," said Rufus. "I simply can't keep someone employed who lights people on fire. It's a liability."

Ursula could feel herself heating up again, and the fever that had been quietly throbbing behind her temples turned into a dull roar. She held onto the door frame for support.

"Well, chin up. I'm sure you'll be able to find another job," said Madeleine, barely containing her glee. "It'll be exciting. A new adventure." She didn't move from the doorframe, obviously savoring the moment.

Ursula felt her temper flare, and she gripped the wood by Madeleine's side. "Are you going to let me leave? Or do you plan to keep blocking the door all night?"

Madeleine gasped, jumping back. She gaped in horror at Ursula's hand—and the smoke that curled from beneath Ursula's fingers.

"Oh my God! What did you do to the door?" Her eyes froze on Ursula's face, and she whispered one word: *"Witch."*

Chapter 3

$\mathcal{U}$rsula skulked along Bow Road, her hands jammed in the pockets of her leopard-print coat, fingers curled up for warmth. With the beer-drenched shirt plastered to her skin, the winter air was brutally cold. At least her feet were warm in her boots, though she'd probably have to sell them soon for cash. She had only one more paycheck coming in, and it wouldn't cover the rent that was due in two days.

Disappointment crushed her. If she didn't figure something out, she'd be homeless soon, sleeping on the streets through the freezing winter. How long, exactly, did it take for a landlord to evict someone? And how long would it take for another homeless person to rob her of her leopard-print coat?

A biting wind nipped at her ears. She could have used a bit more of that fever now. Skint and unemployed, she'd chosen to walk from Brick Lane back to Bow—nearly two miles. She wasn't spending the last her money on a bus. And, more importantly, it had given her time to think. Well, time to stew, really. Her chest ached with a familiar hollow feeling.

She could have done without meeting Madeleine, with her beautifully coiffed blond hair, French-manicured nails, and all the letters she'd have after her name when she graduated.

Ursula shivered. *My eighteenth birthday.* This should have been a night for a celebration, but apart from her flatmate she hardly had any friends left. After her breakup with Rufus, he seemed to have taken her whole clique with him—probably because he could lavish them with champagne and pick up the tabs at fancy restaurants.

Or maybe it was just like Rufus had always said: she wasn't very good with people.

She pulled her coat tighter as she passed the warm lights of a pub, wishing she'd had the foresight to wear a scarf. Break-up aside, she'd been expecting something a little more momentous for her eighteenth birthday. This was the night something big was supposed to happen—she just had no idea what.

Apart from her birthday, there weren't many things Ursula knew about herself. Her background was so outlandish, it was like something out of a soap opera: a rare case of amnesia that had rendered her childhood a complete blank slate. There was simply nothing in her memory before the age of fifteen.

What she knew for certain was that a few years ago she'd turned up in a burnt-out church, with a strange, triangular scar on her shoulder and a piece of paper in her pocket. The paper had read:

On your 18th birthday,
March 15, 2016,
ask for a trial.
- Ursula (You)

She'd started to think of herself as two people: Former Ursula and New Ursula. Former Ursula was a complete mystery, and her one link to Former Ursula was the white stone in her pocket, its surface now worn smooth from constant rubbing. It was a strange little anchor to her old life.

Occasionally, glimpses of a bygone life appeared in her dreams: fields of wild thyme and orchids, skylarks and adders. She had no idea what it meant, except that she'd probably grown up in the countryside.

Here she was, waiting for her life to change by some sort of magic on her eighteenth birthday, but that was obviously a sad joke. At what point in this disaster of a day was she supposed to have asked for a trial? On the crowded bus she took to work, burning with a fever? Midway through losing her job? Or while meeting Rufus's new girlfriend? The whole day had been a series of ordeals, one trial after another, but none of them particularly momentous.

It didn't matter. She'd been gradually losing faith in the idea that her fortunes would magically turn around, that someone or something would waltz into her miserable life bearing a gift of a diamond or a secret bank account.

And now, she had to figure out how to save herself from complete destitution.

She shivered, hugging herself tighter. A normal life would be nice: a family and a steady income. Maybe some childhood memories, and hands that didn't spontaneously ignite.

She stalked past a row of crooked Victorian homes, warmly lit from within. She didn't even want to think about what had happened with her hands. Madeleine had called her a *witch,* for crying out loud. Maybe there *was* a trial in her future.

Her door came into view—the one she could always pick out from the rows of identical houses, by the chipped red paint on the doorframe. She jammed her key into the lock. *Thank God I'm home.*

She stepped inside, hoping to hear a welcoming *Hello* from her flatmate Katie, but the flat was as dark and quiet as a grave. She flicked the switch by the door, but the lights didn't turn on. *Shit.* The electric key must have run out. It would remain dark and cold until she got to the shop tomorrow. She shook her head. Maybe the point of the note was that her whole life was a trial.

Sighing with frustration, she steadied her hand along the wall as she crept down the carpeted stairs.

It wasn't a stunning place—a one-bedroom basement flat—but it was home nonetheless. Katie had the bedroom, since she paid more in rent, and Ursula slept in the living room, tidying up an air mattress every morning. With Katie's help, she'd brightened up the woodchip wallpaper with canary-yellow paint and some posters of wildflowers—forget-me-nots and golden aster—that reminded her of her most soothing dreams.

Ursula pulled out her phone, flicking open a text from Katie.

Happy Birthday Ursula! I'm coming home soon. Let's go out.

A pit opened in her stomach. She was going to have to tell Katie about her little rent problem. She dropped her phone on the sofa, then peeled off her leopard-print coat and the beer-soaked shirt and bra, still shivering, before yanking a black shirt and bra off the drying rack. *Might as well have an outfit to match my mood.*

She slipped into her dry clothes, then crossed to the kitchen, a cupboard-sized space with a tiny vinyl countertop. As she flipped open the blinds, she let a little light in from the streetlamp outside. Crouching before a kitchen drawer, she rifled around for a box of matches.

After lighting two tea candles by the stove, she felt her stomach rumble. When was the last time she'd eaten?

Yanking open the fridge door, she grabbed the last smear of butter. *Bread and butter for dinner.*

Just as she reached for the loaf of bread, the hair on her neck prickled. Someone was watching her. She could always tell when she was being observed. And right now, someone was most definitely lurking in the shadows of her tiny flat.

Slowly, she turned, and her heart nearly leapt from her chest. Moving silently through the living room was a broad-shouldered man, his face hidden in the gloom. Probably her flatmate's latest conquest, but better safe than sorry. She slid open the knife drawer.

Carefully, so as not to alarm the stranger, she gripped a knife's hilt, her hand hidden in the drawer.

The man prowled closer, his movements smooth and almost inhuman.

Ice licked up her spine. Just outside the doorframe, the stranger paused in the shadows.

She swallowed. "Who's there?"

His green eyes seemed to glow in the dark, and the word *witch* flitted through her mind.

"My name is Kester." His deep voice slid through her bones.

When he stepped into the flickering candlelight, she gasped in recognition. Rich chestnut hair, sharp cheekbones, and perfect lips. The hot bloke from the club. *What the hell is he doing here?*

Cold fear tightened her chest. Ursula tightened her fingers around the knife's hilt. "You followed me." A tendril of horror curled around her heart. "Did you just watch me take off my shirt?"

"I averted my eyes. I'm not here to disturb you. I'm just here for your signature." He raised his arms over his head, holding on to the door frame. Candlelight flickered over his golden skin, dancing in his green eyes. Despite his beauty, there was something predatory in the way he stared at her, like he was about to devour her.

"Signature? What are you on about?" Any fast movements, and she'd fling the knife at him. "If you don't leave now, I'll call the police." She couldn't call the police, since she'd just chucked her phone across the room, but he didn't need to know that.

His gaze slid over her, as if he were memorizing her. "I won't linger any longer than you want. I just need you to sign the contract. You must have been expecting me."

"What contract?" Slowly, she lifted the knife in front of her. Only instead of looking at the tip of a blade, she was staring at the soft silicone paddle of a spatula. *Bloody hell.*

He smiled, and white teeth gleamed in the candlelight. "If you want to make me pancakes first, I won't object."

"I don't have the ingredients," she said lamely.

Where are the kitchen knives? They must be dirty. If she could inch over to the sink, she could get a proper blade, one with an edge that could slash his throat.

"Look, I can see you're having a bad night. And I'd truly love to help you." Dropping his arms from the doorframe, he widened his eyes, all sincerity. "But you committed yourself years ago, and it's your eighteenth birthday. All you need to do is sign the contract, and I'll be on my way."

There it was again. How did he know it was her birthday? She didn't know him. Hell, she didn't know anyone remotely like him. There was a strange edge to his plummy voice, one that reeked of old money and private clubs with three-hundred-year-old mahogany bars. Not exactly Ursula's sort of crowd.

She eyed the stove to her right. A dirty cast-iron pan rested on the nearest burner. Perfect for frying sausages, or for smashing skulls, depending on the occasion.

"Ursula. You don't need to be scared," he soothed, his emerald eyes drinking her in. "I'm not here to hurt you."

If he weren't such an obvious nutter, the guy would be seriously seductive. She laid the spatula down on the countertop with feigned casualness. "Look, I've had an awful day. I'm tired, and I want to finish my bread and go out for one little drink with my flatmate, who will be here any minute." She paused. "And she's huge, by the way, and lethal. I'm sure you've got somewhere better to be. I'm advising you to leave me alone. I can be a little... unpredictable when I'm irritated, and I wouldn't want you getting hurt."

He cocked an eyebrow. "Unpredictable? Sounds exciting. But I'm afraid I cannot leave until I get your signature. For Emerazel. Then I'll leave. Unless you want me to stay to attend to your other needs, of course."

"I have no idea who *Emerazel* is. But if you're here because you think I owe you something for helping me out at the club, that's not going to happen. I don't have anything. I can't afford electricity. I can't afford *socks*. My boyfriend just dumped me last week, and then fired me. So on top of all the other shit, I'm unemployed. I'm eating sodding bread and butter for dinner on my eighteenth birthday. So if you're planning on robbing me, have a wonderful time. Take the spatula. Take my threadbare socks. Take the moldy shower curtain. Whatever you desire." She could feel her cheeks burning as anger flooded her. "Then fuck right off."

"I'm not here about the club, and I'm not here to rob you."

"So what are you? Some sort of pervert?" Her body grew hot, her pulse quickening. Pure strength surged through her muscles, and she wanted to break something. If he thought he was going to get his hands on her, she would choke the life out of him.

He opened his palms, eyes widening, all innocence. "Ursula, you're not listening. I'm not here to hurt you. I'm here about that triangular mark you carved somewhere on yourself, the one that gives you the fire. You *do* understand the bargain you made, don't you?"

My scar. So he did see me without my shirt on. There was no air left in the room. "You said you looked away."

"I did. Emerazel sent me, and that's how I know you have a scar. You owe her your signature. It's fine. There's nothing to panic about," he murmured, stepping closer, his voice a dangerous caress. "Everything will be fine, Ursula."

She shook her head. Who was this Emerazel he kept talking about? She had no idea where the scar had come from, or what it meant. All she knew was that only stalkers and serial killers followed women home from work.

Her heart raced faster, adrenaline surging. For some reason she wanted to believe him, but he'd trapped her in her own kitchen. If there was one thing she hated, it was being trapped. She balled her hands into fists, overcome by the need to fight.

She pulled back her arm for a punch, but with a lightning-fast motion, he clamped his hand on her wrist, fingers piercing her flesh. *Not fingers,* she realized with growing terror. *Claws. He has claws. What the fuck?*

Her blood roared in her ears, and she could feel fire run through her, hot and molten. With her free arm, she grasped his shoulder. Her palm glowed. Somehow, her body knew what it was doing—knew how to burn him—and she waited to hear him cry out in pain.

Instead, he stared deep into her eyes. No longer a bright green, his irises now blazed a deep, smoldering red. Terror ripped her mind apart. *What the hell is going on?*

His gaze trailed over her body. "Ursula, my dear. There's no need for fighting. Emerazel's power won't burn me," he purred in a velvety tone. But underneath the softness, there was an edge to his voice—a sharp command. Kester was used to getting what he wanted. "The goddess's fire runs in my veins just as it does in yours. You can't fight me."

His voice was husky, a lethal lullaby. His beautiful gaze hypnotized her, rooting her in place.

A part of her felt tempted to do whatever he wanted just to make him happy. "What do you need me to do?" She rasped, half hating herself as she said it. What was happening to her?

"I'm not here to hurt you." He leaned in closer and whispered, his breath caressing her ear. "Sign," he commanded.

He seemed so sure of himself. Her hand relaxed on his shoulder, and she stared into his fiery eyes. She should be terrified of those preternatural flames, but something about his masculine scent and his beautiful lips was intoxicating. *But the strange fire in his eyes... Is that magic? Do I care?*

His claws retracting, Kester reached into the pocket of his trousers and pulled out a fountain pen the color of bone. Her gaze landed on a tiny symbol carved into the pen—an encircled triangle, just like her scar.

Holding her gaze, Kester popped off the cap, revealing a razor-sharp nib, and gripped her palm. "This will only hurt for a moment," he said, his voice seducing her, sliding over her skin.

As she stared into his beautiful eyes, he pressed the pen into her hand. A sharp pain pulled her attention down, and she watched as the point depressed her skin. Something in the back of her mind rebelled at this imposition. He pushed the nib further, into her flesh, and she snapped out of the spell he'd woven. *What was I thinking, mooning over this posh twat?*

"Ow!" She yanked her arm backward, gripping the cut. Blood dripped between her fingers.

"Apologies for that, Ursula." A seductive smile played over his lips, but she wasn't falling for his act anymore.

He produced a small, yellowed piece of parchment from his other pocket, pushing it toward her along with the blood-inked pen. "Please. I need you to sign."

Her hand throbbed, and she shook it, trying to focus her thoughts. Everything about this man was alluring, but right now only one angry thought burned in her mind: *This entitled wanker thinks he can get whatever he wants. Just like Rufus.*

She blinked, trying to clear her mind. Of *course* she shouldn't trust the psycho who'd stalked her into her kitchen. And did he want her soul? She wasn't signing that away. She had no idea what a soul was for, or even if it was real, but she didn't want to find out what happened when you gave one away.

She glanced down at the parchment, at the faded beige writing. Only a few words were legible in the candlelight, and though the language wasn't English, the looping letters looked strangely familiar. She almost had the sense that if she concentrated hard enough, she could read it. In fact, she could translate a few of the words: *soul, contract, eternal.* The longer she looked at it, the clearer the words became.

"What's this language?"

"Angelic."

"What?" She glared up at the towering stranger. "What happens if I sign it?"

"You've really never been told this?" He seemed genuinely curious. "How did you come to carve yourself in the first place if you don't know who Emerazel is?"

"I have no idea." She nodded at the parchment. "It says something about an eternal contract."

His brow shot up. "You can *read* this?"

"Yes. Don't ask me how. Is this some sort of pact with the devil?"

He exhaled slowly, pinching the bridge of his nose as though marshaling an extreme amount of patience. "No. There is no devil." He gazed up again, a charming smile playing about his lips. "I understand this must be confusing for you. I will leave you as soon as you do what I ask."

She crossed her arms. "Look, I have a little memory problem. I don't know anything about the first fifteen years of my life. You may have heard of me; it was all over the news after I turned up in a burning church in London. The tabloids called me the Mystery Girl." Wherever the scar had come from, that was a secret only Former Ursula could unravel. Not the clueless, unemployed girl trying to eat bread and butter for dinner.

"Mystery Girl? Never heard of you." He studied her carefully, the candlelight flickering over his smooth, golden skin. "I can tell you this. Emerazel is not the devil. Some mortals call her that, but she is a goddess. Her domain is the volcanic magma in the center of the earth and, when angered, she destroys cities. She is neither good nor evil. She is love, power, rage, and light. You cannot fight her. You cannot win this." All signs of softness left his face, and his gaze grew fierce, almost feral. "Do not fight her, and do not fight me. You will not win."

The hair rose on the back of her neck. "Right. According to the crazy bloke who followed me home and broke into my house, I owe my soul to an all-powerful goddess of rage and power." She clamped her hands on her hips, trying to ignore the chill running up her spine. "I'm not signing your stupid paper."

"That's really a shame." Kester tilted his head, almost apologetic. "Then I must reap your soul for Emerazel now."

Ursula forced a smile onto her face. "Whatever that means, it's not happening either." She grabbed the tea candles from the counter, flicking the hot wax in his face.

Kester hardly flinched.

Her panic rising, she grabbed the cast-iron skillet and swung for his head. He reached up to block it, and it slammed against his arm with a crunch. He emitted a low, inhuman growl that rumbled through her gut. As he glared at her, eyes blazing bright green, his forearm swung down at an awkward angle, a mangled mess that should have had him screaming in agony.

She steadied her breath. "I'm not signing your devil's pact tonight. I don't care if you work for Satan, or Emerazel, or if you've escaped from a psychiatric hospital. I'm not giving up my soul. Whoever you are, you need to leave now before I shatter your skull."

Kester's eyes slid to his arm, and he whispered softly—words at once strange and familiar. A chill licked up Ursula's spine.

She stared as Kester's arm straightened with a cracking sound. With the arm fully repaired, he raised his hand again, wiggling his fingers.

Her heart skipped a beat, and the word *demon* rang in her head again.

"That really hurt." His eyes, now the color of blood, met hers.

Her mind screamed, *Not human!*

He unleashed a low growl that trembled over her skin, and she became keenly aware of each of her breaths.

He lunged for her. Instantly, she brought her knee up and into his chest, redirecting his momentum into the cabinets next to the kitchen counter. Wood splintered with the impact.

He started to stand, but she kicked him in the head. Her boot shattered his nose, spraying blood on the kitchen tile. He fell back holding his face.

"Ursula," he purred, slowly getting to his feet. His eyes wild, he unleashed a wicked set of claws from his fingertips, and Ursula's mind screamed with panic. He pressed the end of the pen, and a thin blade protruded from one end. "You should have signed."

He moved so fast she didn't have time to react before he'd pinned her against the wall, gripping her wrists in one hand. The tips of his claws tore her skin, and a low growl escaped his throat, rumbling through her core.

His teeth—his fangs—lengthened, and he pressed in closer, leaving no room for her to kick him. Cold fear stole her breath as she struggled to free her wrists, but this freak was terrifyingly strong. *What is he?*

He leaned in closer, his breath warming her skin. His eyes roamed down her body, and candlelight flickered off his pen's sharp blade. "It's a shame you're going to make me do this. There's something about you I like."

She tried to yank her wrists free. "You don't have to do anything. You can just leave me alone." She could hardly breathe. This was it—the last few moments of her life. *What do I say about a sad life like mine?* She was nothing—a complete loser. No family, no job, no money, no future. Her whole life was just a name, a date, and a piece of paper...

A trial.

Ursula, you idiot.

"I request a trial," she breathed into his neck.

Surprise flickered across his beautiful features, and his fangs retracted. "What did you say?"

"A trial," she said more firmly.

Still pinning her to the wall, he clenched his jaw. "You've *got* to be kidding me." His eyes returned to their emerald green color, and he began muttering in that strange language again. His words transfixed her, soothing her racing heart. A strange sense of calm flooded her body, until her world began to dim.

Chapter 4

$\mathcal{A}$ humming noise woke Ursula, and she cracked open her eyes. The sound grew louder as she pulled herself out of the dense fog of sleep. Her head throbbed, dulling her senses, but there was movement around her—flashes of blue and white in the darkness. For a moment, she wondered if this was the road to the afterlife, but the shooting pain behind her eyes suggested she hadn't yet shuffled off this mortal coil.

When her pupils focused, she saw Kester sitting next to her, his face now clear of blood and his nose unbroken. His hands gripped a steering wheel. *Shit shit shit.*

The only possible explanation for his rapid healing was that... she hesitated to even think it. Could it be that the words he'd whispered had repaired his arm, fixed his broken nose? Could it have been magic?

If that were the case—if he could cast spells—she didn't even want to think about what else he could do. She clamped her eyes shut again, trying to regain control. *No. Magic isn't real.* She'd had a fever tonight, and a psycho had kidnapped her.

Unfortunately, that thought wasn't reassuring either.

Kester focused on the road ahead. The radio blared pop music, and the sound rattled through her throbbing skull. Blue road signs flashed by on the shoulder. *The M4.*

On the plus side, she was alive. On the down side, she'd been kidnapped by a man who'd tried to claim her soul. She didn't know what that meant, but there was a strong chance it involved murder.

"Where are we going?" she managed.

Lazily, his gaze flicked to hers. "You requested a trial, though I have no idea how you knew to ask for that, since you know literally nothing else."

"It was on a note I'd written to myself." She glanced at her right hand, handcuffed to the passenger door handle. "Where does the trial happen? And what is it, exactly?"

"Outside of London."

"Thanks for narrowing it down." *Okay, so he's not going to be helpful with details. Why would he be, if he's about to murder me?* "My flatmate, Katie, is going to be worried about me. She's going to call the police."

"We'll sort that out later."

She glanced at the handcuff again. It wasn't an ordinary manacle. It almost looked like a golden circle of light trapping her wrist. It almost looked like... *magic.* The thought curdled her stomach.

Kester's glowing eyes, her own fire powers, the mysterious attacks, the healing spell, the handcuffs made of light... It was getting a little harder to convince herself that magic wasn't real, and yet she *really* didn't want to be a part of this madness. She could barely cope with her normal life. *Please let me get back to my poverty and unemployment.*

Even though the handcuff didn't burn her, the circle of light held her wrist in a sort of force field. The unnatural sight of it tightened her chest, filling her with a sense of dread. If things like this existed—along with glowing eyes and flaming hands—what *else* didn't she know about the world? She swallowed hard, still trying to free her wrist. "What the hell is this?"

"I can't have you jumping out the door while I'm driving. You're unpredictable, as you so helpfully informed me earlier."

She felt the now-familiar heat and rage begin to simmer insider her, as if her body knew what it was doing. She wanted to burn this thing off of her.

"You won't be able to melt it." Kester continued, his voice bland. "It's immune to hellfire."

If she had to be manacled to get her to this trial, maybe it wasn't something she really wanted after all. Now that she thought about it, trials weren't generally fun events. The phrase "trial by fire" popped into her mind, and she felt a sudden desperation to rip herself free from the car, to tumble into the road and sprint through the dark fields. Suddenly, the impending homelessness she'd been fretting about earlier no longer seemed as daunting as this nightmare.

She glared at him, her pulse racing faster. "Can you at least tell me if I'll get to keep my soul?"

"Maybe. Maybe not. It depends how you do."

Great. With her heart thrumming, she scanned the car's interior, searching for weapons. It was upholstered in deep red leather, intermixed with chrome and instruments the color of gunmetal. The GPS was off, but Ursula could see that the speedometer read 160 kilometers per hour. They were flying down the M4. Even if she managed to free herself, her body would shatter when she flung herself from the car.

"Aren't you going a bit fast?" she asked, her mouth dry.

"We're in a hurry. Besides this is a Lotus. It's not made for driving slow."

Another pop song blared on the radio—Hugo Modes, warbling in a falsetto... The sound grated, the banality of the music such a sharp contrast to her rising fear. The band crooned on, and she could hardly think straight.

But maybe a sense of normalcy could save her right now. Maybe if she got Kester to see her as a person instead of just his victim, he'd empathize with her. Wasn't that what they told the parents of children who'd been kidnapped? Show the human side, tug on the heart strings.

She had the strangest feeling that Kester didn't *have* a human side, but it was worth a shot. She'd only just turned eighteen, and she wasn't ready to die before she'd had the chance to do anything with her life. She took a steadying breath. "Hugo Modes. What's his band called? The Four Points?" She nodded at the radio, trying to keep her voice steady. "I suppose you like boy bands."

"I wouldn't call them a boy band," he snapped. "They play their own instruments."

She tightened her fists so hard her nails pierced her flesh. *This isn't going to work. I can't make small talk about boy bands when I'm about to be murdered.* She seethed with hot anger. She didn't give a shit about the Four Points. What she cared about was that she'd been kidnapped against her will, and she wanted to smash Kester's stupid rich-boy face into the pavement. So maybe her life was pathetic, but she wasn't ready to give up on it. "What the fuck am I doing here?" she shouted in desperation.

Kester let out a low whistle. "You're not really a people person, are you?"

"I'm handcuffed to the door of a car," she snapped. "Don't expect me to be cheerful about it. You broke into my house in the middle of my dinner, attacked me, and abducted me." She gave the manacle one last tug, but it wouldn't budge.

"That was seriously your birthday dinner? Eating bread and butter in a hovel?" He arched a sympathetic eyebrow. "That's just sad. Frankly, I'm doing you a favor. Assuming you survive."

She clenched her jaw, trying to calm herself, and turned to look out the window. *Don't lose your head, Ursula.*

The landscape flew by—a blur of grey branches and patches of snow. Her breath frosted against the window.

A part of her was terrified, but another part knew she'd make it out of this. Her will to survive was too strong. Less than three years had passed since the firefighters had discovered her in the church. That meant she had less than three years of memories— and the most vivid in her mind right now was Rufus, telling her she would never make anything of her life. She couldn't die before she proved him wrong.

Chapter 5

After turning off the M4, they barreled down an empty one-lane road lined with hedgerows. At last, the car slowed, and they turned into a small driveway. A gate stood before them, flanked by stone columns. To the right, tufts of frozen vegetation dotted brown fields stretching out into the darkness.

Isolated, secluded, and alone with a complete nutter. Former Ursula—or F.U., as Ursula was now thinking of her prior self—had a lot to answer for.

She glanced out the driver's window at a small hill with a flattened top. Bare trees protruded from it, like skeletal hands clawing out of graves. She stiffened. The look of this place turned her blood to ice.

Kester turned off the ignition and stepped out of the car, walking around to the back. Ursula watched him, her pulse racing as he rummaged through the boot. Panic rising, she yanked on the manacle, but her hand remained stuck. *He's going to pull out a gun and blow my head off.*

After yanking out a dark grey jacket, he crossed toward Ursula's door, pulling it open. A blast of icy air flooded the cabin, and Ursula's mouth went dry as she looked up at him. She swallowed hard, not yet willing to move. Whatever the trial was, her best chance of survival was probably to get the hell out of here.

He held out his hand. "I'll need your phone."

Still manacled, she jammed her free hand into her back pocket and pulled out her phone with a shaking hand. She passed it to him, watching as he slipped it into his coat. Dread welled in her chest. He was enormous and strong, and she didn't think she could outrun him. She'd have to fight him, though her chances weren't good there, either.

"Wear this." Kester handed Ursula the jacket, then leaned over her, unlocking the handcuff with a gold key. "Don't try anything stupid. You won't outrun me."

Christ. Can he read my thoughts? Stepping out of the car, she slipped into the grey parka, welcoming its warmth. If she was going to fight him in remote fields, she didn't need the added disadvantage of hypothermia. She pulled up the hood, eyeing him cautiously. You didn't give a jacket to someone you wanted to murder, did you? Then again, he was obviously stark raving mad.

A beep sounded as he locked the doors with the key fob. "I'm going to make sure that we're alone. Stay here." Clouds of breath bloomed around his face.

Like hell I'm going to stay here. If she strained her eyes, she could see lights shining on the other side of the fields. There was a faint smell of wood smoke in the air. As soon as he was gone she'd jump the fence, sprint across the field, and run to the nearest house to dial 999. The next time she'd see Kester's pretty face would be on the evening news.

He turned away from her, then glanced back with a wolfish grin. "You should know that if you decide to run, I'll sniff you out before you can get 100 meters. It's only fair to warn you."

Sniff me out? Creep. She shivered, trying not to picture a madman sniffing around her ankles.

Kester faced the berm, tilting back his head. He began to mutter.

What happened next went beyond creepy and right into the realm of pure terror.

As he spoke, his body began to tremble. Panic spread through Ursula as she watched the side of his face transform. His nose protruded, and his clothes disappeared into dark fur. With a sharp crack, his spine lurched forward, bones snapping as they repositioned. Where Kester had been only moments before, now there stood an enormous black hound.

When it turned to Ursula, the beast's eyes glowed green.

Ursula's heart stopped.

She stumbled back toward the car, gaping. *Kester isn't human. It's real. Witches, magic—the fire goddess, my condemned soul.* Her world tilted.

The beast prowled toward her, sniffing the air before emitting a growl than rumbled through her bones.

She tried to steady the shaking in her hands, balling her fingers into fists. *I'm losing my mind.*

Then the hound turned, bounded up the berm, and disappeared into the darkness.

Alone by the Lotus, Ursula felt a cold wind bite through her clothes. Kester's transformation from man to hound had shattered her very understanding of reality, and her blood roared in her ears. For a moment, she wondered if she'd hallucinated the whole scene.

Maybe she'd stolen this car, dreamt up a beautiful dog-man, and convinced herself that her life had a purpose—that she wasn't just a screwed-up, unemployed loser, but was part of a new magical reality.

Or maybe Madeleine was right. Witches were real, and Kester was one of them—just like the monsters who had terrorized Boston.

She watched the snow drifting to the ground, trying to root herself in reality. A sudden ability to conjure fire with her thoughts wasn't exactly normal. Still, she'd assumed there was a scientific explanation she just didn't know about. It wasn't like she'd spent a lot of time in biology classrooms, so maybe she'd missed something.

But magic and werewolves were the stuff of fairy stories. And she didn't want to believe in them, because if magic was real then maybe the gaping-eyed monsters of her nightmares were real, too. A gut-churning image flickered in her memory—a beautiful man with midnight eyes, and a smile cold as death... She shook her head, pushing the image beneath the surface.

Her breath came thick and ragged. *Focus, Ursula. Did I really just see a man transform into a hound? Or have I lost my mind?* The most likely explanation was that she was a mental case—a newly unemployed mental case—with imaginary magical powers. Perhaps she had only just now come to her senses, alone in a field with a stolen car. But mental cases didn't really come to their senses so suddenly, did they?

So what the hell do I do now? Do I run, or will that beast hunt me down and tear the flesh from my bones?

A distant shriek pierced the frozen night, and a moment later the hound bounded down the slope. Blood dripped from its jaws. Her stomach flipped, and panic threatened to overwhelm her.

She stepped back again, her calves thudding against the Lotus's fender.

Panting, the beast retracted its claws, and its snout shortened. As Kester's spine straightened, clothing spread over his body and the fur disappeared, revealing the smooth skin of a movie star.

Her breath came in short, sharp bursts. No, she hadn't finally cracked. People didn't assess their own sanity while they were hallucinating, which meant that Kester was telling the truth. Apparently, Ursula's soul belonged to a fire goddess.

Bloody hell. What the hell had F.U. been doing with her life?

Kester wiped a hand across his mouth. "Looks like we're alone." He followed Ursula's eyes to the blood staining the snow. "Sorry about that. I was hungry."

Her fists clenched tighter, her nails digging into her palms. Who did he just kill? "Did you—" she stammered, "just eat someone?"

Kester smiled wolfishly. "Not a person. What sort of monster do you think I am? Just an old ewe I found on my way back here. Put her out of her misery to be perfectly honest." He scratched his cheek. "She shouldn't have been outside in this weather."

Ursula exhaled. *A sheep. It was only a sheep.*

Kester glanced at her. "We can't talk all night. We have business to attend to, since you wanted the damn trial."

"I have no idea what's going on. F.U. wanted it."

"I beg your pardon?"

"Former Ursula. It's what I call the version of myself I can't remember."

He glared at her like she was the mad one—as if he hadn't just eaten a raw sheep—then crossed toward the car, clicking open the boot. The car lights shone on his dark hair while he rummaged around.

Straightening, he pulled out a long object wrapped in black leather. With a flick of his wrist he yanked the sheath away, revealing an ancient sword. Strange patterns wove and writhed along its iron blade as though it were alive, and the air left her lungs.

Okay. Now I know how he intends to kill me.

Chapter 6

Ursula's chest unclenched a little when Kester shoved the sword back into its sheath. He slammed the boot shut, turning to climb the slope. "Come, my dear. You've got work to do up the hill."

He trudged toward the bank, and she was left with only the sound of the wind rushing across the snow. She glanced one last time at the distant lights twinkling in the night. If she ran in an all-out sprint, she could be sitting before a fireplace in five minutes. But she'd never make it. Kester would hunt her down like the ewe he'd so casually disemboweled.

Dread wrapped its fingers around her heart as she climbed up the slope. *I have to get out of here.* Her best bet would be to convince Kester she was stupid, and then disarm him when he least expected it. In fact, given his condescending tone, there was a good chance he already thought she was an idiot.

If she could get the sword from him, she stood a chance. She was skilled with a sword, even if she had no idea how she'd learned. When she'd been discovered in the church, she had no memories beyond her name. But even though she had no idea *who* she was, the doctors who'd treated her had explained that she still had something called "procedural memory." She remembered how to walk, cut up her food, and speak English. She couldn't type, which meant she'd never learned, but as soon as she saw a piano, she'd been struck by a certainty that she knew what sounds her fingers would make on its keys. She just had no memory of how she'd learned to play in the first place.

When she thought of sword fighting, it was the same. She could imagine herself wielding a blade with precision, each thrust and parry as familiar to her as the movements of walking. As she envisioned herself fighting, a little of the terror seeped out of her chest, and she smiled to herself. In all likelihood, Kester was not counting on her expertise in this area. At least F.U. had done something right for her.

The berm was more slippery than she'd expected, and near the apex she had to scramble on her hands and knees so as not to slide down its side. On the flattened hilltop, she straightened, shielding her eyes as a strong gust of wind whipped snow into her face.

When she'd wiped the snow from her eyes, she found herself standing beside an enormous grey rock, its rough-hewn surface crusted with ice. Two more stones rose from the ground on either side, and if she strained her eyes, she could see the dim edges of more boulders curving off into the darkness.

Kester gripped his sheathed sword. He nodded at one of the rocks. "What do you think of the ringstones?"

She turned to gape at him. *Is he seriously making small talk? And what sort of opinion was she supposed to have on rocks?*

"They're big." She kept her eyes on the weapon that swung by his hips. "But why are we here?"

"A trial can only be conducted in a place of ancient magic." With the sword tucked under one arm, he led her further into the stone circle. As they walked, another ring of giant stones came into view.

She took a deep breath. How, exactly, was she going to distract him long enough to get that sword? He'd nearly lured her into his trap through the power of suggestion, but that really wasn't part of her skill set. Especially not when she was stuffed into a grey parka, half freezing to death.

Then again, men could be simple-minded creatures.

Kester turned to her. "We need to be within the inner circle."

She shivered, gazing out over the dark and empty fields. If she could move in close enough to kiss him, she could ram her elbow into his Adam's apple. He'd drop the sword immediately. And yet, a voice in the back of her mind urged her to follow him.

Maybe, if she survived whatever the hell was about to happen, she could learn the truth about herself, about where she'd come from. If she killed him, she'd be stuck in the darkness forever. There was also the fact that she didn't particularly want to drive a sword through someone's heart, even if he was a psychopath. She'd have to see how this played out before she did anything drastic.

They reached the second circle of stones. Crusted in ice, the monoliths towered over Ursula. Her heart pounded.

His green eyes flashed like storm clouds in the dark. "Wait here a moment."

Cold fear inched up her spine. A few feet from her, Kester pulled the sword from its sheath. Puffs of frozen breath drifted from his mouth as he whispered over the weapon. When he finished, a glowing orb appeared, hovering above his head and illuminating a small patch of snowy grass in the center of the stones. The word *magic* rang again in her head, and her body thrummed with a dark thrill. *It's real.*

Gripping the sword in both hands, Kester raised it above his head, blade pointing toward the earth.

"O' shadow stalker." His voice was firm. "A thane awaits a trial." He stabbed the frozen earth with the blade.

Ursula's stomach clenched. *What the hell is a shadow stalker? And, is this thane supposed to be me?*

The wind died, and a deathly, unnatural silence enveloped them. The orb's flickering glow revealed nothing beyond the stones. In the icy air, each intake of breath froze Ursula's throat.

A snowflake fell on her eyelash and she blinked. Had something shifted in the darkness just beyond the inner stones? The hair rose on the nape of her neck.

She whipped her head around, sensing an unseen danger. "Kester, what—"

He lifted a silencing finger, still holding the sword's hilt. As he raised his eyes, he seemed to search the stones. "Moor fiend, reveal yourself." His grip tightened on the pommel of the sword.

Her heart hammered against her ribs, and time seemed to stretch out as she waited.

Between the stones, she could make out a faint outline—tall and hunched, and nearly as large as the rocks themselves. Her breath caught in her throat. *What is that?*

Kester beckoned Ursula to come closer. "Shadow stalker, I have brought you a thane to battle."

Her mouth went dry, her spine stiff with fear, but she stepped toward Kester. *I can do this—whatever this is. I know how to use a sword.*

He looked at her, one hand still on his sword. "You wouldn't sign the pact," he said in his velvety voice. "This is the third option. If you defeat the wight, you'll become a servant of Emerazel, like I am. You can repay your debt that way."

She took a deep, steadying breath. "I don't really want to do that either. Can't I just go back to my flat—"

"Ursula," he interrupted. "You must decide now. Either sign the contract or defeat the monster. Otherwise, I'll be forced to reap your soul. I don't particularly want to do that. It means you'll die now."

From just beyond the stones, a guttural growl rumbled. A shiver snaked up Ursula's spine. She had a feeling that whatever was out there wanted her soul, too. She gritted her teeth, nodding. *Shadow stalker it is.*

With his eyes locked on hers, Kester released the sword, stepping away. Ursula tried to steady her breathing, stepping toward it.

She inhaled deeply, yanking the sword from the frozen earth. *Lighter than I thought.*

Kester stepped away. "The wight will enter the circle when the light dims. You must defeat him."

As she gripped the sword in both hands, she took a tentative swing. The blade moved easily through the air, and she nearly smiled at the sensation, relief flooding her for the first time tonight. Somehow the sword felt like an extension of her body, like one of her own limbs. F.U. must have swung a sword a thousand times before.

Kester chanted a spell, and as the air crackled with electricity, fur sprouted from his body. He lurched over, bones cracking; with a deep growl, he transformed into a hound. For a moment, he studied her, green eyes flashing, before bounding from the circle.

Above her, the orb began to dim.

Chapter 7

$\mathcal{D}$espite the cold, sweat dampened her brow, and she gripped the sword hard. This blade would be her savior.

She strained to see in the dark, but she could no longer make out the monster's hunched form. The wind picked up again, spraying snow between gaps in the ringstones.

She lifted her weapon, trying to keep the fear at bay. *I'm a sitting duck here.* Her mind raced. She was at a serious disadvantage, since she had no idea where or what this *shadow stalker* was. At least a stone could guard her back. She backed into the shelter of the nearest one.

To her right, something scratched at one of the stones, and she spun to face it. She held the sword in front of her, her breathing ragged. Ice flaked off the boulder, drifting to the ground, and fear stole her breath. Snow crunched behind her, and she whirled again. More fragments, crumbled off the stones. Where was this monster? A low growl spread through the circle, rumbling through her gut, followed by a sharp, scraping sound.

The fiend is sharpening its claws.

Without the orb, darkness enshrouded her. She pressed her back against the basalt rock, her sword wavering as she peered into the darkened center of the circle. How did one see something made of shadows?

In the center of the stones, something whirled—tendrils of black on a phantom wind, deeper and darker than the night sky. *Please let me get through this.*

From two feet above her head, yellow eyes flickered into existence, as large as dinner plates. Panic inched up her spine. The fiend was at least eight feet tall. Following the eyes, its body shimmered into view, shoulders as broad as a ringstone.

A wave of fear slammed into her. Sure, she knew how to swing a blade, but did she know how to fight a giant?

She clutched the sword, pulse racing as the fiend lurched forward. It balanced on the knuckles of a long arm, like a monstrous gorilla. She readied herself for its attack.

It lunged, swiping at her with a clawed hand. She dove to the side, slashing upward, but the blade cut only air. Scrambling to her feet, she searched frantically for the monster, but it was gone.

Bollocks bollocks bollocks. It had only feinted to draw her away from the safety of the stone. She whipped her head around, searching for her opponent—but not fast enough. The creature's arm flew from the darkness behind her, slamming into her side like a cudgel.

The sound of her arm and ribs snapping cracked through the air, and she was lifted off her feet. She slammed into the frozen earth next to one of the blue stones, and pain shot through her like a white-hot knife. She screamed.

A wet, guttural sound drowned out her cries. *Laughter.*

Agony pulled her apart. *I can't die here. I can't die alone, not knowing who I really am.* She gritted her teeth and pulled herself to her feet, lifting her sword. The monster had smashed her left arm, and something warm and metallic dripped from her mouth. *Blood.*

She turned her head toward a movement. The fiend was creeping into the circle again, eyes blazing yellow.

She glared back, her jaw set tight. *If I'm going to die tonight, it's going to be on my terms.* She slashed at its ribs, but despite its enormous size the shadow stalker dodged easily. Fighting this thing was like trying to grip a plume of smoke.

A third option, Kester had called it, but this trial was just a slow and terrifying execution. The moor fiend was toying with her. Kester was probably enjoying every minute of it. He'd sacrificed her to this monster, before she'd even come to grips with the existence of magic.

She tried to block out the pain coursing through her shattered side. *Hell of a birthday.* She'd been fired, stalked, assaulted, kidnapped, and now she'd be mauled to death by a creature made of smoke and wrath.

I didn't even get a chance at life. Rage roiled inside her, simmering away her fear.

"It's my bloody eighteenth birthday!" she shrieked.

As far as she knew, no one had ever baked her a cake. That somehow seemed like the worst offense of all, and anger simmered. *Three years. I only had three years.* As her right hand grew hot, heat burned through her veins. From her palm, fire surged into the sword and flames licked along the blade.

The fiend shrank back, and Ursula stepped forward, emboldened by the flaming sword. *I am an angel of death,* her mind whispered.

The pain in her side threatened to rip her apart, but she held the blade before her like a priest holding a cross to ward off evil. Fire engulfed the whole blade. The few snowflakes that drifted onto the metal sputtered and popped in the heat. *I am wrath.*

The fiend took another step away, pressing its back against a stone. Despite the glow of the fire, the beast's edges were still difficult to make out—a mass of dark hair, muscle, and sinew surrounded by shadows. Its yellow eyes blazed, but no longer just with hunger. She saw fear there, too.

The fiend's shoulders straightened almost imperceptibly, then it leapt. She thrust the sword up just in time to shield herself as the wight grabbed for her. She was ready for it this time, and her blade sliced into its forearm.

Grunting, the fiend slammed its arm into her, sending the sword skittering across the circle. She turned to run for the weapon, but a strong hand grabbed her ponytail and flung her to the ground.

She landed on her broken ribs, and agony fractured her body. *I'm broken.* Gasping for breath, she tried to roll onto her front, desperate to stand, but the fiend leapt on top of her, crushing her lungs and shattered ribs into the icy soil. Long, clawed fingers reached for her throat, and Ursula gasped for breath.

In desperation, she kicked her feet, struggling to free herself, but the fiend slipped its fingers around her throat. It squeezed, like a snake constricting its prey.

Inching toward her face, its golden eyes stared at her with a primitive intelligence. *This is the face of my executioner: bestial and merciless.* Slowly, it opened its mouth, revealing jagged rows of nubby teeth. She braced herself for the bite, until she realized this repugnant display was a smile.

It squeezed harder. Ursula's windpipe flattened with a soft popping noise, and pain splintered her mind.

They say that in your final moments, your life flashes before your eyes—a series of still images projected from your subconscious to your dying mind. For Ursula, it began at fifteen: the firefighter pulling her from the rubble of St. Ethelburga's Church, the flashbulbs as she left the courthouse with her first foster family. The next few scenes were a blur, one family after another, accompanied by a soundtrack of tutting, screaming, and finally shrieks of "I can't take this girl anymore!"

When her lungs were close to bursting, the filmstrip slowed. Her tiny apartment in Bow flickered past. Those two arsehole students fighting in the club. Last of all, Rufus's words reverberated through her skull: "You're a sad cow who won't make anything of your life."

He's right. Because now her shitty life was over in a flash of shattered bones and burning lungs. *Burning.*

A final burst of rage inflamed her—rage at the unfairness and the futility of it all. She hadn't asked for any of this—to be a mystery girl with no family and an infernal fire inside her. Anger flowed, a hot magma in her veins. It erupted from her, broiling and volcanic. She pressed her blazing hands into the wight's shining eyes.

Its hands wrenched off her throat, and she heard her own scream.

Chapter 8

*H*ot blood gurgled from Ursula's throat, bubbling into her lungs. Drowning in her own fluid, she was kept conscious only by the agony wracking her body. Then her vision blurred, and she no longer cared about the injustice of her short life. She just wanted to sleep, to rest peacefully in silence, free of this mind-shattering agony.

But instead of silence, a melodious sound drifted into her ears. Kester, speaking in Angelic again—but she understood the words, something about healing waters and leaching out the pain. Her sight began to clear. She caught a flash of green eyes above her. Kester knelt over her, changing, his brow furrowed with concern.

As he spoke, she could feel her bones shift and slide into place, the pain slowly dulling. Gently, she touched her neck. It still throbbed, but the skin was smooth, healed over. She rolled over, hacking a crimson spatter of blood onto the blackened earth.

Still crouching, Kester quirked a smile. "I imagine this hasn't been the best birthday celebration you've ever had. But you made it."

He'd called up a demonic and lethal creature without warning her, and now he was smiling about it. "Wanker." She choked out the word, her voice box still raw.

"Is that any way to talk to the man who just saved your life?"

Ursula rose to her knees, gasping. Though her ribs and left arm were healed, they still throbbed with pain. "That wasn't a trial. That thing almost killed me." She was fresh out of patience.

"I told you. I'm not in control of these things; Emerazel is. I'm not actually a god, even if I look like one."

Arrogant wanker. She wanted answers. Now. Another foxfire orb burned above them, illuminating the scorched and charred earth around her. At the edge of its glow, something glinted in the shadows. *The sword.* She rushed toward it, plucking it from the frozen earth before whirling to point it at Kester.

"You need to tell me what is going on, or I will slice you in half."

Kester tilted his head thoughtfully. "Fine. I brought you to the Avebury Henge for a trial. To become a hellhound, you must defeat a demon."

She stalked closer, still pointing the sword. Had he said *hellhound*? "I thought fighting the demon—shadow stalker, whatever you call it—I thought that would resolve my debt."

Kester shook his head. "The trial merely gave you the *opportunity* to repay your debt. Your soul still belongs to Emerazel until you pay it off."

The frigid air stung her cheeks and fingers. "So I'm not free?"

"Not free." The tip of his nose had grown pink in the cold. "But on the bright side, you're employed, so that's a step up from a few hours ago. Your new job is to collect either souls or signatures from those who owe a debt to Emerazel. Plus, you're alive, and to be honest my money was on the shadow stalker."

Finally having got an answer, she lowered the sword. "Why didn't you just reap my soul, like you threatened?"

"A request for trial is always honored." His breath clouded

around his head. "And now, we need to go. Sunrise is in an hour, and I don't want to have to explain to a warden of the National Trust why you desecrated a Neolithic monument."

"We're going back to London?" Ursula turned to walk back to the car, but Kester's voice stopped her.

"Not the car, Ursula. We'll be traveling by Emerazel's sigil." He strode toward her and gently pulled the sword from her grasp. Gripping it in both hands, he pointed the tip toward the scorched earth. "And no. Not London."

Ursula jammed her hands in her pockets, trying to warm them. "I don't suppose you're going to tell me where we're going." Apparently that fire had burned the fever right out of her, because her hands were freezing now. Shivering, she watched as Kester carved a triangle in a circle in the snow and soil—the same symbol that marked her shoulder.

Kester slid the sword into its sheath, and reached into an inner pocket of his jacket. With a half-smile, he pulled out a silver flask.

He unscrewed the cap and took a slug, then offered it to her. "Want a sip? It's Glenfiddich, 1937."

Ursula shook her head. "No thanks." She swiped a hand below her eyes. Her eye makeup must be halfway down her face at this point. At best, she probably looked like a drunken KISS fan, but at least she was alive.

"Suit yourself." He poured the contents of the flask into the furrows he'd scratched in the soil. He knelt for a moment, his hand glowing white hot, then flames snaked along the lines in the dirt.

As he straightened, his gaze lingered on Ursula. "You will need to stand right in front of me."

Shoulders hunched in the cold, she edged closer to him. She tensed as he reached for her, pulling her into a tight hug. He smelled faintly of cedar wood—and somehow, the warmth of his body was oddly comforting.

"You'll want to hold your breath," he whispered into her ear.

He chanted an Angelic spell softly, and she listened to the words, understanding each one. He spoke of a portal of fire, and Emerazel's eternal grace. Now, she knew something else about F.U.—she'd apparently been some sort of witch.

As he finished the short spell, the flames blazed high above them. For a moment, her skin seared in an exquisite agony, then she crumbled to ash.

Chapter 9

With the crackling of a thousand cinders uniting, she reconstituted in the center of a circular room, atoms and molecules joining together again with the force of an exploding star. She rested her hands on her knees, her body shaking as she retched. Whatever the fuck she'd just done, she was pretty sure human bodies were not meant to do it.

Her skin crackled with electrical power, and an odd buzzing noise sounded in her head. Each one of her nerve endings blazed in rebellion.

Kester glanced at her. "Are you all right?"

As she straightened, she looked around at the circular room in which they stood. A wrought-iron chandelier, blazing with candles, hung from a towering brick ceiling.

She glanced down. At her feet, a few tongues of flame licked at the edges of an encircled triangle carved into the floor.

Bits of hot ash burned her throat like she'd just pulled too strongly on an unfiltered cigarette. "Bloody hell." She coughed. "What was that?"

"That was sigil travel. You can travel between Emerazel's symbols by knowing the right spell, and envisioning where you want to go, but it's not the most comfortable method of transportation. I recommend actually holding your breath next time."

She rubbed her eyes, still trying to get her bearings. Between three tall windows, the walls were painted with strange frescos of dancing nymphs, satyrs, and occult symbols. On one part of the curving wall stood a mahogany door carved with stars and flames.

Ursula wondered if they might be in some sort of antechamber to the underworld, until the windows caught her eye. Distant lights twinkled through the glass. On the other side of a park, a cityscape glimmered. Entranced, Ursula stepped toward the glass, watching the falling snow that blanketed the treetops and distant buildings. *Where am I?*

She searched for the usual London landmarks: the London Eye, the Thames, or the pointed tip of the Gherkin.

But this wasn't her city. The buildings lining the park were far too tall for London's skyline.

Dizzy, she stepped back from the window. "Where are we?"

"New York City."

She shook her head, trying to clear the confusion. It didn't seem possible—then again, she'd just defeated a demon and travelled through a blaze of fire and ash. Clearly, she needed to rethink what was possible. "So, so..." she stammered. "I'm looking at Central Park."

"Yes." Kester traced a gloved finger over the glass. "It's dark now, but on a clear day you can see the roof of the Metropolitan Museum of Art, and beyond that, Harlem."

She gaped at him, wondering if this was all some kind of dream. "The fire you lit transported us here. With magic." She felt stupid saying the words out loud.

He pulled off his gloves, turning to the sigil. "Precisely. I can call on Emerazel's power with her symbol. With the right spell, it is possible to travel between them."

"I need to let Katie know I'm okay."

"No. There is no Katie anymore. You need to leave your old life behind. I'll take care of the explanations to anyone who knew you."

She eyed him. "You've got to be joking. I can't contact my best friend?"

"You don't want to test me on this. There are worse things than death, and they'll be waiting for you if you defy that order." His voice sent a shiver over her skin, putting an end to that conversation.

Her skin felt hot, and she pulled off the coat Kester had given her, trying to think of what to say next. *I was burnt to ash, and then I traveled to New York through a flaming sigil. Magic, demons, hellhounds...* Her mind raced in a jumble of confused words that she couldn't process. *F.U., you were a raging lunatic.* "Where are we standing right now?"

"This room has been properly prepared to receive those who travel by Emerazel's fire," he said, pointing at the markings on the walls. "It's on the top floor of the Plaza hotel."

"The Plaza Hotel. Right. And witches and demons are real, and you eat raw sheep and steal souls."

"We don't say 'witch' in our world. 'Philosopher' or 'mage' are the preferred terms. And I am your new mentor, so you'll need to watch that unpredictable attitude, or you'll find yourself on the wrong side of my wrath. Are we clear?"

She choked back a retort, forcing a smile. "Clear as day."

"Good. Come with me." He pulled off his jacket, tucking it under his arm as he walked through the door. "I think you'll find this place an improvement over your usual haunts."

She followed Kester down the hallway and into a cavernous main hall. *Bloody hell.* She let out a low whistle. The place looked like some sort of medieval castle. *Is this where he lives?*

High above, the ceiling's arches gave the room an almost cathedral-like quality. Persian rugs carpeted the floor, and rich taupe velvets upholstered the sofas. A baby grand piano stood in a far corner. Above the fireplace hung an antique portrait of a beautiful ivory-skinned woman, her raven hair threaded with wildflowers. On a small plaque pinned to the bottom of the gilt frame was the name *Louisa.*

Fancy as it was, a musty smell hung in the air. Dust coated the floor, and flowers in a vase had dried into drooping husks. This place had clearly been unused for quite some time. *What a waste.*

Kester waved a hand. "The living room."

"Who lives here?"

"We'll get to that."

"It looks... fancy." She glanced around furtively, feeling like an intruder in a rich person's home. "But how do you get out of here?" Admittedly, escape routes were a bit of a preoccupation, but since she'd been attacked by two different creatures tonight, she thought she could be forgiven for a little neurosis.

He pointed to a doorway. "The elevator is through there, but the Plaza's security is excellent. No one is coming in here unless you want them to. You're perfectly safe. Come with me."

Ursula followed him down a hallway, gaping at the vibrant paintings of pale, ecstatic women dressed in gold and crimson gowns. The place was decadent, but intensely beautiful.

He stopped by an open door, flicking on a light switch. "This is the library."

Ursula peered inside. Distant streetlights flickered through a single window at the opposite end, and a comfortable window seat nestled under it. A small table stood in the center, and dark bookcases lined the walls, their shelves filled with leather-bound volumes. She had a sudden desire to lock herself in the room and page through each book for the next month. "I love this room," she breathed. Maybe she wasn't much of an intellectual, but the room's coziness called to her.

"You'll have time to look around later. There's more to see," said Kester. He strode to the end of the hall, and she followed. Though another door, he pointed out an enormous kitchen with marble countertops.

This was a kitchen made for something a little more delectable than buttered bread. Her stomach rumbled, but Kester had already moved on.

Down the hall, he flicked on a light through a doorway. "The armory."

Ursula's pulse quickened. *Weapons.* She'd grown quite fond of that sword tonight.

She peeked inside. The armory was as large as the main hall. A mirror lined one wall, and beige tatami mats covered the floor. A wooden sparring dummy stood in a corner. Across from her, a magnificent collection of daggers, swords, and spears hung on wooden racks. Grinning, Ursula hurried across the room to inspect them.

"Take your time," said Kester. "I'm going to see about some food. I can hear your stomach rumbling from here."

Ursula's eyes went wide at the gleaming collection. There was a Viking sword like the one she'd so recently used to fight the shadow stalker, pointed blades for puncturing hearts and lungs, stubby Roman swords, and even a Scottish claymore. But it was the rack of Asian weapons that most drew her eye: a sword for chopping the legs off of charging horses, a pair of daggers, two long spears, and a wicked-looking katana. She had no idea why, but these swords called to her.

She bit her lip, fighting the urge to steal a few daggers. She didn't know where she'd be resting her head tonight, but sleeping with a cold blade by her side might not be a bad idea. Especially since her new mentor had the disturbing tendency to grow claws and fangs. Maybe he was being civil to her now, but he was clearly dodgy as hell.

She reached for the katana. Black silk wrapped the hilt, and the guard was forged in the shape of a dragon. The blade shone like a viper's tooth.

It was perfectly weighted. She hurried to the center of the room and sliced the blade through the air in a practice swing, thrilling at the feel of the steel. She swung again, and the muscles in her shoulders loosened. *Home. This feels like home.* Her arm still throbbed where the shadow stalker had broken it, but with the sword in her hand, the dull ache began to ease.

Turning toward the mirror, she caught a glimpse of herself and winced. Her auburn hair lay matted to her head. Blood and dirt stained her shirt and jeans, and her black eye makeup formed two dark semi-circles below her hazel eyes. *I look like a goth clown—definitely worse than a drunken KISS fan.*

At least the sword was beautiful. With a faint smile, she raised it above her head. She sliced downward with a yell, halting when the blade was parallel to the floor. As she lifted her arms to take another swing, Kester's voice interrupted.

"I see you're making yourself at home." He leaned against the door frame, staring at her. "I would ask how you learned to wield a sword like that, but I'd wager you have no idea."

"You'd wager right." She turned and pointed the sword at him. He stood ten feet away, and she could be there in two steps.

Before he'd have a chance to blink, she could bury the sword in his chest. After stopping his heart, she'd just take the elevator to the ground floor and disappear into the New York City night. Would it be so hard to start over as a waitress in New York?

But something stopped her. It wasn't just his pretty face. As insane as he sounded, Kester had actually been telling the truth. *Magic is real.* She'd seen him transform into a hound, summon a shadow stalker, and whisk them to New York through a flaming sigil. She felt it when she lifted the sword, and what was more, some sort of magical fire now flowed in her veins. And if Kester was telling the truth, that meant there was no escape from Emerazel and her infernal flames.

She lowered the blade, wiping the makeup below her eyes on the back of her other wrist.

If Kester suspected that she'd just run through the pros and cons of stabbing him to death, his face didn't show it.

He nodded at the sword. "I see you've acquainted yourself with my friend Honjo Masamune. I know he's quite charming, but he can wait until morning. Dinner is served."

With a heavy sigh, Ursula crossed to the racks, placing the katana in the empty spot. *Until we meet again, my friend.*

Chapter 10

$\mathcal{K}$ester led her down the hall, past the sigil room, and pulled open the door to a dining room. A domed ceiling arched impossibly high above them, painted with a fresco of dryads and centaurs. Mahogany cabinets displayed antique porcelain and crystal glassware. In the center of the room, a silver candelabra cast warm light over the rich wood of a banquet table. Two place settings lay in one corner, along with a pair of domed silver trays.

Ursula's back stiffened. *I'll just have to pretend that I don't normally eat a dinner of beans and toast in front of a TV.*

Kester crossed to the head of the table. "Have a seat."

Instead of sitting in front of the tray, she pulled out a chair on the opposite side, giving herself a clear view of the door. She needed to know if anyone else was going to slip in here.

He arched an eyebrow. "A little nervous, are we?"

Reaching across the table, she dragged over the other place setting. "I like a view of the door."

"In case an intruder comes in?"

"Wouldn't be the first time tonight."

"What is *that?*" He nodded at her hand.

She hadn't even realized that she'd pulled out her white stone and was rubbing it between her thumb and forefinger. "It's my good luck charm."

"What is the point?"

"There's no point. I'm just attached to it." It was the one constant thing in her life.

"Good luck charms are for the desperate."

"I'd say that describes me perfectly."

"May I?" He asked, holding out a hand.

Reluctantly, she handed it over. "I suppose you're going to tell me it's something magical."

He sighed, rolling it around in his fingers. "No. It's ordinary hecatolite. Completely uninteresting."

"It has sentimental value." Though what it tied her to, she had no idea.

He eyed her. "I thought you had no memory."

"I don't, but I always assumed F.U.'s life was better than mine."

"You're a very strange person, you know that?"

"I saw you turn into a dog and eat a live sheep," she sputtered. "I'm not sure you have a great handle on normal behavior."

"You still seem cranky. Have some dinner." He pulled the dome off her tray, revealing a beautifully plated steak, a bowl of cauliflower soup, and a small watercress salad.

Her mouth watered at the rich aromas. "Where did this all come from?"

"Room service here is fast and Michelin rated." He filled her wine glass. "Hopefully, some filet mignon and red wine will placate you."

She picked up her knife and fork to cut the steak and took a bite; it was as soft as butter. For the time being, she could almost forgive Kester for kidnapping her in the middle of her slice of bread.

"I hope you like it here," he said.

"It's... fancy. Empty, but very grand."

"You don't find it comfortable?"

She cut another piece of rich meat. "It's not what I'm used to. It's amazing, but I was about two days away from being homeless, and it just seems like it's a waste for a place like this to lie empty when there are probably families freezing outside." She frowned at him. "You're not eating?"

"I filled up on lamb."

It took Ursula a moment to realize that he was talking about the ewe he'd devoured. "Right." The image of his gore-covered teeth almost put her off her food. "What exactly are you? Some sort of werewolf? Am I going to turn into a wolf now that I work for Emerazel?"

"A hound. I'm a hellhound, and so are you. But you won't transform for a number of years."

"Are we..." She struggled to get the word out. "Witches—I mean, mages? Like people are talking about? The terrorists who slaughtered people in Boston?"

Kester shook his head. "We are mortal demons, compelled by our marks to work for the fire goddess. I know magic as well, but you needn't learn it. I just need you to learn to fight and to collect souls."

She nearly choked on her wine. "I'm sorry—did you say I'm a demon?"

"I did." His tone was matter-of-fact. "And your job is to find those in Emerazel's debt. Force them to sign the contract, by whatever means required."

She took a deep breath, trying to process the word *demon*. "I'm having a hard time with the demon concept. Surely demons are scaly creatures with pointy tails and claws." She stopped herself. "I mean, you have claws, but no scales." She shook her head. She was babbling like a loon now. "Demons are monsters. I don't look like a demon, do I?" She gripped her knife so tight she thought the silver might bend.

"Right now you do."

"It just sounds like madness." She sucked in a deep breath. "I'm not sure when you last spent time around normal people, but normal people don't talk about demons. They don't fight monsters in ringstones, or eat live sheep, or travel across continents by incinerating themselves."

Kester leaned back in his chair. "But you're not normal. Normal people don't have severe retrograde amnesia, and they can't light things on fire with their hands. Given the rest of your life, the fact that you're a demon shouldn't be much of a surprise." His green eyes gleamed. "What exactly was your explanation for your powers?"

"Genetics," she blurted. "A mutation. I have no clue. I've hardly taken any science classes. And anyway, it just happened for the first time tonight so it's not like I've had time to think about it."

"You think a random mutation in your DNA could allow you to do this?" He held up his silver fork. For an instant his hand glowed incredibly hot, like he'd pulled the door to a furnace. Then the fork collapsed on the table in a molten lump.

She felt dizzy, overwhelmed by a strange sense of vertigo. "I have no idea. I don't understand any of this." Maybe he was right, though. Only the supernatural could explain everything she'd seen. "I need to know more specifics about this new job."

"You track down people who've struck a bargain with Emerazel, people who've traded their soul for fame and wealth. You need them to sign the contract to bind their soul to the goddess when they die. Very rarely, you might meet another such as yourself who has carved Emerazel's mark in their body. But there aren't many around with these." He unbuttoned his shirt collar, and her eyes landed on the familiar scar in the center of his athletic chest. "Emerazel's strength can only be granted through one of her blades, and there aren't many in the world." He buttoned his shirt again, and she tried not to think about his body.

"I don't even know how I got my scar," she said.

"You really have no idea?"

"Nope." She swirled the wine in her glass. "What happens when someone signs their soul away?"

"Each god has their own hell. Emerazel's is the inferno. The debtor's soul will go there once they die."

Suddenly, she was no longer hungry. "And the soul burns forever? Does it hurt?"

"I assume so. That's why I've been keen to avoid it."

She stared down at the lump of meat on her plate, fighting a growing sense of nausea. "I can't do that to people. I can't send them to hell."

"My darling, you don't have a choice. It's you or them. You won't win in a fight against Emerazel. You'll come to understand that over time. Anyway, the debtors agreed to the bargain. It was their choice."

She rubbed a knot in her forehead. "How do I know where to find them?"

"Emerazel will tell you." He leaned closer. "You know the symbol we travel through?"

"It's familiar, yes, since it burned me to a crisp a half hour ago."

Kester ran his fingers over the rim of his wine glass. "A sigil of fire can also be used to contain demons. Even gods. We can summon Emerazel within it."

"I light the symbol, and Emerazel appears with instructions?"

"Precisely."

Whatever Emerazel was like, it couldn't be much worse than working for Rufus. "And I suppose I need to find a new flat?"

"This apartment is your new home."

Her jaw dropped. "There's no possible way I could afford to live here."

He shook his head. "This apartment is paid for. You don't have to worry about rent. And of course Emerazel pays an annual stipend of ten ingots of gold."

She stared at him. "Gold what?"

"Gold ingots are 400 ounces each, and the price of gold is about $1,500 an ounce." He looked at the ceiling, muttering calculations. "That's six million dollars a year, or about four million pounds. Give or take." He dabbed the corner of his mouth with a napkin.

She gaped at him. *This must be a dream.* There was no way she could be making that much money. "Six million dollars a year," she repeated. The amount was so far out of her frame of reference that it almost had no meaning. "What would I do with six million dollars a year?"

His cheek dimpled as he flashed a smile. "Oh, I'm sure you could find a worthy anti-gentrification cause to fund."

"Uh-huh." *Definitely better than working for Rufus.* She took a long sip of her red wine. She had no idea what kind it was, since Rufus's club never got any more specific than *red* or *white*. "So why was this place empty? Who used to live here?"

"Another hellhound. But he's moved on to other things."

"And he has a scar. Just like ours?"

"Exactly."

"How did you get yours?"

He reached down, twisting a silver cufflink. For the first time she saw a hint of vulnerability, when he didn't meet her eyes. She liked this side of him better. He swallowed, still examining his cufflinks. "Everyone has their stories."

Wow. That was amazingly...vague. "Right, but what is your—"

"Oh, I almost forgot." Reaching under the table, he lifted up a silver bucket that held champagne and crystal flutes. He looked at her again. "It is your eighteenth birthday."

Chapter 11

She sniffed the champagne, waiting until Kester took a sip of his before she put the glass to her lips, just in case it was poisoned. It tasted fruity and crisp, like fall apples.

"This is delicious," she said.

"It's a 1928 Krug. One of my favorite vintages. I keep a few bottles around for special occasions."

"Champagne from the '20s. This glass probably cost more than my annual wages," she mused.

"Things have changed for you." He stood, a champagne flute in one hand and the bottle in the other. "Shall we see the rest of the apartment?"

"There's more?"

"There's the second floor." He stepped out the door.

She rose, gripping her champagne as she followed him into a large foyer with a marble staircase. He pointed to a set of double doors. "The elevator, which should satisfy your paranoid tendencies in case you need to make a fast escape." He flicked a wall switch. Above, a chandelier sparkled with a hundred tiny lights. "The bedrooms are on the upper level."

As she climbed the stairs with him, her shoulders tensed. Maybe magic was real, but that didn't mean he wasn't a pervert.

She glanced at him. If he attacked her in some way, she could smash the champagne flute and stab him with the stem. "Before you try anything funny, you should know that I'm pretty good at brawling."

He shot her a sharp look. "Charming. First, you will not beat me in a fight. Not ever. And second, I promise you there's no need for me to force myself on unenthusiastic women when there are many willing participants to choose from."

"Is that so?" It was the only retort she could come up with.

"Do I need to remind you again that I'm your mentor?" That cold, commanding tone had entered his voice again. Gone was the whole soothing charade he'd plied her with earlier in the dining room. Obviously, persuasion was part of his hellhound skill set.

She loosed a sigh. "You don't need to remind me." As she climbed up the stairs after him, she ran her fingers over the brass railing. "This is all part of the hotel?"

"The upper floors of the Plaza are all private residences. A former hellhound purchased this apartment in the twenties for a pittance. The Plaza tried to reacquire it in the thirties but... well, let's say we have our ways of getting what we want."

They reached the landing at the top of the stairs, and a hallway stretched out in either direction. Kester crossed to a door, pushing it open and flicking on a light. "Bedroom one. The greenery room."

Ursula peered inside. This bedroom appeared to double as a botanical conservatory. A wrought-iron scaffold supported glass panes, enclosing half the room. A small day bed stood in one corner. It was pretty in a way, but rotting orchids and cacti lined shelves, and a smell of decay filled the air.

She stepped out. "Interesting. Maybe I'll get into gardening."

"I'll have the cleaning staff come through in the morning," said Kester, closing the door.

He continued down the hall, gesturing through a doorway. She stuck her head into a grey-tiled bathroom. An enormous claw-foot bathtub stood in the center, with a shower in the corner. *Beautiful.* She'd never had a proper shower before, just grimy tubs with handheld sprayers that emitted a sad trickle of water. "I'm really going to enjoy that shower."

"I thought you'd like it. Come. There's more." Kester led her to another room. When he entered, he muttered in that strange language, and candles blazed all over the room. Shadows danced over high, arched ceilings and stained glass windows. In the center stood a four-poster bed with a black canopy. Shelves lined the walls, filled with jars of potions and animal skulls. "The master bedroom."

Stunning—but creepy. Not unlike my new mentor. "Great. Maybe I'll sleep here."

There was no way she was sleeping with the skulls. She'd sleep in the living room.

"There's one more." He walked to the end of the hall.

She stepped inside. This room was smaller than the others. A twin bed with a cream coverlet nestled below a window, and an antique dresser stood in the corner. Kester muttered the spell again and the lantern that sat on the bedside table flickered to life, bathing the room in warm light. On the ceiling, someone had painted the zodiac—gold on midnight blue. It was perfect. It just needed a few finishing touches, maybe a bit of color, to make her feel at home.

"I love it." If Ursula had brought a bag she would have tossed it on the bed to claim it as her own.

"There's one more thing you need to know." He stepped back into the hall, pointing to a door across from hers. She couldn't believe she hadn't noticed it before.

Made of rough oak studded with iron nails, it could only be described one way: *creepy as hell.* It looked like something you'd find in Vlad the Impaler's castle. A pale yellow glow surrounded its frame, the exact color of the shackles Kester had clamped on her wrist in the Lotus.

"In case the spikes didn't make it clear enough, that room is off limits."

Suddenly chilled, she hugged herself. "What's in it?"

Kester glared at her. "You don't need to know that. And now, I'll leave you to that shower. Alone, of course."

He turned to leave, but she touched his arm. "Kester. What happened to the last hellhound? What did he move on to?"

He stared her down. "That's not for you to worry about, Ursula. You have enough to take care of. Get some sleep."

His response didn't do anything to put her mind at ease.

Kester let himself out, leaving Ursula to rifle through the drawers and cupboards on her own. After a glorious hot shower to wash off the remnants of the Muppet's stale beer, she picked through the apartment again, one room at a time.

In the kitchen, she discovered a chrome espresso machine and coffee grinder stowed in a closet. She dusted them off, moving them to one of the marble countertops. *I love coffee. I belong in America. Would it be strange to pay for coffee beans with gold ingots?*

Returning to the library, she read the spines of every book in the room. There were first editions of all the modern classics: Melville, Poe, Dickens, and Brontë. She even found older works by Chaucer, Dante, and Shakespeare—many of them written on parchment and beautifully illustrated in the margins.

Strangely, a lower shelf seemed to be protected by the same golden glow that blazed from the door upstairs. When she reached for the books, her hand was repelled by an invisible force. So of course, those were the ones she most wanted to read. Gold lettering looped up their faded blue and maroon spines: *Fasciculus Chemicus*, *Iconologia*, and *Picatrix*. She had no clue what any of that meant, just a strong desire to do whatever she wasn't supposed to do.

After giving up on the enchanted books, she rose to take one last peek in the armory. When she stepped into the room, she caught a glimpse of the clock mounted above the mirror. It was past midnight. That was, what, five or six a.m. in the UK? She really needed to get some rest.

She trudged up the stairs to her new bedroom and crawled under the coverlet. As she lay in the darkness, she closed her eyes, trying to calm the thoughts blazing through her mind.

Muppet's singed shirt, Kester's fiery eyes and clawed fingers, the moor fiend's leering grin.

She'd never fall asleep with these thoughts whirling in her skull. She imagined one of her favorite places: a ruined church near the tower of London, its crumbling stone walls covered in ivy. But even with that serene image in her mind, Kester's words rang in her head: *You're a demon.*

The concept was horrifying. She'd always known she was different, but... a demon? A mortal one, no less. You'd think that one of the benefits of demonhood would be immortality, but no. Not only was she an abomination and a bringer of death, but she had to die, just like everyone else. She rubbed her white stone between her fingers, but it wasn't giving her comfort tonight.

She pulled her bedsheets tighter. She hadn't asked for any of this. At least, she didn't *think* she had. As long as she could remember, the strange scar had marred her shoulder. Who knew how she got it? She was a Mystery Girl all right—a Mystery Girl who'd made a terrible decision she couldn't even remember. And now she was stuck in a foreign country, permanently cut off from her best friend.

That was the thing that really bothered her. More than anything, she wanted to find a way to phone Katie, just to hear a friendly voice again. But she really didn't want to find out what Kester's threat meant. And what could she even say to Katie without sounding like a complete and utter lunatic? Heat rose in her chest, and sweat beaded on her face.

She rolled onto her back, staring up at the blue ceiling flecked with gold stars. There was something oddly comforting about the night sky. At times like this, when the world seemed to suffocate her, she felt like she wanted to throw herself into the freezing night air, to drift along in the wind, riding a night storm...

Basically, she was a lunatic, trapped with her own thoughts.

And as if they weren't enough to keep her awake, a glowing, spiked door lurked just outside her room.

She threw off her covers and rose from the bed. Shivering, she returned downstairs and snatched a dagger to slip beneath her pillow.

Chapter 12

$\mathcal{A}$s her nails dug into her palms, Ursula stood by the empty reception desk of Ostema, a hair salon near the Plaza Hotel. Around the room, tall mirrors gleamed over bamboo countertops. The air had a faint citrus sent. The place was designed to lull customers into a sense of peace, but Ursula's head was a war zone. Her mind burned with everything that had happened in the past twenty-four hours: her newfound wealth, Kester's hound form, a soul that was no longer quite her own.

And her new, icy companion wasn't doing anything to calm her nerves.

That morning, Kester had brought with him a slender young woman named Zemfira. With platinum-blond hair cut in a chic bob, and a patterned mini dress, she looked like some sort of retro supermodel. Ursula, on the other hand, wore the same black clothes from the day before, her red hair pulled into a messy ponytail. She'd been too overwhelmed to care how she looked this morning.

Before Kester had left, he'd explained that Zemfira—or Zee, as she called herself—would be getting Ursula settled. And, at Zemfira's insistence, their first *crucial* stop was a hair salon.

"Try to look cool," said the girl, her accent faintly Russian.

"I don't even know what that means." *Be nice, Ursula*. This girl was frosty, but if Ursula could get on her good side, maybe Zee would be a little more forthcoming than Kester. Like, about what had happened to the last guy who had Ursula's job.

Working at Rufus's bar, Ursula had met glamorous girls like Zee before. They *loved* to gossip.

Zee leveled cobalt blue eyes at her. "I don't enjoy being seen around the city with someone who looks like she drank twenty wine coolers at a skanky art student party last night."

Or maybe not. For some reason, Zee had decided she hated Ursula. Something had obviously struck a nerve, and Ursula needed to figure out what it was. "That's how you'd describe me? A drunk art skank?"

"I suppose." Zemfira's eyes flicked to her steel-grey nails, as though they were the most fascinating things in the room. "But Luis is a master with hair. He'll be able to help you with... the thing you've got going on with your head. Is it a British thing?"

"Is *what* a British thing?" Ursula asked, no longer trying to hide the irritation in her voice. Zee was a nightmare.

"Having your hair plastered flat to your head like that. Like it wants to escape its miserable existence on your head, and you won't let it."

Ursula gritted her teeth. She would find a way to be nice to Zee, even if it killed her. She could do this. "I don't know, but your hair is pretty." She'd been trying for a compliment, but with her jaw clenched like that, it had somehow come out sounding like a threat. Like she'd just proposed scalping Zee and wearing her platinum hair as a wig.

"It is pretty," Zee agreed cautiously.

"Absolutely. Very... straight. And blond."

"At least you noticed. Kester did not."

Aha. "Oh. Is he your boyfriend?"

Zee cut her a cold look. "He is not. He likes to pick up strays. Women who are beneath him." Her narrowed eyes implied that this included Ursula.

And I've just found the raw nerve. "I hope you don't think *I'm* one of his strays. We've only just met, and he's my mentor. I work with him, as of last night, but our relationship is purely professional. In fact, I'm fairly certain he doesn't like me." That was certainly true.

"Right. Like he 'worked' with that orange-skinned girl from Hoboken he met at Tatty O'Rourke's. And yet he doesn't seem interested in 'working' with me. Because he likes *skanks.*" She picked up a magazine, flipping a page with a ferocity that suggested she had a vendetta against paper. "He likes slumming it."

"I wasn't using 'working' as a euphemism. I mean actual *work.*" Sure, it involved reaping souls and traveling through a fire portal, but it was work all the same. "Do you know what we do for work, by any chance?"

"Of course I do." Zee arched a thin eyebrow and snapped her magazine shut. "Ah. Here is Luis."

A dark-haired young man approached them, his crisp white shirt vibrant against his bronze skin. He was nearly as big as Kester, and he'd accessorized beautifully with a gold watch and chunky glasses. He peered over them, staring at Ursula's hair. "Hello, gorgeous."

Ursula straightened. *Odd behavior for a hairdresser, but okay.*

"Keep your hands to yourself, Luis," said Zee. "She works for Kester."

"I'll behave." He smiled at Zee. "So glad you could bring in this beauty. I love redheads."

"Beauty?" Zee glared at Ursula. "Her head is an aesthetic crime scene. I was hoping you could clean it up. I told her you were the best. And very discreet, of course."

Luis brightened and waggled a finger. "I never tell Emerazel's secrets."

Ursula raised an eyebrow. *Does everyone know about Emerazel but me?*

"Of course you don't tell our secrets. You wouldn't want to land on the Headsman's bad side."

The Headsman. A shiver crawled up Ursula's spine. She didn't like the sound of that. Of course, life among the demons was bound to be unnerving.

Luis pursed his lips, studying Ursula. "The cut is all wrong, but her auburn hair is simply delicious." He reached out, wrapping a tendril of her hair around his fingers. He stared at it, licking his lips in a way she could only describe as lascivious, as a glazed look overtook his eyes. *What the hell?* He took a shuddering breath before dropping the lock of her hair, his eyes becoming alert again. "A treatment with my Brazilian conditioner will really bring out the color." He beckoned her to a room in the back, his gaze still lingering on her hair.

He seated Ursula in a soft leather chair, easing her head into a shampoo sink. Warm water trickled through her hair, and his fingers lathered her scalp with sensual swirls. "Red hair is my favorite."

Ursula almost thought she heard Luis moan, but she shut out that disturbing thought.

Zee plopped into the chair next to her. "Oh, Luis. You and your redheads. As if you don't get enough of them at Oberon's."

Ursula had no clue what they were talking about, but she breathed in the calming aroma of the pineapple-scented shampoo. Maybe she could get used to this life if she absolutely had to. As soon as she left the salon, she was going to buy paints to brighten up her new bedroom. She'd paint bluebells and aster, to make herself feel at home again.

Then again, there was that whole *Headsman* thing. Whoever that was, he sounded terrifying.

She opened her eyes, glancing at Zee. "Zee. Did you say something about a *Headsman*?"

Luis stopped lathering her hair.

Zee let out a long sigh. "Oh. That's Kester's nickname."

Goose bumps raised over Ursula's skin. "Why the Headsman?"

"It means *executioner*. He's Emerazel's most senior hellhound. Kester gets the most difficult cases, and his numbers are unparalleled. He has sent more souls into Emerazel's flames than you can imagine. He's lethal, and practically like a god himself."

And she'd fought him last night. She was lucky to have survived her eighteenth birthday at all. No wonder he'd warned her that she wouldn't win in a fight against him.

Luis's fingers resumed their massage.

At least I got Zee talking. What she was hearing was terrifying, but at least she was hearing something. "So what you're saying is that I'm in good hands?"

"As long as you stay on his good side. You'll need his protection, you know." Zee sighed loudly. "All this effort to make you look presentable, and you'll probably just be shredded anyway."

Ursula's pulse raced. *This is getting worse.* "What do you mean, *shredded*?"

Zee straightened, peering over at Ursula's face. "You mean Kester didn't tell you why there was an opening in New York?"

Her stomach clenched. "No, he was a little quiet on that point."

"Ugh, it was ghastly. Someone gutted the last guy, and strung his entrails over the trees in Central Park. They looked like Christmas tree ornaments, only made of flesh." Zee smiled sweetly. "And now you have his job."

Bloody hell. Pictures of bluebells and asters won't be nearly enough to help me sleep soundly tonight.

Chapter 13

*I*n the armory, Ursula faced herself in mirror, staring at her glossy locks. Luis hadn't cut off much—just enough that her hair now fell above her shoulders. He'd been a little creepy—in fact, he'd pressed his cell phone number into her palm and demanded that she call him for a scalp massage—but at least he'd done a wonderful job with the cut.

She was already feeling much better about her insane new life. After she'd returned that afternoon, she'd finished painting a small mural of wildflowers on her bedroom wall, making it feel a little more like home. And when she'd strode downstairs, covered in smudges of periwinkle and honey-hued paints, she'd found bags of clothes waiting for her on the living room floor.

Inside one of the bags, there was a handwritten note from Kester explaining that she'd need the clothes for work. Whoever had bought them had exquisite taste. Apart from some gorgeous dresses they were, unfortunately, all black—not exactly her thing. But still, she wasn't going to complain about Louboutin boots and Burberry trousers.

If only she could have ignored the whole *eternal torment* thing—not to mention the *shredded hellhounds* thing—she'd be having a wonderful time in New York.

As she gripped Honjo in front of her, she pointed the blade straight at the mirror, her feet planted in a fighting stance. She now wore a new pair of black trousers—real leather this time—and a black tank top. She looked like some sort of American action hero.

She sliced the katana to the side, eviscerating an imaginary assailant. She resumed the ready position with the blade parallel to the floor. As she watched her form for precision and balance, she slowly raised the sword above her head. She slashed it down. *Thanks ever so much for the work clothes, Kester, but did you forget to mention that bit about the entrails in the park trees?*

Beyond the evisceration and public display of intestines, Zee had known no more about who or what had killed the last hellhound. She didn't know if the murderer was still a threat, or if he was likely to come for Ursula.

The steel glinted in Ursula's hands. If someone was after her, she'd be prepared.

Footsteps echoed behind her, and she turned to find Kester standing in the doorway, dressed in a fitted black suit.

She gripped the sword's hilt. "When were you planning on telling me the last fellow was gutted in Central Park?"

A muscle worked in his jaw. "Zee has a little problem with discretion. And tact." His green eyes lingered on her a little too long; something feral flickered in them. "You clean up nicely. Black suits you."

"It does not suit me." At the carnal look in his eyes, heat burned her cheeks. "I'm more of a spring colors girl."

"You're not a 'spring colors girl.' You're a gods-damned demon. Do you understand that? You're going to have to kill people."

Dread tightened her chest. She hadn't really thought about that. "Speaking of killing people..." She strode across the room and pointed the blade at his chest. "I want to know what's going on. Why was the last hellhound murdered?"

He didn't flinch. Apparently, even when she was armed with a katana, he didn't view her as dangerous. His eyes flashed with anger. "I don't know why he was murdered. You're here to help me find out, once you've calmed down a bit."

"I'm perfectly—"

In a fraction of a second, he'd moved behind her, swift as the wind—one powerful arm wrapped tightly around her, and the other hand gripping her sword arm. Heat from his body warmed her. He squeezed her wrist, and she gasped at the pain, dropping the sword. "Don't take on an opponent you have no chance of beating, Ursula," he whispered in her ear. "Not unless you have a really good plan."

Her frustration lent her boldness. "Oh, right. I hear you're 'the Headsman.' Quite the nickname you have." Her heart raced. She shouldn't be prodding this beast, but she wasn't so sure she could cope with being a hellhound. What did she really have to lose at this point? "Your colleague was gutted, his intestines strewn about like holiday decorations, and you have no idea why?"

He loosened his grip on her, slipping away. "It could have been any number of things. Some demons enjoy dispatching their prey with a dramatic flair. Sometimes a curse can rebound, injuring the caster. A lot of things could have led to Henry's demise."

Demons. Curses. All in a day's work around here. "Hellhounds use curses, too?"

"We do what Emerazel tells us. Usually it's signing pacts and reaping souls, but sometimes she has more specific requests."

"Such as?"

"When you get one, you'll know." Something wicked glinted in his eyes. "And if you must know, I really don't mourn Henry's loss. He was something of a psychopath."

She narrowed her eyes. "Speaking of psychopaths, Headsman, why are you in my apartment?"

He flashed her a wolfish smile. "I couldn't resist your warm and inviting company."

She crossed her arms, eyeing the sword on the ground. "Seriously. What did you come for?"

"I left a box of gold ingots on your kitchen table—your annual stipend—and I'm here to teach you how to summon Emerazel." He turned toward the hallway. "Follow me."

She snatched Honjo from the ground, returning it to the rack, and stalked after Kester.

He spoke over his shoulder. "When you meet the goddess of passion and wrath, please don't mouth off. She can compel you to do whatever she wants, including throwing yourself through a window, so I'd advise you to be pleasant and charming." He slid a cold gaze her way. "In other words, don't be yourself."

"I'm perfectly charming to people who haven't abducted me and threatened my life," she shot back.

"You asked for this." They stopped at the door to the sigil room, and Kester continued. "Summoning her is simple. You just need three ingredients. The first is her symbol."

"The encircled triangle. I've got that one memorized." She followed him into the sigil room, glancing out the windows at the snow-covered city. She was about to meet an immortal goddess of fire, yet her blood had turned to ice. She hugged herself tight.

Kester pulled the rug aside to reveal the symbol on the floor. "The second ingredient is fire." He produced a box of matches and the small silver flask from inside his jacket.

He unscrewed the top, taking a swig. "Glorious." After pouring a few ounces of scotch on the sigil, he struck a match and dropped it. His voice took on a professorial tone. "If you're using alcohol, be sure that it's high enough proof to take a flame. You don't want to be caught with your hand on a pact and a sigil that won't light."

"High proof. Got it." It didn't have to be expensive, just alcoholic.

"Lastly, you need to intone the summoning spell." Kester reached into his pocket and produced a small scrap of parchment. "I've memorized it, but here's a copy so you can follow along. You'll need to repeat after me."

Ursula looked at the paper. Spidery letters crowded its surface. Kester started to speak, and though she didn't know the name of the language, she found she could read it phonetically. F.U. was just full of surprises.

As they worked their way through the spell, the words began to roll off her tongue.

When they finished the final line, fire blazed like an erupting volcano, and Ursula shielded her face from the heat. The flame died abruptly, revealing a dark, smoky form crouched in the sigil's center.

A feminine figure rose. Dark tendrils of smoke curled off her, and her eyes burned like supernovas. Wincing, Ursula looked away before her retinas burned out.

A raspy voice, crackling with fire, spoke. "Is this the girl you told me about?"

"This is Ursula."

Ursula shielded her eyes, but Emerazel's heat filled the room. Plumes of smoke wafted through the air like tentacles, encircling the two hellhounds. Outside, Ursula thought she caught a glimpse of Central Park now blazing with spewing lava and ash. *That isn't real, is it?*

She couldn't breathe. What had happened to the air? She wanted to get the hell out of here. Ash seemed to fill her lungs. It was too hot.

"Interesting," whispered the goddess. "Very interesting. I see something in her."

"She is... feisty," said Kester.

"There's something else. Something I didn't notice before, the day she carved herself."

The day I carved myself. Does she know me? Nausea welled in Ursula's gut. Something felt wrong. It was too hot in here—too bright. She needed the cool night air, needed to slip into the shadows, to ride the dark wind into cool, quiet space. Her body trembled, and she clamped her eyes shut. She wasn't sure she could speak, even if she wanted to.

"You remember her?" asked Kester. "She doesn't know where she came from."

"That's for the best," Emerazel spat. "I want to see her kneel before me."

The words rang in Ursula's head, and without thinking, she fell, her knees cracking against the floor. Her body trembled. Emerazel had complete control over her, just as Kester had told her she would.

"A loyal subject to do with as I please. How delicious." The goddess's voice hissed like water on a hot stone.

Ursula had no reply, couldn't meet the goddess's eyes. Nausea and dread wound through her, curling around her thoughts. *I don't belong here.*

"Tell me you're my subject," whispered Emerazel.

Ursula felt her mouth moving. "I am your loyal subject," she intoned. "I am yours."

A deep laugh rumbled through the room, shaking the floor. "You burn for me."

With a great force of will, Ursula dared to raise her eyes, though not high enough to meet the goddess's shining gaze. She stared instead at Emerazel's lips, cracked into a cinder-flecked smile. *She knows something about me.* If Ursula had had any control over her own body, she'd have asked what it was.

"Do you remember when she carved herself?" Kester pressed.

"I remember the day, though I didn't know who she was then. So many souls came to me that day. It was glorious." An ashy smile played about the goddess's lips. "That's all you need to know. I have an assignment for my sniveling little subject."

Ursula fought against the urge to scream. Her skin was on fire, and she was in the center of a volcano. Pain ripped her mind apart. Why didn't Kester mind the heat? How could he stand this?

Emerazel's smile widened. "The target is a particularly delectable soul. He allied himself with me a few months ago. You might have heard of him—Hugo Modes. You're to collect his soul for me. Do not disappoint me. Kester, give her a ledger. One thousand pages. One page for each task, until the book is full."

Ursula's body trembled. *Did she say a thousand pages?*

Kester nodded. "She's had no training, so I will go with her on her first assignment."

"No," Emerazel bellowed. "I want to see what she can do on her own. And, Kester, when you train her, make sure she remains submissive. Do not go gentle on her. I want this one to obey."

"Of course," he said, his tone flat.

"If she needs to die," Emerazel mused. "Be sure you bring her to me first. I will dispose of her myself. In fact, I rather look forward to it." Emerazel's lips began to crumble, and her body collapsed into a pile of ash.

Ursula gasped as cool air filled the room, and the icy winter day returned through the windows. Shaking, she hunched over on her hands and knees, fighting the urge to vomit. Her body twitched uncontrollably. A strong taste of creosote filled her mouth, and sandpaper seemed to line her eyelids. Coughing and gagging, she blinked, trying to force some moisture from her tear ducts.

"That was awful. You didn't tell me it would be that awful." She hated the way her voice broke. She didn't want Kester to see her weakened like this. He already had far too much control over her life.

"Gods below," said Kester, his voice low. "Your first lesson is never to look directly at her."

He held out a hand, lifting her up. "Are you all right?"

Too tired to care about her pride, she leaned into him. "I won't make that mistake again," she managed. She needed a cool bath, and a long sleep.

Kester slipped an arm around her waist, holding her up, and studied her. "I didn't know that would happen," he said quietly. "I've never seen her act that way before. And her flames shouldn't burn one with the mark. I don't feel her heat when she appears. You were in agony."

"I thought I was dying."

"You've certainly earned that *Mystery Girl* nickname."

She straightened, pulling away from him as the nausea subsided. "I don't suppose I can convince Emerazel to tell me what she knows about me."

"She clearly hates you for some reason, so no."

Trapped in the constant desperation of trying to pay her rent and buy food, she'd ignored the most fundamental question for so long: *Who am I?* And now it blazed in her mind like Emerazel's terrifying eyes. "Why would she hate me? What did I do?"

Kester's gaze bored into her. "I can tell you that your Angelic incantation was very clear. In fact, your accent is perfect. You were a scholar, once. How can you remember Angelic if you can't remember anything about yourself?"

"Same reason I can speak English and know how to use a knife and fork. It's a different type of memory." She frowned. *Scholar* was not a word she'd ever associated with herself. "But an Angelic scholar? Where would I have learned it?"

"No idea. I guess that's what makes you the Mystery Girl."

She swallowed hard. "What did she mean by a ledger?"

"Every hellhound has a book—a ledger to track your progress. One page per task. When it is full, your soul is free. I'll have one ready for you when you return from your assignment. I haven't even begun training you, and I honestly have no idea why Emerazel has given you an assignment already. You're not ready for it. But she has it in for you, so you'd better get it right, because it seemed like she wanted to kill you."

Cold dread bloomed in her mind. *My assignment. Right.* "I was in too much pain to focus when she was talking. I almost thought she was talking about Hugo Modes—the lead singer of Four Points. But that can't be right."

Kester quirked an eyebrow. "She was. You'd best pick out one of those dresses I bought you. Charm is one of the best weapons we have, though I don't get the impression it comes naturally to you."

Chapter 14

Ursula sat in the back seat of a Bentley, staring out the window at a line of shivering club-goers. She wore a silky cocktail dress that felt gorgeous against her skin. Black—of course, since Kester had picked it out. With her nerves frayed beyond recognition, she'd arrived at her first assignment twenty minutes early.

Outside, snowflakes drifted through the air. A few had melted on the car's warm windows where they reflected the neon lights of Brooklyn like tiny jewels. In the front seat, the driver hummed tunelessly to the radio, a Mets cap on his head.

"You think the Mets will be any good this season," she asked. She wasn't even sure what sort of sports she was talking about, but she needed a distraction, some sense of normalcy.

"Yeah," he said.

So much for small talk.

She drummed her manicured fingernails over her bare thighs. *Hugo Modes.* She was supposed to claim the soul of Hugo Modes. Could she really send his soul to a fiery afterlife? And what, exactly, did Emerazel plan to do with it down there?

Honestly, if his music was anything to go by, he didn't have much of a soul. His songs were the melodic equivalent of a white-bread and margarine sandwich. In fact, if she were ever tasked with designing her own personal hell, it would involve listening to The Four Points song "Girl, You Got a Magic Body" on a loop.

Still, it wasn't like she wanted to murder him for it.

And yet, there were only two options: get the contract signed, or reap his soul. "Just stab him right in the heart with the blade of the pen," Kester had explained, like it was nothing.

Soul-reaping didn't seem to bother him. Of course, someone with the nickname *the Headsman* probably didn't have normal, human emotions. Over a glass of wine, he'd casually declared, "By the way, you can't contact any old friends, since you're officially dead. The police notified them yesterday. I say 'friends'—really it was just the flatmate and an ex-boyfriend. Kind of a sad life you left behind. Anyway, the papers have already reported the Mystery Girl's overdose. Heroin and crack. Naughty girl."

Just like that, Kester had told her only friend of her demise.

Three years was the sad sum of her life, according to the tabloids. Found in a church, couldn't handle the fame, shifted from one foster home to the next. "Unstable," her former boss Rufus had reported. "Couldn't be trusted around customers. I had to fire her after she attacked someone."

The British tabloids now speculated that she'd started the St. Ethelburga fire herself. Though, now that she knew about her fiery hands, that might not be a million miles from the truth.

Bloody Kester. He couldn't have orchestrated some kind of heroic death.

She tightened her fists. Two minutes before her first mission was no time to get emotional. She needed to keep a clear head. She had a soul to collect, and she wasn't going to screw it up, because it sort of seemed like the fire goddess really wanted to slaughter her.

She pulled out the new mobile Kester had given her, and flicked open a web browser, searching for "Hugo Modes" to get a refresher on his face. He grinned at the camera, all white teeth, pink lips, and large brown eyes—virtually indistinguishable from the three other mop-haired boys in his band.

Kester had been clear on the plan. She and Zee were supposed to approach Hugo together. Keep a low profile, and stay in the shadows. That part was easy enough. She liked shadows. It was just the whole *killing* thing that made her uneasy. Hopefully it wouldn't come down to that. She might be a mortal demon, but she wasn't a murderer.

Someone rapped on the window, and Ursula jumped. It was Zee, clad in a belted white coat, her breath clouding around her face. Ursula opened the door, stepping into icy air that nipped at her bare legs.

"Zee." Ursula shut the door behind her. "Thanks for meeting me here."

The Russian stepped back, surveying Ursula's black coat and tan heels. "You don't look as gross as you did before."

"Thanks." She hugged herself. "What do you do for Kester, anyway? Are you his employee?" *Or do you just do what he says because you fancy him?*

"I have certain skills for which Kester pays me. That's all you need to know. For one thing, I can get us in anywhere." Her eye makeup shone gold in the tungsten streetlights. "This place is like my second home." Behind her, gold-plated lettering read *Club Lalique*.

Ursula's teeth chattered. "I'm freezing. Shall we get in line?" She stuffed her phone into a small clutch the color of smoke. *Wyrm skin*, Kester had said. Dragon hide was invisible to normal humans, which made the clutch perfect for what she had to carry into the club.

"Come with me." Zee looped her arm through Ursula's, leading her to the front of the line.

"Are we just going to jump the queue?" Ursula whispered. She felt like a tit cutting in front of everyone, and she could feel their angry stares burning into her.

"Of course."

A ruddy-faced bouncer in a long heavy coat stood behind a red rope. "Good evening, Zemfira."

Zee smiled. "Just my friend and me tonight."

The bouncer lifted the rope, then pulled open a black door. It led into a short hallway lined with pale marble tiles, and once she was inside its warmth Ursula's stiff shoulders began to relax. They walked through a narrow hall to a set of gold-plated doors.

Zee pushed a button, and the doors opened to reveal an elevator's mirrored interior. They both stepped inside.

Ursula took a deep breath. *Calm down. All you need to do is give Hugo the parchment, and ask him to sign. He should be perfectly reasonable about it.* What Emerazel wanted with his soul was a mystery, but she supposed Kester would probably just tell her it was none of her concern.

As the elevator silently climbed fifteen stories, she glanced at a CCTV camera in the corner. This place was probably littered with cameras. A bit tricky to stay in the shadows.

At the top floor, the doors opened to reveal a vast room dripping with opulence: platinum, muted gold, and vibrant amber. It was like something out of a Russian palace before the revolution. No wonder Zee liked it here.

A few patrons clustered around a circular bar, while others lounged in cream leather booths. Above the bar, a gold column branched out like a metal tree, and crystal lights sparkled among its boughs. But the most eye-catching aspect of the room was the view: across the East River, Manhattan's buildings jutted into the sky, a glittering, steel forest. This place was so far from Rufus's club that it might as well have been on another planet. *You've come a long way, Ursula.*

A grey-haired man in a black sweater approached them. "May I take your coats?"

"Yes, please," said Zee.

Zee wriggled out of her white coat, revealing a pale cocktail dress that hugged her delicate curves. A pearl necklace draped around her neck, and she gripped a small, indigo clutch that matched her shoes.

The man turned to Ursula. "Miss?"

Ursula slipped out of her coat. The black Prada dress hugged her body perfectly. Short and A-line—good for running if she needed to slip away fast. She handed over her coat.

Zee appraised her outfit. "Black. Sophisticated. Very nice."

You're not the only one out here who can pick out a dress. "Thanks."

"I don't know about you," Zee continued, "but I'm dying for a cocktail." She headed to the bar, nabbing the last gold-cushioned seat. Ursula had to stand awkwardly behind her.

Within moments, a blond bartender leaned across the wooden bar. "The usual, Miss Zemfira?"

"Yes, but make it two." She turned to Ursula. "You like champagne cocktails." It was less a question than a directive. *Drink it or else.*

"Sure. Whatever." With her nerves blazing, Ursula wasn't really in the mood for drinking, but it would help her blend in. Champagne wasn't so alcoholic as to get her drunk, and she could slowly nurse it.

"Great." Zee smiled. "Save my spot. I have to pee."

After Zee hurried off, Ursula slipped into her seat, watching as the bartender put together their drinks. After dropping two sugar cubes into a pair of champagne flutes, he retrieved a bottle of Angostura. He dropped the bitters onto the cubes— deep red drops, like blood on snow. As he filled the glasses with champagne, Ursula shivered for a moment, thinking of the last hellhound, and the entrails that had decorated a tree.

The bartender slid the glasses across the rich wood.

"Thank you." When she took a sip, the bubbles tickled her nose.

A thin hand snapped up the other drink. "Just in time," said Zee.

"When do you think Hugo will get here?" Ursula whispered.

"Soon, I suppose. He's a regular here." Zee leaned in close. "I can't believe he's your first target."

"How is it that you know all about this? About what I do?"

Zee's blue eyes sparkled. "I take it Kester hasn't told you very much about me."

Of course not. He hadn't told her very much about anything. Before Ursula could asked her what she meant, Zee shushed her. "Hugo's here."

"Where?"

"In the corner booth. Three o'clock. No wait. Nine o'clock? Whatever. To your left."

Ursula shifted in her seat.

"Don't look. He's seen me. Did you see him? Don't look!" Zee paused for what seem like a minute, but was probably only a few seconds. "Ok, you can look now, but don't be obvious. He's with a brunette. A lingerie model. I recognize her." Zee took a sip of her champagne. "Shall we chat with him?"

Zee's onslaught of directions had left Ursula confused. "Now? I was planning on cornering him here at the bar."

"He has bottle service. He won't leave his table." Zee slipped off her stool and started toward Hugo's booth. After smoothing down her hair, Ursula followed. Apparently, they were just going to walk up and introduce themselves to the superstar.

Hugo slouched into the pale leather of a large U-shaped booth. A bottle of champagne sat in an ice bucket shaped like a golden egg. Just to the side of the table hovered an enormous bald bodyguard, with a face the color of raw meat. A snake tattoo curled around his scalp. Even with fire magic on her side, Ursula didn't want to learn how she'd do in a fight against him. She'd have to find a way to leave the hulk behind, and get Hugo on his own.

She stopped just next to Zee at the edge of the table, clutching her champagne. She tried to loosen her shoulders so she didn't look quite so much like a grim reaper on a death hunt. *Except that's pretty much what I am.*

Zee plonked her champagne on the table, flashing the group a dazzling smile. The model grinned, throwing her hands in the air and trilling in a French accent, "Zee! I'm so glad you're here. You look amazing, as usual." She wore a tiny, beaded white dress, so delicate that it reminded Ursula of dew drops on a spider web. The woman draped a thin, tan arm over Hugo's shoulders.

She knows Zee. Zee didn't mention that.

The bodyguard turned his head. "Good to see you again, Zee. I was hoping we'd see you tonight."

And the bodyguard, too? Ursula frowned, staring at her companion. If Zee was a regular here, maybe she'd know the doorman, the coat man, and the bartender. But what were the chances she would happen to be close friends with a French lingerie model and Hugo Mode's bouncer?

Is this magic, too?

Chapter 15

Only Hugo seemed immune to Zee's spell. Over a pale green cocktail, he narrowed his eyes. Up close, his features were less plastic than they appeared in the music videos, and his dark blue irises glittered in the dim club's lights.

The model twirled the stem of her Manhattan glass. "Please. Join us, Zemfira."

Zee scooted in next to the model, while Ursula took a spot next to Hugo. Yanking a thin straw from his drink, he flicked tiny droplets over the table. "I was in the middle of a story."

Zee took a sip of her cocktail. "Don't let us stop you, Hugo."

Hugo shifted in his seat, looking around the table. "I was explaining why I had to dump Madison. I'm sure you saw it in the papers." He raked his fingers through his hair. "So my PR guy sent me Virginie here. We're supposed to go to the opera tomorrow. Like, to be seen together."

Virginie smiled.

"Oh?" Zee cocked her head, feigning sympathy. "What happened with Madison?"

Hugo frowned. "She bought a one-piece for our vacation in Saint Kitts. And there were going to be paparazzi there, obviously." His clipped accent and soft Rs suggested he had some history in a British boarding school, but also that he'd lived in the US long enough to give his voice a nasal quality. He sounded a bit like a 1920s radio announcer. Hugo turned to Ursula, dark eyebrows raised. "Do I look like the kind of guy who would date a girl with a one-piece?"

"I don't even know what that means."

"A one-piece bathing suit. A swimming costume." He spoke slowly, like she might have a head injury. "Like, not a bikini."

"Yeah, I get the bathing suit concept. I just didn't know there was a recognizable type of man whose girlfriend—"

Zee kicked her hard under the table and Hugo glared at her. *Shit. I'm supposed to be charming.*

She smiled, widening her eyes. "But of course I never wear swimming costumes—I mean bathing suits."

"You don't swim?

She licked her lips in what she hoped was a seductive gesture. "I only swim *au naturel.*"

Hugo shifted toward her, suddenly interested. "What else do you do *au naturel?*" His gaze rested firmly on her breasts before moving to her face.

"Oh, you know. *Things.*" She said it softly, gently placing a hand on Hugo's knee where Virginie couldn't see. Hopefully the knee-touching would distract him from the fact that she'd just tried to say "things" seductively.

Hugo stared into her eyes, and little smirk played around the corner of his mouth, before he abruptly looked away, slapping his hands on the table. "I need to go for a slash."

He pushed his leg against Ursula's, indicating that he wanted to get up from the table. Ursula scooted out, watching as Hugo and the bodyguard disappeared into the crowd. She took a sip of her champagne cocktail. *Charm him and isolate him. One point for Ursula.*

Her cell phone vibrated in her purse and she pulled it out. Zee's name popped up.

> r u going to follow him????
> should I?
> he wants u 2. now is ur chance.

Virginie was gushing to Zee about her upcoming opera date—as if the Russian ice princess were the warmest, friendliest person in the world. *Definitely magic of some sort.* Ursula would have to ask Zee about that later.

Straightening her short dress, Ursula stood and strode toward the bathrooms. She'd read somewhere that British soldiers were given a rum ration before they went over the trenches. She downed the rest of her cocktail. In Club Lalique, champagne would have to do.

She glanced down at the wyrm-skin purse tucked under her arm. It held a credit card, 250 American dollars, a tube of red lipstick, her lucky stone, and her cellphone. But most importantly, it contained a small parchment pact and a bone-colored pen with a razor-sharp nib. All she had to do was remind Hugo of his contract, jab his palm, and get him to sign in his blood. *Simple.*

The dance floor had begun to fill, and Ursula wove her way through the crowd of lithe, glittering women and besuited men. She tried not to think about the pen's second function. Kester had shown her a button hidden in its side that, when clicked, extended the nib into a small blade. That was the soul-reaping blade.

But she wasn't going to use that. Even by the Headsman's standards, that was a worst-case scenario. No one would agree to these bargains if word got round that Emerazel's hellhounds murdered everyone on their eighteenth birthdays. In order for the system to work, they needed signatures, not corpses.

In one of the corners, a gold-plated letter *M* hung above a dark alcove. Hugo's bodyguard stood just next to the entrance. As Ursula approached, the bodyguard gave her a wink. *Good. Hugo's definitely expecting me.*

She pushed open the door and slipped inside. There was a short, curly-haired man by the sinks with a white towel in his hand. A silver tray of cologne, Club Lalique matchbooks, and breath mints were arranged on the counter behind him. "Miss, this is the men's—" he started to say, but he fell silent when he glimpsed the one-hundred-dollar bill in Ursula's outstretched hand.

"Can you give us a few minutes?" she whispered.

He nodded silently, pointing to the end of a row of black stall doors.

Ursula's heels clacked over the tiles. Steel urinals lined the left wall under tall windows that granted a view of Manhattan. Any man taking a piss in Club Lalique could imagine that he was urinating on all the poor sods below. *Ugh. If the revolution came, I'd be on the wrong side of the palace walls.*

As she took a deep breath, she tapped the last door. "Hugo?" *Seductive. Sound seductive.* "It's Ursula," she breathed.

He cracked the door open, and she slipped inside, gripping her purse in anticipation. A window filled one entire wall, with only a thin black curtain covering the lower half for discretion. She could only hope no one was spending their evening scanning the Lalique bathrooms with a pair of binoculars.

Hugo pressed himself flat against the window, loosening his shirt collar. "Who are you?"

Ursula tried tossing her hair, but with the awkward jerk of her head it probably came off more like an involuntary twitch. "I'm Ursula. Zee's friend."

A cold sweat beaded on his forehead. "But I don't know who Zee is, or why my date seemed to know her. When I asked my bodyguard, he couldn't remember where he knew her from either."

Zee had *definitely* used some sort of spell on them. Time to dispense with the pleasantries. "You've just turned eighteen. I'm here about your pact with Emerazel."

He wiped a hand across his mouth, staring into her eyes. Emerazel's fire now blazed behind his indigo irises. "No one came on my birthday. I thought I'd gotten away with it."

She exhaled. So he knew the drill and this wasn't too much of a shock. "Sorry, no. You didn't get away. And now it's time to sign the papers." She stepped closer, pulling the pen from her bag and popping off the cap.

"And after I sign... I'm just a little fuzzy on what I'm agreeing to."

"When you die, Emerazel will take your soul to burn in the inferno for eternity." *Bollocks. I might need to work on my pitch a little.*

Hugo's blue eyes bulged. "I don't want to do it anymore."

"Of course you don't. It's awful—" Ursula sputtered. "—Not ideal, but you don't have a choice. The deal was, you gave your soul in exchange for—" She pulled the parchment out of her purse. "What was it you asked for? Fame?"

He swallowed hard, eyes open wide. "For people to hear my music and think it's amazing."

She thrust the contract toward him. "Hmmm... Well I guess it only works on a portion of the population. Anyway, you made the deal verbally. And now you get all the French models, Grammys, and green cocktails you can consume until you die. Considering most of the world has to live on $6 a day, you're getting quite lot. I mean sure, the eternal torment—"

"It's the soul part that concerns me." The pink had vanished from his cheeks. "It was just a lark with my mates. I thought it was a fairy story."

Was she going to have to act as a therapist with all the supplicants? She wasn't very good at this hand-holding stuff. How was she supposed to convince him this was a good idea? This was an *awful* idea. And even if he was a knob, she didn't want him to burn until the end of time. Bloody hell, she wasn't a psychopath—she definitely wasn't cut out for this gig. Still, she'd have to put forth the effort if she didn't want to face slaughter at Emerazel's hands—or perhaps Kester's.

She squared her shoulders. "Well, chin up, and all that. Here's the pen." She forced a smile onto her face. "Please sign, and everything will be fine... for a while." She couldn't bring herself to outright lie about it. She was a terrible liar.

"I'll have to spend eternity burning in the inferno," he sputtered.

This tidbit would likely be a bit of a sticking point in these negotiations. "From what I understand, the other option is starting your sentence now, and I'm sure you can see that's worse. You're young. Death is a long way off. Unless you refuse to sign, and then it's a very short way off."

Hugo's shoulders hunched. "What do you mean?"

Ursula gazed into his indigo eyes, trying to convey the gravity of the situation. "If you don't sign, I have to reap your soul now, and then it's straight to the fires. The torment can start now, or later." *God I don't want to be doing this.*

Hugo swallowed hard, his body trembling.

She depressed the button on the knife and the blade popped out with a snapping noise. She pressed the button again, retracting the blade. Hugo's eyes bulged.

"Of course, Emerazel doesn't want me to reap your soul now. It's bad for business if you guys don't get anything in return for eternity. She needs to keep the bargains coming, you know?"

Hugo tightened his lips, reaching for the pen with a resigned look on his face. But just as he was about to take it, he swung an elbow at her head.

Chapter 16

$\mathcal{U}$ rsula dodged, but not before Hugo's elbow grazed her cheekbone. She stumbled into the side of the stall. He followed his elbow with a wild haymaker, but she saw it coming. As she ducked, she struck upward with the sharp nib of the pen, slicing into his forearm.

Hugo let out a shrill scream, gripping his wrist. "You cut me."

"You're lucky I haven't killed you yet." She thrust the bloody pen toward him. "Sign. Now."

She was losing control of this situation. Kester had told her not to call attention to herself, that she was supposed to work in the shadows, but she had a hysterical pop star on her hands. Just as she thrust the parchment at him, Hugo lowered his shoulder and charged.

She tried to sidestep, but the stall was too narrow. He knocked her backward through the door and onto the marble tiles. Her head smacked against the floor, and pain exploded in her skull.

Clutching his arm, blood dripping between his fingers, he stood looking down at her. "Unbelievable," he said, then sprinted from the bathroom.

Ursula clenched her teeth, forcing herself to stand. Little flecks of light sparked in the periphery of her vision, and she held onto the edge of the sink for support. She rubbed the back of her throbbing head. *I can't let Hugo get away.* She had royally cocked this up, but at least the bathroom was still empty.

Outside the door she could hear Hugo shrieking, "A crazy woman cut me! Call the police!"

Shit. How was she supposed to get out quietly now? This place was littered with CCTV cameras, and everyone would be looking for her. If she screwed this up, Emerazel was going to take pleasure in personally executing her, for reasons Ursula did not even understand.

Think, Ursula. If she ran through the door, she could make it past Hugo's guard, but some well-meaning club patron would surely tackle her before she made it across the room. What about a diversion? If she used Emerazel's fire, she could set off the sprinklers and the fire alarm. In the ensuing chaos, she might make it to the elevator, but likely not much further before a bouncer caught her. She tightened her fists. *F.U., you bloody maniac, you dragged me into a hellish world I don't even understand.*

She needed to escape now—before anyone came in.

Outside the door someone shouted, "She's still in there, right?"

Sodding hell. So much for working in the shadows. In a few moments, Hugo's bodyguard and the bouncers would be in here. Her heart raced, heat blazing from her hand. If she didn't control herself, she'd be lighting something on fire. Or worse—she'd be lighting *someone* on fire. She glanced down at her hands, at the black smoke curling from her fingertips.

Then it came to her. She rushed to the door, gripping the doorknob. She closed her eyes, willing the heat from her hand into the metal. It was just enough to warp the latch shut.

Someone banged on the door, shouting and trying to turn the knob, but it wouldn't open.

Okay. I've locked myself in. But how was she supposed to get out? There were windows over the urinals, but they were sealed shut. And even if she could break one, she was fifteen stories up. She hadn't exactly brought a parachute. *Magic. I need to use magic.*

She grabbed a bottle of cologne and a matchbook from the attendant's tray. Gripping the bottle, she smashed off the top on the steel edge of the sink before pouring it on the floor in the shape of Emerazel's sigil. She struck a match and dropped it. Flames blazed around her.

What was that transportation spell Kester had chanted? He hadn't taught it to her. *Bollocks bollocks bollocks.*

An authoritative voice boomed through the door. "Is she still in there?"

She closed her eyes. *It's in my brain, somewhere.* In her mind's eye, she was back in the stone circle. Kester held her against his chest. She could almost feel his heartbeat next to her cheek. He'd intoned the strange magical words about a portal of fire, and Emerazel's grace. She repeated after him, and the spell slipped from her tongue, as though she'd known it all her life—which, perhaps, she had.

The bodyguard pounded on the door, shouting. But the fire was raging all around her, and she dissolved into ash.

Chapter 17

Ursula blazed into the sigil room before doubling over with a coughing fit. Hot soot seared her lungs, and her body burned with preternatural pain. *I really need to remember to hold my damn breath.* At least she'd escaped the club in one piece. Granted, she didn't have Hugo's signature on the pact, and she'd left Zee behind, but neither was she in handcuffs in the back of a police cruiser.

Footsteps sounded in the hall, and Kester appeared at the doorway. "What happened? How did you get here?" He paused, sniffing. "Did you douse yourself in cologne?"

She'd never thought the sight of his strange green eyes would be a relief. "Sigil spell. Forgot to hold my breath." She wiped tears from her smoke-stung eyes. "And I had to use Giorgio Armani as the accelerant."

"You look gorgeous." Candlelight danced in eyes, and his gaze trailed over her short dress. "But I still don't understand how you got here. I never taught you that spell."

"I remembered what you said."

He stepped closer, narrowing his eyes. "Impressive as that is, I'm a little alarmed that you felt the need to use it. You collected Hugo's signature, right?"

Ursula brushed ash off her dress. "Things got messy. Hugo made a scene."

A muscle clenched in his jaw. "You didn't get his signature? Then why are you here?"

"I had to escape." *How do I explain this?* "Hugo ran away and started shrieking that I wanted to stab him." *The truth again, I guess.*

Kester moved closer, irises burning. Had she really found his face a welcome sight? He looked—terrifying. "We're supposed to work in the shadows. If your face becomes known, Emerazel will destroy you. If you fail to get a target's signature, as you have, Emerazel will destroy you. She hates you, for reasons I don't understand, and she seemed very eager to reap your soul. I told you the importance of getting this right."

Oh, God. I can't escape the lectures about my own failure, even among the hellhounds. "You told me the importance, but that doesn't make me any more experienced. You and I both agreed it was insane that Emerazel wanted to send me off without training. I don't know why you're suddenly surprised that it didn't turn out well. And you know what? I still don't understand what she wants with everyone's souls. What does she do with them?"

"It's the stakes that mattered. You couldn't afford to fail." Ignoring her question, he rooted her in place with his gaze, and stepped closer. "I don't know why you didn't just sign the pact like I told you to in the first place. Then neither of us would have to worry about this mess."

She crossed her arms, taking a step back, until she was backed up against the wall. "I don't know—why didn't I sign that pact?" She touched her finger to her lips. "Oh yeah, I guess I was a bit put off by the 'burning in eternity' thing. It sounded unpleasant— which, by the way, is why I'm not going to be a great salesman for this deal, because only a psychopath would want someone to burn forever. Hugo gets some cash in exchange for everlasting torture? And I'm supposed to convince him that's a good deal? It's insane. I'm not a monster, Kester."

"Oh, but you are," he snarled. "And so am I." He pressed his palms to the wall on either side of her head, boxing her in.

Adrenaline surged. "I never wanted this."

"You and I don't get the luxury of morality and soul-searching. You asked to be just like me when you wanted a trial, and now you're one of the demons. And I notice you quite happily accept the lodging and the payment for your work."

White-hot anger burned her cheeks. "All I wanted from life was a normal job, enough for food and rent, and a couple of normal friends. I was happy in my hovel of an apartment. It was my home, before you told everyone I overdosed. I don't need three bedrooms in a mansion, or a four-hundred-dollar haircut. And I don't need gold ingots. For fuck's sake."

His eyes bored into her, and for a second, she thought he might tear into her neck like he'd slaughtered the ewe. "Has it occurred to you that there might be worse monsters out there than hellhounds like me?"

Her fingernails dug into her palms. "Worse than agents of perpetual agony? Is that so?"

"There are monsters who would torture you without your consent, who prey on the innocent—unlike hellhounds, who approach only those who've agreed to the bargain. Whether you remember it or not, you agreed to serve Emerazel, and so did Hugo. So did I. Now we all reap the consequences. That's life."

"And you're fine with that?"

A low growl escaped him, and she caught a glimpse of lengthening fangs. He was going to murder her. "Don't you get it? It doesn't matter if I'm fine with it. You can't fight it. Emerazel is as old, as powerful, and as immovable as the stars. If we don't reap the souls, she's more than capable of taking them herself. Hugo's soul will be collected whether you do it or not. But if you defy the goddess, you will join him in the inferno. In fact, Emerazel will want your soul now for your mistake."

A hollow opened in the pit of Ursula's stomach. "For one cock-up?"

Kester's face was stony. "Hugo is internationally famous. Your image will be plastered across the news. If I don't tell Emerazel about your failure, she'll slaughter me along with you."

Ursula fought the urge to vomit. *Of course.* There had been CCTV cameras all over the club, recording her image. She could already imagine the headline: *Insane Mystery Girl Fakes Death, Attacks Hugo Modes.*

"Maybe no one remembers me," she said, her voice breaking.

An eternity in the inferno. Kester was going to give her up to Emerazel. Her heart pounded. She needed to get out of here. Glancing around for an escape route, her eyes landed on the chandelier. She could leap up, kick Kester in the face, and bolt into the elevator. But it wouldn't be on her floor, and she'd have to stand there waiting for it to arrive while Kester summoned the goddess of fire and brimstone. *Bollocks, Ursula.*

Could she make it out a window? Did windows in penthouses even open? Even if she did escape, the goddess had total control over her mind and body. There was no way to run from her.

Raw panic flooded her body, and she began pacing like a caged animal.

Kester's phone buzzed, and he stepped away from her, yanking it from his pocket. After a moment, he exhaled, his shoulders visibly relaxing. "You are *very* lucky Zee was there."

"Why? What happened?" Hope bloomed in her chest.

He shoved the phone in his pocket. "Zee was able to glamour everyone at the club. They won't remember you."

"How?"

"Zee's a fae. That's one of the reasons I sent her along."

"Fae? I don't even know what that is." She was still vibrating with panic; her statement came out as an angry shout.

"The fae can influence people's thoughts. Luckily for you, she convinced the security guards to hand over the tapes of your panicking face."

Ursula loosed a long breath, steadying her nerves. She slid her face into her hands, trying not to imagine Hugo burning in hellfire. "A relief from my death sentence. I could kiss Zee. And now I just need to find Hugo. I heard him saying he was going to the opera tomorrow night."

Kester smirked. "You see? The prospect of your own torment clarifies your thinking, doesn't it?"

She glowered at him. "I don't need you to gloat about it."

"Obviously, you need training. I can give you until tomorrow night to collect Hugo's soul, but beyond that I'll have to report to Emerazel. Even this amount of leniency is risking my own skin." His glacial voice chilled her blood. "And do not create a scene again, or we'll both end up in flames. You have one thousand pages in your ledger—a thousand souls you must collect. Don't give Emerazel the pleasure of reaping your soul before you get through them."

He pivoted, stalking out of the room, and Ursula was left on her own to stare at the cold vastness of New York.

Chapter 18

*U*rsula hugged herself and crossed into the cavernous living room. The apartment felt noticeably colder without Kester in it.

On an oak coffee table, an uncorked champagne bottle rested in a bucket of ice, two empty glasses next to it. She sighed. Kester had obviously been planning a little celebration, assuming she'd somehow succeed.

Instead, she was left on her own. Again.

Her sense of loneliness threatened to crush the breath out of her. She had no one—not in a world where people kept their secrets closely guarded, disclosing only the tiniest glimmers of truth.

She poured herself a glass and collapsed onto the stiff crimson settee. Might as well make use of this.

She tried to ignore the ache of isolation gnawing at her chest, and flipped open her phone, scanning the news. A story about a crazed fan at Club Lalique was the top story. Fortunately, Zee had apparently glamoured everyone into believing the assailant was a blue-haired man with a tattoo of a spider on his cheek. It was a bizarre enough description that it wouldn't lead to any false arrests. Only Hugo would still remember the truth.

Kester was right. She needed to find him as soon as she could, or the truth would get out.

And yet, Kester's secrecy made her blood boil. The man was full of mysteries: the death of Henry, the truth about Zee, his own mysterious past, the locked library books—even the forbidden room upstairs.

At this point, she was entirely dependent on him to tell her about this bizarre new world, yet the guy clearly wasn't trustworthy. He was *the Headsman*, for crying out loud. He'd even referred to *himself* as a monster. How could she trust anything he said? What if all of this was a lie, and there was another way out?

Moreover—what was it he was so desperate to keep from her, that stood locked in her own apartment? He'd said this was her place, but he sure didn't act that way. There were rooms she couldn't enter, while Kester was free to swan in and out whenever he pleased. She drained another glass of champagne. She was going to start finding out secrets on her own.

She refilled her champagne flute and rose. Clutching the glass, she hurried upstairs into the hallway. As the bubbly took hold of her mind, her mood brightened. *I'm not a screw-up. I just have a normal aversion to sending people to hell.*

At the end of the dark corridor, the forbidden oak door shone with an otherworldly light.

Slowly, she approached the door, its surface punctuated by iron spikes. It certainly didn't look inviting, but maybe some kind of answers lay inside. She was done with secrets. She gripped the doorknob, cursing when it wouldn't twist open. Kester hadn't lied when he said it was locked. She'd need to find another way in.

She stalked down the hall to the botanical room, which stood adjacent to the locked door. She inhaled deeply. *Oranges, rosemary, and marigolds.* Kester hadn't just had the place cleaned—he'd had the whole greenroom replanted.

She stepped inside, shutting the door behind her. In the frost-covered panes, Manhattan's lights appeared hazy and distorted.

She gazed down at the yellow taxis and the few pedestrians foolhardy enough to brave the winter night. What were they doing, with their normal human lives? Hurrying to their parents, their spouses, their lovers? Maybe just slipping down the block for last call at the bar?

Still agitated, she took a long slug of her champagne. She'd grown sick of all secrets and mystery. She didn't want to be the bloody Mystery Girl. She wanted to know where she came from, who her parents were, and how she'd ended up with Emerazel's mark carved in her shoulder. But short of that information, she at least wanted to know what lurked in the locked room in her own apartment. *Is that too much to ask?*

She glanced at the windowsill. A little brass handle protruded from the iron rail, and she pulled at it, cracking it open. *I guess that answers my question about penthouse windows.*

If she was going to break into the locked room, her only hope was to climb along the outside wall and through one of its windows. She drained the last drops of her champagne. She'd need a little Dutch courage for this.

A hard push was enough to open the window wide. A frigid breeze blew into the room. Ursula held tight to the sill, leaning out, and peered to her left, at the windows of the locked room just eight feet away.

A small stone ledge jutted from the wall a few feet below, barely large enough for her to stand on. A giddy thrill bubbled through her—one which turned terrifying when she looked past the ledge at the streets below. She was at least fifteen stories up.

She edged back into the safety of the conservatory. She needed a plan. One slip on the ledge would send her plunging to her death. Crawling would be safest. On her hands and knees she'd be more stable.

Still, she would need a way to pry open the window of the locked room. A crowbar would be ideal, but it was too late for a trip to the hardware store. A small blade might work, and that was something she had.

She hurried to her bedroom, snatching the dagger from under her pillow.

Her pulse raced as she returned to the conservatory. The window was still open. She held her breath and crawled through it and onto the ledge, keeping the knife clenched between her teeth.

A thick layer of crusted snow covered the ledge. A strong gust of wind blew up her skirt, pushing it up over her waist and exposing her tiny thong. If any eagle-eyed New Yorkers were watching from below, they'd catch a wondrous view of her arse. *Why didn't I change into trousers first?* Her bare knees were freezing against the ice. She'd been too charged up to think this through, as usual.

Another gust of wind blew her hair into her eyes. She wanted to brush it away, but she couldn't lift a hand from the ledge without slipping.

Her heart hammered against her ribs. As she inched toward the window, she did her best to ignore the auburn tresses slapping her cheeks. She crawled forward, and the ice on the ledge thickened. She glanced down at the street fifteen stories below. The falling snow obscured most of the details, and it looked as though she was peering into a bottomless void. *What the hell was I thinking? This is insane.* She started to edge backward, but her knee slipped from the ledge, and she scrambled to press herself close against the building.

She gasped, and the knife almost slipped from her teeth. She didn't want to move forward or backward at this point, but she obviously couldn't stay here. *I really am a first-class idiot.* She'd failed at holding down a job, keeping a boyfriend, achieving any sort of education or achievement. Tonight she'd screwed up her hellhound job, and now she was stuck on an icy ledge fifteen stories above Manhattan's streets. No one would really care if she lived or died. Her only contribution to the world so far was her ability to light things on fire.

Although... A thought sparked in her mind. Maybe she could channel Emerazel's fire and melt some of the ice.

But how to do it? Before when she'd used the fire, she hadn't uttered any Angelic to call up the fire. Neither, as far as she could tell, had Kester. It had just sort of been there when she needed it, burning her veins and channeling into her fingers until they glowed, white-hot. Maybe she just needed to envision it.

She imagined her palms burning, her fingertips blazing like candles.

She glanced at her hands. *Nothing.*

As she closed her eyes, she envisioned a raging forest fire. She peeked at her fingertips, frozen to the ledge. A frigid gust of wind blew up her skirt again. How did you explain to a hospital how you'd got frostbite on your arse?

Bollocks. Imagining fire couldn't be it. And when she thought about it, she hadn't even known she had this ability when she'd burned Muppet in Rufus's club.

Another snow squall whipped by her ears. Her hands were freezing against the stone. Damn it, this had been a terrible idea.

And then she felt it: a distant trickle of heat. Almost as soon as it was there, it flickered away again.

Ok, what did I just do? The wind blew, I looked at my freezing fingers, I swore. That had to be it. The fire came from anger. She could do anger.

Ursula closed her eyes, imagining Rufus and Madeleine cuddling on his sofa, surrounded by empty wine bottles and expensive cheese. The familiar warmth flowed in her veins. This was a start, but it wasn't going to clear a path anytime soon. She didn't really give a fuck about Madeleine. She needed more heat.

In her mind's eye, Rufus leaned over his desk. "The problem, Urse, is that you have no goals—no vision," he whinged.

The heat poured out of Ursula like liquid metal from a crucible. The ice in front of her melted with a hiss and a burst of steam.

Rufus continued to play his part in her imagination. "You're just a sad cow who will never make anything of your life."

Flames burst from her palms pouring along the ledge. Sparks fell toward the street below in a waterfall of hellfire. Ursula watched the fire, entranced by its beauty, until a great gust of freezing wind snapped her out of her reverie. *Get a grip.*

One the plus side, the ice had fully melted. Ursula inched forward over the stone. When she reached the forbidden room's windows, she pressed her face against the glass, but all she could see were heavy curtains. She wouldn't learn any secrets unless she actually broke into the room.

She kneeled flat against the wall, the dagger still clenched between her teeth. Gingerly, she released it into her hand, careful not to slice herself with the sharp edge. Holding it firmly, she slipped the blade into the crack between the window and the sill. A twist of the dagger's hilt ratcheted the window open.

Slipping her fingers into the gap, she pulled it open further. Crouched on the ledge, she didn't have the leverage to open it all the way without leaning dangerously close to death. She would have to clamber in as best she could.

Chapter 19

*T*eeth chattering, she squeezed through on her stomach, tumbling onto the floor of a pitch-black room. She crouched, clutching the dagger, and listened. All she could hear was a soft hiss of air from the window behind her head. Otherwise, the room lay silent as a tomb.

She rose to her feet, holding the dagger defensively. She still shivered, and it shook in her hand. When nothing leapt at her from the darkness, she pulled open the curtains, letting light fall on the room.

She almost dropped her knife when she saw what lay before her.

The interior looked like some sort of alchemical laboratory, with a rib-vaulted ceiling that arched high above. A small forge stood in a hearth, and shelves of strange glassware lined the walls: rows of delicate Alembic flasks, Dimroth condensers, Thiele tubes, and Thistle funnels.

How in God's name do I even know these words?

Tentatively, she crossed the room to the shelves, reading the hand-written labels on the flasks. They bore names like *nigredo, aqua regia, dragon's blood*, and *philosophic mercury*. She sniffed the air. *Stale creosote.* This laboratory hadn't been used in a long time.

She turned, surveying the rest of the room. The walls were painted a deep indigo blue, patterned with golden astrological symbols and strange alchemical glyphs that twinkled and drifted like stars in the sky.

Ursula crossed back to the window, pulling it closed. If she left it open, Kester would know she'd been in here. With no breeze, an eerie silence descended and the tension returned to her shoulders. Ursula let out a slow breath. She could hear her heart thrumming in her chest. *Why am I so nervous? There's no one here.*

Slipping the dagger into her belt, she crossed to another rack of shelves. A thin layer of dust covered the flasks. She slid her fingers around one of the containers, picking it up. As she blew off the dust, she held it in the pale of light of the window. Her face reflected in its surface, and behind her the laboratory. Even an old bed, tucked into the shadows.

A cold chill slithered up her spine. In the glass's reflection, it almost looked like a dark shape lay on the bed. *A body.*

Ursula hardly dared to breathe. She turned, placing the flask back on its shelf as quietly as she could. Slowly, she drew the dagger from her belt again.

She approached the bed, gripping her weapon. An enormous, muscled man lay atop a deep crimson bedspread. He was huge. *Bloody hell, is he even human?*

"Hey?" she called out in a low whisper.

He didn't move.

"Hey!" She said it louder this time, but he remained motionless.

She moved closer, hardly daring to breathe. The dagger trembled violently in her fist.

His eyes were closed and raven black hair framed his face—his perfect, sublimely beautiful face. He had the most stunning features Ursula had ever seen: sharp cheekbones, a strong jaw, and perfect, kissable lips. His body was strong and muscled, and his skin had a deep Mediterranean tan, rich and warm, even in the faint light. Her dagger stopped its frantic shaking.

He must be asleep, right? Surely I don't fancy a corpse. At least, his warm olive color suggested that he lived.

"Hello?" She shouldn't be here. She should turn around, wrench open the door, and never come back into the forbidden chamber again. But something drew her toward him. Maybe it was his thrilling masculine allure, or maybe it was simple compassion. What if he needed her help?

She stared at the stranger's chest. It neither rose nor fell, and the only sounds of breathing were her own anxious breaths. "Who are you?" she whispered, more to herself than to him.

Muscular arms lay crossed on his chest, and his feet were bare. He looked like an effigy carved on a medieval tomb. He wore dark jeans and a grey t-shirt. Thin iron chains snaked around his body. When she looked closer, she could see tendrils of dark air curling off him, like black smoke.

What the hell is that?

If he was dangerous, at least he was bound, but she still clutched the dagger in case he sprang to life, desperate for her blood.

Slowly, she reached for his wrist, tracing her fingers over his warm skin. As soon as she touched him, something sparked like an electrical charge. It coursed through her body—a thrilling vibration of dark and ancient power.

She exhaled, trying to focus. *Definitely a magical creature.* She touched his wrist again, trying to ignore that rush of magical energy. The man had no *actual* pulse.

You don't feel dead, but you don't breathe, and your heart doesn't beat.

Her mind turned over the possibilities. He could be a fresh corpse that Kester had stored after a recent kill—but the warmth of his skin and that energy that radiated from him seemed so alive. Plus, there was a certain tautness to his muscles, a look of composure in his perfect face.

Perhaps he was a vampire? Heartless, strong, and gorgeous. With the way things were going, vampirism didn't seem like such a stretch, but it was the middle of the night, and weren't vampires nocturnal? Maybe he'd been subdued with some sort of sleeping spell, and he wouldn't awake until the right person kissed him. Tempting, but if the corpse scenario turned out to be accurate, there wouldn't be enough soap in the world to clean off her mouth.

She took another step closer, studying the man. With a burst of horror, she realized the crimson wasn't the color of the bedspread beneath him. Her heart threatened to gallop out of her chest.

It was blood. Gallons of dried blood.

Ursula leapt back from the bed, almost tripping on the rug. The blood stained the sheets in a crimson halo. She scanned the body for wounds, but whatever had injured him had left no visible mark. Something very bad had happened to the stranger, but she didn't know what. Maybe the Headsman had murdered him.

A terrifying reality settled over her like a burial shroud: she was in way over her head.

Gripping the dagger, she moved to the door. She could see no sign of the magical lock and she desperately hoped that meant it would open from the inside. She twisted the handle and relief washed over her when it turned in her grasp. A gentle push cracked the door open and she slipped out, shutting it behind her.

She crouched in the doorway of her bedroom, watching the door. Her eyes were beginning to water, but she didn't blink. The dagger remained ready at her side.

Even though his chest didn't rise and he had no pulse, the beautiful man had felt alive when she'd touched him. His warm skin had seemed to exude a powerful, shadowy magic. If he was alive, then she had to consider the possibility that she might have disturbed his slumber. What sort of a creature could lose that much blood and live? She'd actually been able to *feel* the intensity of his power. Hadn't Kester said something like "there might be worse monsters than hellhounds?" She had a bad feeling that she might now know what he was talking about.

The stranger could burst through the door at any moment and rip her to shreds. In fact, maybe he was the monster who had slaughtered the last hellhound. Then again, if he was such a threat, Kester would have locked the door from the inside too. Her pulse began to slow. She was probably safe for now.

Ursula slid the dagger into her belt before she got up from her crouch and walked to the conservatory. Her hands were still shaking as she shut the window and collected her empty champagne flute. She couldn't have Kester discovering her unsanctioned nocturnal activity, or he'd send her straight to Emerazel.

She closed her eyes, and for a moment, her mind flashed with an image of her body burning in hellfire, her skin blistering and blackening. She shuddered, shoving her fingers into her hair. *I'm going to lose my mind.*

Maybe Kester was right about her. Maybe she'd quickly shove her moral qualms aside to do what she needed to save herself. After all, she only had herself to rely on in this world.

She tightened her fists, sighing. Tomorrow, she would hunt down Hugo Modes at the opera, even if it meant she'd become a monster herself.

Chapter 20

$\mathcal{U}$rsula poured herself a cup of coffee, her mind rejoicing in the rich aroma. An old rock song played on the radio—Iggy Pop, *The Passenger*. She loved this song, and even through the fog of exhaustion, part of her wanted to dance, just to feel human again. Clearly, she was running on some kind of insane adrenaline at this point, trying to drown out all thoughts of the man or demon upstairs.

She'd gotten a few hours of sleep—if fitfully rolling around, trying not to think about impending doom, was considered sleeping. There'd been just one period of rest between two and six a.m., until the sound of her dagger falling to the floor woke her with a shout.

Morning's arrival had been a blessing, restoring some sense of normalcy. After she'd climbed from her sheets, she'd slipped into a pair of thin grey trousers, her thigh-high boots, and a bright blue top—one of the few bright things Kester had bought her. She'd pulled up her hair into a high ponytail, and carefully applied her eyeliner. Monsters be damned, she would wrench back some sense of control and normalcy over her own life.

She took a long sip of coffee and cast an approving glance at her reflection in the chrome coffee maker. *So maybe I live in a hellish new world of monsters and headsmen because F.U. sent me here. I'm not going to let myself fall completely to pieces.*

The caffeine rejuvenated her. With the radio on, she almost felt like herself again, and she let her hips sway to the music, dancing along as Iggy Pop sang about stars coming out in the night sky. She loved that part...

Footsteps clacked over the floor, and she whirled, nearly spitting out her coffee.

Kester stood in the doorway, wearing a black T-shirt and dark jeans. It would have been a perfectly sensible ensemble, if it weren't for the sheathed sword at his waist, and the strange alchemical tattoos covering his forearms. "I like the way you move."

She narrowed her eyes. "You can't just stride in here whenever you want."

"What are your plans to find Hugo?" he demanded.

"Is there any way you can start knocking, or at least calling first?" What she really wanted to ask, but resisted, was *Hey, can you tell me about that gorgeous and terrifying man upstairs?* The Headsman clearly wasn't in a mood for insubordination from a novice hellhound today.

"What is your plan?" he repeated.

"I'm pouring you some coffee first. You seem cranky." She grabbed a ceramic mug from one of the cabinets, filling it with coffee. "I'll approach Hugo at the Metropolitan Opera this evening. He's going with some French model. I'll get his soul." She slid the coffee across the table.

"And you think he'll be more agreeable tonight?" His gaze roamed over her fitted blue top.

Is he checking me out? "My plan is to do whatever it takes so I don't have to burn for eternity." She hated what she was becoming, but self-preservation came first. She'd have to sort through the ethics later. "And I was hoping Zee could come again and use her fairy magic."

"Of course." Kester arched an eyebrow, pulling out his cell phone. "Gods know you'll need some help." He tapped on his phone, then took a sip of his coffee.

"Seriously, though. You need to knock. I could have been in my underwear."

For the first time in two days, he flashed a smile. "That's hardly going to put me off."

"Do you want me busting into your apartment?"

"Fine. I'll knock next time." His phone buzzed, and he flicked open a text. "Zee says she'd love to go to the opera. She'll meet you at seven p.m." Kester put his phone back in his pocket. "Right. Now that that's settled, I believe we have some training to do."

☙ ☙ ☙

Barefoot, Kester stood in the armory, inspecting the blades. "Choose your weapon."

She picked up Honjo from the rack. Ursula's gazed flicked to his powerful arms, tattooed with the same glyphs and astrological signs that covered the walls in the sleeper's room. "Why are we training with blades? Am I supposed to force Hugo to sign at knifepoint?"

"If that's what it takes," said Kester. "But this isn't for Hugo. He's not the only thing you need to worry about."

"What do you mean?"

He leveled his green eyes on her. "We're not the only monsters out there, Ursula. There are legions of demons who want us dead, and if they ever scent your fear, they will tear you to shreds. For whatever reason, Emerazel won't allow me to accompany you on your mission, but I'm going to make sure you don't die. And that means you need to know how to protect yourself. Understood?"

Ursula raised her eyebrows. "That sounds comforting and ominous at the same time."

"I'm your mentor. Whatever Emerazel's problem is, you're my responsibility, and I'll keep you alive. I've seen you use a sword, and you look like you've had some serious training already. It's a good place to start."

Maybe he was on her side, even if he was the Headsman. She really had no clue at this point. "When you said there are other monsters out there... " *Do you mean monsters like the bleeding guy across from my room?* She was desperate to ask about the sleeping stranger, but she bit her tongue. "What types of monsters do you mean?"

A muscle tightened in his jaw. "I forget how little you know."

"The only things I know about this world, I've learned from you. Which is basically fuck-all."

"We don't have time to go into the whole history, but I can tell you this. Light demons have been warring with the dark ones for a hundred thousand years. Our gods are in a race to collect souls, and that means you're a prime target for the shadow demons."

A shiver crawled up her spine. *Is that what is sleeping in the room across from mine?* "What makes them dark? Are they more evil?"

"No. It's just how the universe keeps magic in balance, with equal amounts of light and dark magic, like day and night. Only the fae are neutral. What you need to know is that you can kill shadow demons with certain weapons—especially those made with iron. They must be charmed with the right spells."

She suppressed a shudder, thinking of the sleeping man upstairs, and the ancient magic that coiled off him in electrifying midnight tendrils. "And some of these shadow demons might be after me tonight?"

"Perhaps. And that's why you need to learn to fight them." He pulled a small glass jar full of amber liquid from his pocket, then a handkerchief. He poured some of the oil onto the cloth. "I'm going to anoint your sword with Zornhau's oil. It's a salve that protects a blade from damage. Also prevents you from seriously injuring your opponent—limits the chance of an accidental *coup de main* considerably."

He held out his hand for the sword, and Ursula handed him the hilt. Kester rubbed the blade with the cloth, holding Honjo with a casual confidence that told Ursula that he was an experienced swordsman. Once the katana glistened with gold, he handed it back to her. "Just remember to clean the sword thoroughly when we're done. The steel is useless with the oil on it."

Backing into the center of the room, he drew his own sword from the sheath at his waist. It was the same blade Ursula had used at her battle with the Moor fiend, already glistening with amber oil. "Are you ready?"

Ursula gripped the Katana, planting her feet in a fighting stance. "Whenever you are."

Kester lunged, his sword striking hers like the fang of a venomous serpent. Ursula deflected his blade with a deft parry, but he stepped back before she could counter. She danced closer, looking for an opening, but he sidestepped, staying just out of range. Their swords clashed, though Kester didn't break a sweat.

He pushed in, striking. "I spoke with Zee about your encounter with Hugo."

"Oh?" Apparently Kester was planning on incorporating a bit of chit-chat into their bout.

"She told me you argued with him about bathing suits." His tone was somewhere between a joke and an accusation. She slashed at him, but he parried easily. He was trying to throw her off her game by bringing this up now.

"Yes, Hugo was saying that he broke up with his girlfriend because—"

But before she could detail Hugo's misogynistic attitude towards woman's swimwear, Kester cut in. "I don't care what he said. My point is: you need to lure people in. Make them think they can trust you, that they want to please you." He flicked his blade, and she had to leap to the side to avoid being skewered.

"He seemed to like it when I told him I prefer to swim nude."

She caught a flicker of interest in Kester's eyes. *Two can play at the distraction game.* She hadn't failed to notice his eyes lingering on her cleavage whenever he got the chance.

"Nude?" He parried, and a thin sheen of sweat covered his forehead. "Is that so? You like the feel of the water against your bare skin?"

You've got him, Ursula. Keep going. "Yes, and I eat ice cream nude, because I like when it melts and drips down my breasts."

Nope. That was just weird. Really, really weird.

Weird or not, Kester faltered. With him off balance, Ursula stabbed at him. He dodged, but not before the tip of her katana nicked his ribs.

"Touché," Kester swiped the blood from the hole in his shirt and sucked it off his finger. He lifted his sword again. "We're not done."

"You want more of that?"

His sword clashed off Honjo. "You got off on the wrong foot with Hugo." He began to circle her, fire flashing in his eyes.

"Is this some sort of interrogation?"

"Yes."

Kester feinted at her head and then slashed at her knees. Ursula just barely deflected the blow with a downward swipe. He moved out of range before she could counter. She couldn't keep up with him.

His fiery gaze was hypnotic. "To succeed as a hellhound, you need both steel and silk, weapons and charm. You can't always force a signature. Sometimes you must lure in a debtor, convince him it's in his best interest to sign over his soul."

She thrust her sword at him, but he dodged. "You think I can't do that?"

"Zee said you have all the social graces of a water buffalo."

What. A. Bitch. "That's a load of bollocks." Ursula said it confidently, but inwardly she knew he'd touched on something. How many foster families had she been through? Four? Five? She'd lost count. Even the people she'd loved had told her the same thing.

Rufus's voice rang in the hollows of her mind: "The truth is, you're a sad cow who won't make anything of your life." Hollowness welled in her chest. Worst of all was the dawning realization that this character deficit might explain her amnesia. Was she some sort of magical reject? Forced to forget her past and then cast aside because she put everyone off? Was it possible that no one had ever loved her?

She felt tears prick behind her eyelids. *Bloody hell, Ursula. Do not cry. Do not cry.* Not in front of Kester. She needed to prove she had both the skill and character to be a hellhound, or she could forget about that whole "self-preservation" thing.

"So—" Kester held up his hand and then laid his blade on the mat indicating that the sword-play was on hold. "Prove it."

"Prove what?"

Kester stared at her like she was off her meds. "Prove that you know how to charm people. Look approachable."

She scowled. "How am I supposed to prove that?"

"By not making that face, for one thing."

She lowered Honjo and straightened. She pushed out her chest, smiled and cocked her head.

"Much better, but your smile doesn't look genuine. You'll need to soothe him. Keep him from panicking."

Ursula felt a familiar heat rise within in her. First, she had to force people to sign away their souls. On top of that, she had to condemn them with a lullaby, cooing at them as she consigned them to hell? How much would she end up hating herself if this was the person she was to become? But she couldn't say that out loud—not to Kester.

"Put down your sword." Kester stepped closer, his green eyes drinking her in. "Ask me to sign the pact."

She tucked her sword in the corner of the room before straightening her shoulders. She tried to force a pleasant smile onto her face. "You just need to sign here." She pointed to an imaginary pact in her hand, using a firm but gentle voice, like she was a police negotiator convincing a suicidal man to step away from the edge of a bridge.

Kester answered in a perfect impression of Hugo's posh British accent. "No I don't want to sign. This must be some sort of stunt. Are you having me on?"

"This is not a stunt. Hasn't your career taken off since you asked Emerazel for her power?" The content was good, but Ursula stumbled over the last few words.

He continued to ape Hugo's accent. "I'm not doing it. I'm not giving my soul away."

"You have to. You agreed to the bargain."

He shook his head. "Relax your shoulders. You're supposed to look alluring."

"How did you do it, when you broke into my kitchen? I was ready to bash your head in with a frying pan, and then the next thing I knew, I wanted to do whatever you wanted."

"Some of that was my natural charm, but some of it was magic. It's taken me a long time to learn how to bend people's wills, and I've honed the skill well. You were surprisingly resistant to my influence. I don't encounter that often."

"I'd had a very bad day." She eyed him warily. "You can mind-control me?"

"It's not something I use unless I must. In any case, you don't have that skill, so you'll have to rely on your charms." A smile played over his lips.

"And my razor-sharp wit."

"Right. Get on with it."

She closed her eyes, trying to remember how Kester had approached her in her kitchen. His intense eyes had slid all over her body, like he was memorizing each one of her curves. He'd somehow managed to project strength and temptation at the same time. Gazing at him, she stepped closer, letting her eyes trail over his strong arms, and down the front of his shirt for a moment. Just inches from him, she stared up at him, eyes wide and innocent.

He leaned in, whispering in her ear. "Closer."

She pressed forward, relishing the heat that radiated from his body, and his delicious scent—cedar and fresh earth. It wasn't hard to feign attraction.

She stared into his eyes. "If you sign now, you'll get everything you ever wanted. Everything you could desire for the rest of your life." She had no idea what possessed her, but she traced her finger down the front of his chest, feeling the hard body underneath.

His breathing sped up, and he grabbed her hand, his fingers burning. "That's good. But you don't need to touch him. Not if you don't want to. You only need to lure him in."

Her body grew hotter, and she could feel her cheeks flushing. "I guess I've got the silk thing covered."

"Good. Now I want to see how you can use your fire." He stepped away, picking up his sword. This time when he faced her, his smile had turned predatory; hellfire flashed in his eyes. Ursula's stomach lurched.

His blade whipped at her gut in a blur of metal, but she dove out of reach. "Use your fire," he said, his voice husky.

Her sword clashed against his, and her heartbeat raced. He was going to disembowel her. "I don't know how."

His sword flashed again and she was only just able to deflect it above her head. The sound of clashing steel rang in her ears.

"Use your fire," he commanded, louder this time, eyes burning with hellfire.

She tried to envision flames blazing through her body. "I'm trying." She had to leap into the air to avoid losing her legs as his sword passed clean under her.

"Try harder." He struck at her, and she parried. Immediately he struck again. She deflected, gasping for breath. Sweat broke out on her brow. His attacks grew faster, driving her across the room. She had to call up the flames, but she could hardly focus her attention with Kester's sword threatening to rip her to shreds.

She stepped back, banging against the wall. Retreating was no longer an option. Kester struck again, locking his sword with hers, and slowly pushed his blade closer and closer to her face. His breath was warm against her cheek, fueled by Emerazel's flames.

Her arms burned with exhaustion. She hadn't been training, and her muscles weren't ready for this. Kester's blade pushed closer, grazing her cheek. *He's going to cut my face off.* As panic flooded her, an image burst into her mind: a blood-soaked floor, a crumpled body, twitching fingertips. What *was* that? She didn't recognize the images, but a hollow opened in her chest all the same, a void so deep and cavernous it could never be filled. Her heart ached.

Kester's eyes were incandescent, the heat from his body overwhelming. He was going to kill her. She was certain of it. "Get away from me." Fire kindled in her core, filling the void with a burning sensation. Almost instantly, it turned violently hot, like a dying star. Strength burned through her nerve endings. *I am hellfire, and I will bathe the world in flames.*

Fire blasted out of her body, knocking Kester away.

He dropped his sword, holding out his hands. "Get it under control."

Glorious flames poured from her body in waves. She was no longer standing in the armory. She was in the center of a volcanic maelstrom, blessed with the power of a god.

Distantly she heard a hissing noise. Within moments, the inferno was gone, replaced by snow, and she coughed. But this snow wasn't cold; it was suffocating. She couldn't breathe. She fell to her knees, gasping.

Kester stood above her. "Use Emerazel's fire for strength. Don't burn down your apartment."

"Something snapped in me when you held that blade to my cheek." Whatever spell Kester had used stung like hell, and it tasted awful. The room smelled of burnt straw, and the tatami mats lay scorched. As she turned toward the wall-length mirror, she caught a glimpse of herself covered in white powder.

"I was trying to teach you to use your power. It doesn't burn me, but it will be burn the shadow demons."

"It looked like you were about to cut my face off." She rose, shaking off the powder.

"Why would I do that?"

She cocked a hip. *I don't know. Why did you leave a man to bleed out across from my bedroom?* "Maybe you wanted to wear it on your next mission because of my considerable allure."

"I'm pretty enough as it is. And I was trying to teach you how to use your power to fight. Remember, Zornhau's oil won't let me hurt you." He raised his sword, wrapping his fingers around the razor sharp blade. With a grunt of pain, he yanked the sword from his fist. Blood poured from his fingers, and Ursula gasped. But when he opened his hand, the wound had already healed. "It still hurts, but you can't seriously injure yourself. But if you don't learn to channel the hellfire, you'll find yourself trapped in a burning building."

"I think I need a lot of practice." She wiped the white foam off her cheeks. "What kind of spell did you cast on me?"

"Not a spell," he nodded at a fire extinguisher.

"Ugh. I'm going to make use of that shower." She turned to walk out of the room.

"Ursula. You did well, at least until you exploded. Use that charm on Hugo tonight, and everything will be fine. But if anything happens—if you need me, just use that mobile I gave you."

"I thought Emerazel wasn't letting you help me."

"I can help you. I just can't go with you."

"That is good to know." She flashed him a tentative smile.

Even with her aching muscles, as she strode up the stairs to the bathroom, she felt a little better than she had that morning.

Chapter 21

$\mathcal{U}$rsula leaned against the balcony's railing and looked down into the crowd, ten minutes before the start of Act One. She wore a long gown, the slate-grey color of a winter sea, which slid silkily against her bare legs. She'd accessorized with a necklace of black pearls, and finished off the ensemble with a spray of lavender perfume. The scent should have encouraged a sense of calm, but it did nothing for her nerves right now.

She closed her eyes, inhaling deeply. Just before she'd left for the opera, Kester had stopped by her apartment again—knocking this time—and had cast a long, approving glance over her outfit, that carnal look sparking in his eyes again. *If only he weren't a psychotic headsman with boundary issues, he'd be my kind of guy.*

She opened her eyes, scanning the lobby. From her perch on the upper level, she had a view of the lower floor and the marble stairs, curving below like the inside of a sea shell. Her hand rested lightly on the wyrm-skin purse, Emerazel's pen and a pact tucked safely inside, along with her white stone and opera glasses. *Not to mention the small dagger.* Silk and steel were her weapons, just as Kester had said.

In theory, she had everything she needed—except Hugo. *And where the hell is Zee?* She'd arrived early with the hope that she might extract Hugo's signature before the opera began, but as the minutes ticked by that became less likely. Closing her eyes, she inhaled deeply, pushing out all thoughts of hellfire and shadow demons. Tonight, she needed to focus, or she'd have to face Emerazel and submit to those horrific flames again. The thought curdled her stomach. Maybe someday she'd figure a way out of this—maybe even a way to save Hugo—but right now, she had more immediate problems. Like avoiding the wrath of a bloodthirsty goddess.

Someone brushed her elbow and she moved to make room.

"Thanks miss," said a melodious voice.

She glanced at her neighbor, and found herself staring into the face of a gorgeous, man, immaculately dressed in a black tuxedo. Golden skin and pale grey eyes contrasted with his dark hair, and he flashed her an inviting smile. This was the kind of gorgeous man she should be lusting after—a normal, human man who wouldn't attack her with swords and tell her friends she'd overdosed on heroin.

The man adjusted his cufflinks, and the way his eyes raked over her body made her want to blush. "My name is Abe. It's a pleasure to meet you."

"Ursula," she said, trying to keep her eye on the lobby.

"Is this your first time at the opera?"

With a great deal of effort, she pulled her gaze away from his beautiful face. She wasn't here to socialize, and she needed to focus on her target. "First time. Yes." She stared at the lobby, desperate for a sign of the pop star.

"You seem a little overwhelmed."

Act normal, Ursula. "Just excited, and a bit preoccupied by work." *Condemning people to hell isn't a walk in the park, you know.* Her hands tightened around the railing.

He kept his gaze fixed on her. "Well, I think you'll find the opera is the perfect place to set aside life's anxieties and experience something extraordinary."

"That's what I'm hoping for." If only she could set aside her anxieties—her overwhelming fear of Emerazel's flames, the gnawing guilt at her new role. And what *were* those images she'd seen when she thought Kester was going to slaughter her—the crumpled body on the floor, drenched in blood? She shuddered.

Whatever they were, this wasn't the time to delve into it. *Focus, Ursula.*

The crowd below quieted, all turning to look at the entrance. Ursula's heart skipped a beat as she watched the crowd part. Hugo and Virginie stepped into the lobby, flanked by three security guards. Ursula's breath caught. This was her moment to save her own life.

"Ah," said the man by her side, tapping his fingers on the railing. "A celebrity has joined us." The lights above flickered, and the lobby quieted. He turned to her. "I think that's our cue. I do hope you enjoy the show."

But as she thought of what she needed to do tonight, her blood roared in her ears. She'd come to condemn a man to hell.

Ursula hurried through a warren of red carpeted hallways before finding her seat. Enormous chandeliers hung from the gold-leaf ceiling, glimmering like icy fireworks.

Although the opera was sold out, Kester had managed to buy an entire set of box seats on the second level. Since Zee hadn't bothered to show, Ursula had it entirely to herself. She plopped into a seat in the front row.

From here, she had an expansive view of the opera hall. Beneath her, patrons in suits and gowns filled rows of red velvet seats. Ushers directed a few stragglers down the aisles. Next to the stage the orchestra readied itself with trills, scales, and arpeggios.

Ursula dug around in her purse and found the set of opera glasses. The miniature brass binoculars would give her a view of Hugo, and she'd be able to intercept him after the first act. With Zee's help to distract Virginie, Ursula could blink her eyes and lure him into signing.

She took a deep breath, trying to relax. *But where the hell is he sitting? And where is Zee?* She lifted the binoculars to her eyes, scanning the room, but only found row after row of stuffy older couples.

As the chandeliers began to dim, the hall fell silent. In thirty seconds, the entire room would be dark. *Bollocks.* Everyone had stared at Hugo when he'd arrived, but now he'd gone invisible.

She bit her lip. Perhaps they'd still be staring at him.

She glanced at the box to her left. A woman in her fifties, crammed into a red corseted dress, focused her binoculars on an upper balcony.

Ursula followed her gaze. Sure enough, there was Hugo, his cheeks slightly paler than they'd been when she first met him. Maybe he knew what waited for him—that death had come for him at the opera tonight, scented with lavender and dressed in a gown of grey silk.

She loosed a long breath. She'd found her target. Now she just needed to wait for the first act to end, and then she'd sidle up to him and try her whole *silk* routine, all verbal caresses and whispers of eternal happiness.

Only, there weren't many private places for a tête-à-tête in this place. Was she going to have to follow him into the loo again? When Kester had told her she would need to "keep a low profile, and stay in the shadows," she hadn't realized that meant working next to urinals.

The hall was completely dark until, after a few moments, a spotlight beamed onto the orchestra, illuminating a grey-haired conductor. He bowed, and the audience roared with applause. Then, turning to face the orchestra, he raised his hands. With a flick of his wrist, the musicians were off.

As the first notes sounded through the hall, an enormous gold curtain lifted to reveal the set. She'd been expecting something opulent, but saw instead a stage set with a shabby room—a hovel, as Kester would call it.

But the music itself was as lush as the theater, and the violins and trumpets washing over Ursula in a glorious wave. As the music swelled, she leaned forward in her seat. A man with dark hair walked to the center of the stage and began to sing in a rich baritone, full of passion. Another man strode onto the stage, joining him in a clear tenor voice. *If only I knew what they were singing about.*

By their costumes, she could tell the characters were poor, but the way they sang to each other suggested warmth between them. As the music flowed around her, she thought of Katie, and how they'd spent their weekends exploring London's forgotten canals, too broke to do anything else. She'd been happy enough then, right? Perhaps, in her isolation, she was romanticizing, but at least she hadn't had a bounty on her head and a goddess of hellfire who wanted to torture her to death. And, moreover, at least she'd had Katie. Right now, her loneliness threatened to swallow her whole.

On the stage, the tenor was joined by a young woman, wrapped in a woolen shawl and rubbing her arms as he serenaded her. *Amore.* That was a word she recognized: love. The tenor's emotional outpouring held no artifice, no silk or steel—he simply bared his soul. The music built, and Ursula nearly forgot to breathe, her chest aching.

As the aria reached its climax, she couldn't help but imagine someone looking at her the way the tenor looked at his beloved. For just a second, she closed her eyes, and an image rose from the back of her mind—a painfully beautiful man with star-flecked eyes, deep and dark as the night sky.

With a jolt, she realized exactly who she was picturing—the injured demon who lay asleep in her apartment.

What the hell?

Chapter 22

$\mathcal{U}$nnerved she glanced around, exhaling slowly as she caught a glimpse of Zee slipping into the row, dressed in a crimson gown. *About time she showed up.*

As Zee took her seat, she studied Ursula with an expression that fell somewhere between annoyance and concern. "Are you having another bad day?"

"What are you talking about?" But even as she said it, Ursula realized that a few tears had slid down her cheek. She started to wipe her eyes, but Zee pulled her hand away. "You'll ruin your makeup," she whispered. "Let me do it."

Zee opened her purse, pulling out a tissue, and she dabbled Ursula's cheeks. "I also cried the first time I saw *La bohème*," she whispered.

"You're an opera fan?"

"I love the romance. Puccini understood how it felt to get swept away by love." There was something wistful about the way she spoke, and her eyes glistened. The ice princess had disappeared for just a moment, until her clear gaze focused again. "But we're not here for the music. Where's the target?"

"Up there." Ursula nodded at the box on the upper level, where Hugo still sat whispering with Virginie. Maybe this was going to be easier than she'd anticipated.

The first act ended, and Ursula sucked in a long breath. *It's now or never*. She turned to Zee. "Can we approach them in the booth? Would you be able to glamour his girlfriend again?"

"Of course."

Zee slipped out of the box, and Ursula followed. In the hall, patrons mingled with glasses of wine. Zee slipped between them, like a deer weaving between trees in a forest, and Ursula hurried along behind her.

"Thank you for helping me, Zee."

"Of course. It's what I'm paid for." She stepped into a curving flight of stairs. "But you must relax. You look nervous."

"I'm not nervous. I'm dreading my part in this."

"Oh. The whole *eternal torture* thing. Well, Hugo asked for it."

"Do you think there's another way out, without me collecting souls?"

Zee shot her a sharp look. "Keep your voice down. And, no. What Kester says is the truth, or he'd have freed himself ages ago. You think he likes it any better than you do?"

"You trust him?" Ursula desperately wanted to ask Zee about the bleeding man in her apartment. What if he needed help—and what if Kester had put him there? She choked down the questions for now.

"Of course I trust Kester. I've known him a very long time." They reached the top of the stairs—Hugo's level. "I don't think he likes collecting souls any more than you do. But there is no other option, believe me."

They strode down the hall toward Hugo's box, and Ursula clutched her wyrm-skin purse. "Do you know why Kester carved his mark?"

"Yes, but it's not for me to tell." Zee paused at a door. "I think this is Hugo's. Do you want me to go in first?"

"I think that's a good idea. It's likely to alarm him when he sees his own damnation coming for him." Plus, Zee could glamour everyone around him. Ursula pulled her pen from her purse, ready to charm the pants off Hugo.

Zee open the door, and Ursula lingered in the doorway, keeping in the shadows—just like a good hellhound.

"Oh hi, Zee!" Virginie trilled, throwing her arms in the air. "I didn't know you were going to be at the Opera tonight."

"Hi, Virginie." Zee's glamour was utterly convincing. Too bad Hugo wasn't there.

Zee's hand flew to her chest. "Where's your gorgeous date?"

"He went to the little boy's room."

Ursula began to slip away. *Of course. That's where I have all my traumatic encounters with pop stars.*

The theater's lights flickered, signaling the end of intermission. *Show time, Ursula.* She turned, hurrying through the hall, the bone-colored pen clutched tight in her fist.

A few stragglers rushed back to their seats in the corridor. At the end of the hall, Ursula spied a door labeled *Men* in gold lettering. *No bodyguards—good.* That would simplify things.

Ursula swallowed hard, trying not to think about fire. She glanced behind her to make sure no one was around, then slipped inside.

Gilded moldings and pictures of famous opera singers decorated the walls.

"Hello?" she called out in her most soothing voice. "Hugo, darling?"

Only the sound of dripping water greeted her, and the faint swell of violins from the orchestra. *Shit.*

Ursula's mind raced through the possibilities. If he'd returned to his box, she would have seen him in the corridor. He wouldn't have just left Virginie alone at the opera while he went somewhere else, would he?

Actually, that did seem like something he'd do. This was a guy who'd dumped his girlfriend for wearing the wrong swimsuit.

But, no—his jacket had been hanging on the back of his chair in the box. He *had* to be here.

Maybe he'd gone out for a smoke? She turned, catching a glimpse of herself in the mirror. Her auburn hair was piled on her head in a glamorous up-do, a few tendrils cascading over her pale shoulders. If she couldn't lure Hugo into his own damnation looking like this, she'd never get anyone to sign.

She turned, eyeing the stalls. The doors reached the floor, so she couldn't peer under them. Instead, she began pushing them open, one by one. The doors creaked as she opened them. "Hugo, my love. I've been wanting to see you again." *Creak.* "I thought perhaps I could explain things better." *Creak.* "Maybe over some wine—"

From the furthest stall, a sucking sound interrupted her investigation. *What the hell?*

"Hugo, darling?" she said in her most soothing voice. "Is that you?"

The noise stopped, replaced by the muffled voice of the tenor singing on stage.

"Hello?" She softened her voice into a low caress, walking toward the final stall, heels clacking on the floor. "Are you there? We got off the wrong foot before, I know. I'm here to make everything better."

No response. As she stood before the final stall, the hair rose on her arms. Something felt *wrong*—the air felt a little too cold, almost electrified. Was it just a draft, or was that dark magic crackling in the air around her? She flicked out the blade of the reaping pen. Dread rose up her throat, and she leaned closer, knocking on the door. "Hugo, my darling. It's not as bad as you think." *Lies. Horrible, evil lies, tumbling from perfectly-glossed pink lips. She was a monster now.*

She took a deep breath, waiting for his response, but she heard only shuffling in the stall, and a low moan.

She stepped back. Her heels wouldn't be good for running, but she could still kick down a door. She hiked up her dress and slammed her foot into the wood. Her kick snapped the lock, sending the door smacking open.

A rush of fear ran over her skin. The man she'd met earlier—the one with the pale grey eyes—stood, cradling Hugo in his arms like a baby. As soon as the man's eyes locked on Ursula, he dropped Hugo onto the toilet seat, and the pop star's head smacked hard against the stall's wooden walls. His skin had taken on an unhealthy sheen.

Ursula swallowed hard. *What. The. Fuck.* "What are you?" she breathed.

Abe stepped toward her in a single flowing motion, like smoke rising from the wick of an extinguished candle. The air temperature dropped at least ten degrees. He fixed his otherworldly gaze on her, his eyes gunmetal grey.

He moved closer to her. When he smiled, fear twisted in her gut—but something else, too. She couldn't stop staring at his smooth, golden skin.

"Hello, pretty girl." His voice whispered over her body. When he spoke, it almost felt as though he were touching her with a feather-light stroke. "I was wondering if you'd stop by."

She tore her eyes away from him, glancing at the crumpled pop star on the toilet. Nausea welled in her stomach. This was all wrong. "Did you kill him?"

"I may have been a bit greedy with him. His soul tasted delicious."

"You devoured his soul?" Horror slithered over her skin. She had a dizzying feeling she was facing one of those shadow demons Kester had mentioned. And what would Emerazel do when she learned Hugo's soul had been stolen?

Abe's cheek dimpled as he smiled. "Nyxobas needed more souls. I know you understand." He reached out, stroking her cheek, and his touch sent a thrill racing through her body, pushing out all of her dread. "But of course, you are the real prize this evening. You're the most beautiful woman here, and it's not every day I get to consume a hellhound's soul."

Chapter 23

*H*er body was growing hot, and sweat beaded on her neck.

"Look, I don't know who you think you are, but I've become quite attached to my soul, and I plan to hang on to it." His lips looked full and soft, but she forced herself to tear her gaze off them, stepping backward toward the sinks. A strange ache was beginning to fill her body, and she couldn't stop looking at him.

Slowly, he moved closer, his eyes trailing over her shoulders, her cleavage, her hips, as if he could see right through her dress to the lacy pink bra and panties underneath, and the thought sent a strange thrill through her belly. *What is he doing to me?* With a trembling hand, she lifted the blade of the pen toward the center of his chest. "Don't get any closer. I won't hesitate to reap your soul." *I need to burn him, but I can't remember how.*

"You silly little thing." His eyes blazed with desire. "Do you have any idea how powerful I am?"

A battle raged in her head—carnal desires warring against the corner of her mind that wanted to bash his head into the tiles. Some traitorous part of her wanted to rip off her dress right there and invite him closer, while the rest of her knew she should stab him with the pen. *I need to get out of here.*

She could yell for help, but Emerazel would surely slaughter her for calling attention to herself.

Abe prowled closer, licking his perfect lips. Ursula let the silky strap of her gown fall lower. She wanted him to see all of her, wanted his hands on her bare skin.

Just inches from her, he ran a finger over her collarbone, and heat blazed through her. He leaned in, and she arched against him, desperate to feel his lips against hers. "I wish I could take you to Oberon's. It would be so fun to show off a gorgeous human pet like you, with your perfect breasts and ass..."

Fuck. Hadn't Zee and the hairdresser said something about Oberon's? But it hadn't sounded nearly as tempting as when the word rolled off Abe's tongue. Whatever Oberon's was, she wanted to go with him. What *was* she doing here? She was here for him, wasn't she? Here to please this god of a man. She felt her legs opening, and her hand slid up his chest. There was something she was supposed to be doing, but her mind was a blank.

He slipped his hand around the back of her neck, his eyes trailing down her heaving chest. A pleasurable heat radiated from his body, and she could think of nothing but his touch.

He lowered his mouth to hers, and for one glorious instant an inferno of euphoria flared—until it died as quickly as it had arrived, replaced by a gnawing emptiness and overwhelming sense of revulsion.

Abe pulled away from her, his face contorted with disgust—just like Ursula felt. He wiped the back of his hand across his lips, as if trying to wipe away her taste.

"Ugh." Infuriated, he glared at her, gripping her wrist. "What the hell *are* you?"

Rage simmered in her chest. She was getting sick of being treated like a toy for the demons to play with. "I'm a hellhound." Free of his spell, she could feel the fire rising through her arms, hot and molten. Abe jerked away from her, and she threw a hard punch at his pretty face, thrilling at the smack of knuckles against bone.

Abe's head snapped back, and he growled. Faster than a storm wind, his hands were at her throat, and his cold stare hypnotized her. He opened his mouth, sucking in air from her body. As he did, a deep void filled her chest. She kicked his shins, but his eyes remained locked on her, unflinching.

Her blood rushed in her ears, her limbs tingling and weakening. *What is he doing to me?* She was going to die in the men's bathroom at the hands of a pervert she'd just kissed. This was worse than the fake heroin overdose. Abe's fingers dug into her neck, his icy eyes flashing with cold light.

Her vision grew dark, and she could hear her own heartbeat growing weaker as he sucked the life from her. Panic exploded in her skull. *He's killing me.* Lights flashed before her eyes. Her lungs were going to implode, as the fire inside her guttered and dimmed. A tiny lick of flame danced in the recesses of her mind, and as her energy drained from her body, she tried to stoke it to life, but it sputtered and died. Something else was filling her mind now—a memory: a gleaming sword in the sunlight, in a field overgrown with wildflowers, a smaller sword in her own hand. The blade cut through the air, glinting in the sunlight, as she was taught to wield it.

Fight, Ursula.

Someone, long ago, had wanted her to be a warrior.

Fight.

She blinked, trying to refocus her vision, and she made out the blurred outline of her attacker. She needed to—

Thwak! Something hit him in the side of the head, and he released his grip.

Abe let her crumple to the ground, and her head smacked against the floor, the nape of her neck pressing against the bathroom tiles—cold, just like her body. She felt as though a heavy weight pressed on her, crushing the life out of her. Nearby, Abe was fighting with someone—a woman—but Ursula's limbs were frozen, drained.

"Ursula!" they shrieked. *Zee?*

She licked her lips. She needed to warn Zee away—Abe's kiss was death—but she felt herself drifting away, a cold wind whispering over her skin.

I need to help Zee. She willed herself to get up. She would fight him, smash his pretty face into the tiles.

With a great force of will, she forced her eyes open, staring up at the ceiling. Abe had drunk so deeply from her it took virtually all her remaining strength to roll to her side. She blinked, her vision coming into focus. Abe, a few feet from her, stood clutching Zee like a rag doll.

If she'd had any of Emerazel's fire still within her, she would have tried to scorch him, burn him to ashes, but he'd sucked her dry. She needed to hurt him another way.

Her eyes flicked to Emerazel's pen, glinting in the yellow lights just a few feet away. Slowly, like she was moving through quicksand, she reached for it until her knuckles brushed its bony cylinder. She tightened her fingers around it, pulling it into her grasp.

Zee's blond hair hung down as Abe held her in his arms, her black high heels dangling over the floor. Ursula inched closer, shivering at the chill that emanated from him. Had she actually been *attracted* to this monster?

Gritting her teeth, she rolled closer and stabbed the pen's blade into his heel with all the strength she could muster.

He wrenched his foot away with a muffled grunt, then tottered for a moment before crashing to the floor, the knife protruding from his foot. She yanked out the pen, its blade stained with blood.

"Gods below," he sputtered.

A small smile curled her lips. She wasn't going down without a fight.

He rose, lunging for her like a lion attacking its prey. She stabbed him again; she'd aimed for his heart, but the blade lodged in his stomach instead.

On his knees, Abe threw back his head, roaring, the bony pen shaking where it protruded from his gut. He clawed at it, as the wound started to smoke. The smell of burning flesh filled the room. *Emerazel's weapon.*

Abe leapt to his feet in a blur of motion and staggered toward the exit, blood and steam bubbling between his fingers.

She rose on her elbows, trying out one of her new seductive smiles. "For such a little thing, it's got a hell of a bite."

"Bitch," he spat before flinging open the door and disappearing into the hall.

Chapter 24

*U*rsula lay on her back and stared at the eggshell-white ceiling, trying to will herself to move.

But the first step was peeling herself off the bathroom floor. Her legs tingled with pins and needles, and she almost cried with relief when she moved her toes. She pushed herself up, onto her hands and knees. She crawled closer to Zee, panting. Hadn't Abe said the opera was the perfect place to put aside one's anxieties? *Wanker.*

She crouched next to Zee, her heart tightening at the sight of her. The fae girl's chest hardly moved. Blood stained her dress and matted her hair, though Ursula was pretty sure that belonged to Abe.

She reached out, feeling for a pulse on Zee's neck. It was faint, but blood flowed gently beneath her translucent skin. If she could only get her outside, there was a Bentley waiting for them by the Met's entrance.

Thank God Abe hadn't killed her, but she wasn't about to walk out of here. *How the hell do I wake her up?*

Once, she'd seen someone come back from the dead. Braden, a boy in her first foster home, had a nut allergy, and he'd chowed through a packet of almond macaroons without realizing. He'd passed out in less than five minutes, but an EpiPen had completely revived him.

That was what epinephrine did, right? It sent hormones racing through your veins. She just needed to get her hands on one. Her pulse raced. This was *not* a good situation.

She panted, still trying to catch her breath, her knees pressed into the cold tile. Maybe this was a good time to call Kester.

As she glanced around for her purse, she heard the door creak open. She lifted her head, bracing for another fight—not that she *could* fight at this point. A silver-haired opera patron, dressed in a beige suit, stood in the doorframe. Ursula blinked through the fog of exhaustion, trying to make sense of this new player in the game.

Half-conscious, her first thought was *What sort of knob wears a cravat?* And her second was *He's going to call the police.*

For a moment, his eyes locked on hers, and she recognized the horror in his face. "Good god!" He shouted. "What did you do?"

With a tremendous effort, Ursula sat up. Her eyes flicked to Zee, whose jaw hung open like a corpse's. Of course the man was panicking. He'd just discovered two women on the bathroom floor covered in fresh blood, one of them apparently dead. It was a small mercy he couldn't see Hugo's corpse slumped over the toilet in the stall.

She imagined how the next twenty minutes would go down. First, Silver-Hair would alert security and call the police. They'd find Hugo's carcass. None of the authorities would believe her when she described Abe's death kiss, and as the only conscious person in the room, she could find herself accused of the pop star's murder, as well as some sort of assault on Zee. Her heart thrummed.

"I'll get the police," he stammered. "Security."

So much for staying in the bloody shadows. I'm getting sent straight to the inferno when Emerazel learns of this. In a few minutes the bathroom would be full of security guards. If she'd had any energy, she'd have lit the place on fire to give herself enough time to escape, but she could feel her embers dulled.

"Wait," she said, holding up a hand. She couldn't let him leave.

There were two options: she could create a diversion using hellfire, or she could find some way to attack the man and get out of here with Zee. Only, she couldn't manage either of those things without energy.

Shit. What would a normal woman do in this situation? Probably not thinking about lighting things on fire and stabbing people, for one thing.

A normal person would cry.

"Wait," she repeated. She let her eyes fill with tears, and pouted, choking out a sob. "She wasn't feeling well," she sniffed, letting the strap of her gown drop again. "I told her not to order the salad. She didn't have her EpiPen. Or her inhaler. And I tried to take her to the women's room, but she said she couldn't make it. So we came in here. And then she slipped on the tile and cracked her head. She's my dearest friend. Please help us." She let a tear roll down her cheek. *Please, please, please, convince him.*

"Oh. That's awful." He pulled out his phone. "I'll call an ambulance."

"No!" she shouted, before letting her face soften again. "It will take too long for them to get here. If she doesn't get an EpiPen now, she'll die."

His face blanched. "Where do I get an EpiPen?"

"There are three thousand people in here. One of them is bound to have an allergy."

He cleared his throat. "Shall I... shall I interrupt the performance?"

She let the genuine desperation show on her face. She didn't know how long Zee would have before her heart gave out. "Please hurry, before it's too late."

The man turned, flinging open the door and breaking into a run. As Ursula was left with her own thoughts, she could feel some of her energy returning. She could call Kester now, but she didn't want to bring him into this until she'd already gained control of the situation. She didn't need to call him just to tell him she'd become entangled in another disaster.

She reached down, feeling Zee's pulse again. Still there, but growing fainter. Panic twisted through Ursula. She couldn't let Zee die. Maybe this *was* the time to call Kester. She turned, reaching for her purse that lay on the tiles, when Silver-Hair slammed the door open, a green tube in his hands.

"I've got it!" he said, beaming. He rushed across the tiles and handed it to Ursula.

"Thank you so much. You've saved her life." She popped off the blue cap, sliding the EpiPen out of its tube and scanning the directions.

"We should call an ambulance," said the man.

"Let me concentrate." It came out harsher than she'd meant it. "Please."

She pulled off the blue safety, reared back her arm, and jammed the pen into Zee's leg. She counted to ten, watching as Zee's eyelids fluttered.

"See, she's getting better." She couldn't believe this had worked. "You saved her. You're an amazing, beautiful man." *Too much, Ursula. Rein it in.*

He cleared his throat. "She's not awake yet. I really think we should call that amb—"

Ursula slapped Zee in the face as hard as she could, and when the fae's blue eyes opened, Ursula leaned over. "Zee, you had a reaction to the salad. It was the hidden walnuts."

Zee's gaze met hers, registering understanding.

Ursula leaned in close and whispered: "You need to *tell* this man you're OK." *I really hope she can still glamour them.*

"I—I'm OK." Zee's voice wavered, but Silver-Hair nodded.

Silver-Hair stepped closer, leaning over her. "Let me help you up."

Zee shot up, grabbing the man by his collar. "I'm feeling much better now. You are no longer needed. Get the fuck out, and don't tell anyone about me."

In a daze, he rose and tottered out the door.

"Calm down, Zee." Ursula sat back on the tile, letting out a long breath. "I asked you to glamour him. Not assault him."

Zee's eyes were wild. "What did you do to revive me? I feel like I want to kill something."

"Epinephrine."

Zee shook her head. "What is epinephrine?"

I really have no clue. "I think it's some kind of life-giving hormone. Anyway, it fixed you. Let's get out of here."

Scowling, Zee lifted a hand to her cheek. "Did you slap me?"

Ursula shook her head. "Nope. Just an effect of the epinephrine, I think."

Zee narrowed her eyes before glancing down at her dress. "Whose blood is on my Valentino?"

"Abe. I think he was a shadow demon. He tried to kill us. Look, we need to get out of here. Can you walk?"

Zee slowly stood, smoothing her hair. "I can't believe that prick ruined my dress."

Clutching her wyrm-skin purse, Ursula rose, unsteady on her feet. Zee shot her a sharp look before slipping her arm around Ursula's waist. They staggered into the corridor, and Ursula kept her gaze on the floor, hoping to remain unnoticed. *Nothing to see here, folks. Just two chicks in opera gowns, drenched in demon blood.*

Chapter 25

$\mathcal{S}$tepping out of the cold winter air, Ursula folded herself into the soft seat of the Bentley like a bird settling onto its nest, and Zee followed, shutting the car door.

Zee clutched her chest, shrinking into the corner. "I don't feel so good."

Ursula rubbed her arms, trying to warm herself. "Holy fuck. That was a close call."

"My heart is racing," said Zee.

"Are you okay?"

The fae took a deep breath, staring out the window. "I'll be fine. Where are we going?"

Ursula glanced at the driver. "Take us to my place, please. The Plaza Hotel." Just as she was letting out a sigh of relief, she realized she wasn't out of trouble yet. Her target's soul had been claimed by a shadow demon, and that meant Emerazel would murder her slowly. Dread raced up her spine.

The driver turned on the engine and tried to edge into the stalled traffic.

Outside, the wind beat against the sedan's windows. Ursula rubbed her temples. "What the hell kind of demon was that? I think I'm in huge trouble."

Zee didn't answer, instead staring out her window. But something was wrong with the angle of her neck—she wasn't moving. Ursula moved closer, touching Zee's shoulder. The fae's head slumped to the side; her mouth hung open and her eyelids fluttered.

"Zee!" Ursula gripped Zee's shoulders. She slapped her cheek again, but this time Zee didn't wake up—didn't even flinch.

Horror tightened around Ursula's heart. "Driver! We have a situation." She dug around in her purse until she found her mobile. With trembling fingers, she scrolled to Kester's number. He picked up after a few rings.

"Kester?" she shouted, pulse racing.

"Is everything okay?" Apparently the cell phone had no trouble conveying the panic in her voice.

"Zee's unconscious." The words poured out of her. "And I think Hugo's dead. Something called Abe kissed me and he sucked out my fire. And then he kissed Zee, but I stabbed him. I gave her an EpiPen—"

"Slow down. Hugo's dead?"

Ursula took a deep breath, trying to steady herself. "I went to the men's room to talk to Hugo. I didn't think he was there at first, but then I found him in a stall in the back. He's dead. I think. Abe was kissing him, and said he'd drunk too deeply."

"What *exactly* did Abe look like?"

"Tall. Gorgeous. Golden skin. Grey eyes. His touch was like ice cubes. He made me feel—" Her stomach clenched. She wasn't going to go into the whole arousal scenario. "Do vampires exist?"

There was a long pause. "He made you feel *how?*"

Ursula thought she detected a note of anger in his voice. "He made me think I wanted to kiss him." That was both a euphemism and a secret she had no desire to share with Kester, but maybe it would help identify whatever the hell that thing was.

"Not a vampire," he snarled. "Where are you?"

"In the Bentley. Outside the Met. Should I come back to the Plaza?"

"No. Tell Joe to take you to the Elysian. Tell him to floor it." He hung up.

Ursula glanced at Joe. "Elysian. He said to floor it."

Without responding, Joe stepped on the accelerator, cutting into traffic. They raced up 10th Avenue and turned onto West 66th street, weaving between taxis. She clung to Zee, trying to keep her from bouncing all over the car—there hadn't been time to think about seatbelts. For a few moments, a city bus blocked their path, but Joe swerved around it like he was driving a Formula One race car, until—at last—he veered wildly into an empty parking lot by the Hudson River. Frantic thoughts ignited Ursula's mind—Zee's poisoned body, her own skin blackening in a fire.

The car skidded to a halt, and Joe popped the locks on doors.

"Where are we?" Ursula asked, shuddering at the sound of the wind howling and keening against the car windows.

Joe simply tapped his fingers against the steering wheel.

"Thanks, Joe. That's really helpful." She turned to scoop the diminutive fae into her arms, clumsily pulling her closer. As she grasped Zee's waist and shoulders, someone yanked open the door behind her, and an icy wind rushed into the car.

Kester stood in the dim street lights, the wind tearing at him like a wild animal. Despite the cold, he remained perfectly still, oblivious to the frigid air. He stood barefoot, wearing only a pair of boxers, his strong chest covered in menacing tattoos. Wordlessly, Kester gathered Zee into his arms, eyes blazing.

"Will she be okay?" Ursula asked, stepping out of the car into the freezing air.

"Come with me," he said, as Joe drove away.

So he's not going to answer my questions. She was obviously in trouble—big trouble. He'd warned her that if she screwed up, he'd have to send her to Emerazel.

She rubbed her arms, trying to burn some warmth into her skin. "Is she okay?" she repeated, clutching her purse to her chest. *Please wake up, Zee.*

Silently, he pressed on over the icy pavement.

Ursula's heels clacked over the asphalt as she followed him, and her body burned with fatigue. From the river, the wind whipped off the tops of the waves, blowing a freezing spray that coated everything in a thin layer of ice. Ursula hugged herself, shivering in her flimsy dress.

He led her toward a dock that jutted into the water. Despite his bare feet and state of undress, he navigated the slick planking with ease. Swirls of steam rose from the ground as his fiery body melted the icy ground. Ursula trailed behind, clutching a frozen rail.

At the end of the dock, a paint-chipped tugboat floated in the water, tied to a post. Its stern had been painted with gold lettering: *ELYSIAN.* Not exactly what she'd expected of a place with such a poetic name. It looked like a large, shabby version of a child's bathtub toy. *Is this where he lives?*

Kester slipped over a narrow gangplank, disappearing inside. Teeth chattering, she followed, treading carefully to avoid falling into the churning water.

The boat's warmth washed over her as she stepped inside. Although the tug's exterior had suggested a state of total disrepair, the inside was immaculate. Books lined tall wooden shelves between a row of portholes. A wooden table nestled into an alcove, and a fire crackled in an iron stove that stood in the center of the cabin. She eyed a green velvet sofa, fighting the urge to give in to her aching body and rest. The only thing unusual about the place was the dark mark of Emerazel on the floor—another sigil.

Kester held Zee's unconscious body, examining her face. "I won't be able to heal her." His eyes flicked to Ursula's, burning with accusation. "Were you so enthralled by the incubus that you let him feast on Zee, after you failed at your task for a second time?

"Incubus?" He was clearly accusing her of something, and his words stung. "I don't know what an incubus is, but I think you well know that whatever powers he used on me were magical and therefore hard to resist. Abe was attacking me, and Zee came in to stop it. Hugo had been sucked dry before I even got in there."

"Abe." He spat the word like a curse. "You said he had golden skin and grey eyes?"

"Yes. And dark brown hair. He seemed perfectly charming at first."

"Abrax," he choked out the word, laying Zee down on the table. "I can't believe you succumbed to his charm. I want to flay his skin from his body."

Holy hell. "Who is he?"

"He's an incubus. He works for Nyxobas, the god of night." He crossed to her, his body crackling with fiery magic. "There aren't many incubi in the world, and this one is pure evil."

Dread crawled up her spine. "What, exactly, is an incubus? And what makes him so evil?"

"Incubi like him have the power to drain people. They can drain energy, magic, even souls to give to Nyxobas. That's what he did to Zee. And an incubus can inflame sexual energy and take power from that. I'm guessing that's how he transfixed you."

She cleared her throat, listening to the sound of the howling wind batter the side of the boat. God, she was freezing. "There's no point rehashing what already happened. It's over. What do we need to do *now*?"

"It's amazing to me that you dismiss tonight's events so quickly." He stepped closer, boxing her against the wall, his face burning with fury. "You failed to reap Hugo's soul, and you let a shadow demon claim it. You do realize what this means?"

Fear tightened her chest. *He's going to send me to Emerazel.*

Chapter 26

$\mathcal{P}$reternatural power flickered in his eyes.

Adrenaline flooded Ursula's veins. *I need a weapon. He's going to kill me.* She still clutched her wyrm-skin purse, but Abe had run off with her blade lodged in his gut.

She scanned the room for something sharp, her eyes landing on an old cutlass that hung above a porthole. But with Kester blocking her path, she wouldn't be able to get to it.

He inched closer. "I should never have let you go on your own."

"Emerazel said you *had* to send me alone, and I know you can't disobey her." Anger tightened her chest.

His eyes flashed. "That's one of the few sensible things you've ever said."

Frantically, Ursula's eyes darted around the room. Since the cutlass was out of reach, she needed to identify an escape route if he was going to sacrifice her. "And she said you need to send me to her if I screwed up again."

He stepped closer, bare feet padding across the deck, until he stood so close she could feel the heat rolling off him, and smell his earthy scent. His eyes trailed over her shivering body, like he was sizing up the value of his sacrificial victim, and her muscles tightened at his gaze.

Her heart thrummed. There was no way she could take on someone with his strength, not when she'd been drained by the incubus. And yet, she had no other choice. An image flashed in her mind—swords shining in the moonlight as someone trained her. *Fight, Ursula.*

Just as he took another step closer, she dropped her purse, throwing a hard punch to his jaw. He flinched, but didn't move. With a racing pulse, she threw another, but her aim was off. He caught her fist in his hand, his grip iron-clad.

Spinning her around, he pulled her arm up behind her back, pushing her up against the wall. The splintered wood pierced her silk dress, and she fought to catch her breath.

"I told you," he purred in her ear, his breath hot on her neck. "You can't fight me. Let me—"

Like hell I can't. She elbowed him hard in the stomach, and he stumbled. She tried to race for the door, but he caught her by the hair, yanking her head back. He slipped his other arm around her body, holding her tight, and growled. "What is wrong with you?"

"I don't want to die. Or burn. I don't want to suffer for something F.U. has done, and I don't want Zee to suffer because of her either. If I could murder anyone, it would be F.U., but that would create a paradox..." She let her thought trail off. She was babbling like a nutter now.

His strong body pressed into her back. "I wasn't going to kill you."

With one of his hands tightly fisted into her hair, and the other grabbing her shoulder, she wasn't going anywhere. His arm heated her skin through her dress, warming her breasts.

"Are you talking about yourself in the third person again? It's really strange."

Relief flooded her. "You said there was no point fighting Emerazel. Just like there's no point in me fighting you."

He loosened his grip on her. "I should kill you. I won't pretend it didn't cross my mind."

She stepped out of his grasp, hugging herself. Away from his warm body, the air chilled her skin. "But you're not going to?"

Golden lantern light bathed his chiseled body. "I should, but no."

"Why?"

He shrugged, confusion and anger warring across his features. "I don't want to kill you."

"I thought you did whatever Emerazel told you to."

"Mostly, yes." He looked away, his face suddenly sad. "But I loathe her."

Ursula shook her head. "I don't understand. I thought you were her Headsman. Why would you do whatever she wanted if you loathe her?"

Flames glinted in his eyes. "I hate that name. And the rest of it isn't for you to worry about now." He clearly wasn't ready to bare his soul.

Shivering, Ursula hugged herself, eyeing the inviting sofa that called to her aching body. "Fine. But what is the point of all of this? Why is she so obsessed with claiming souls anyway?"

"Rest for a minute," he said, nodding at the chair. "Maybe it's time for you to learn something about your world before we hunt down Abrax."

She collapsed into the chair with a sigh, letting the soft cushions embrace her. Her muscles sang with relief.

Kester ran a hand through his hair. "The souls of men are what give gods their power. Emerazel's fire is fueled by the souls of her supplicants. Nyxobas's magic works the same way. The gods are constantly warring over this human currency, and long ago they formed factions of shadow and light to fight against each other. When Abrax drained Hugo, he stopped us from acquiring the soul. He also steals any magic that Emerazel had invested in Hugo." He eyed her with concern. "Like how he drained your fire before Zee stopped him. Honestly, it's a miracle he didn't take your soul."

"It was odd. We became repulsed by each other as soon as his lips touched mine."

He stared at her, surprise flickering across his features. "Really?"

She nodded. "But that means he stole Zee's soul?"

"Half of it, at least."

"Shit." Ursula took a deep breath, trying to push that horrific thought out of her mind. "If incubi work for Nyxobas, what god do the fae work for? Is there a god we can appeal to for help?"

"No. Unlike every other magical creature on earth, they're unaligned. They're descendants of angels who chose to come to earth long ago."

"Why would they want to live on earth instead of in the heavens?" She ached with exhaustion, but this was the first time someone was actually telling her something, and she needed to get as much out of it as she could.

"The fae are simply hedonists. They enjoy earthly pleasures."

Ursula glanced at Zee, whose arm dangled limply over the side of the table. "We can save her if we find Abe."

"Abrax." His eyes blazed. "And maybe we can get Hugo's soul back from him, too, so Emerazel doesn't need to claim your soul. Then I'll crush the life out of him."

"What happens if we don't get the rest of Zee's soul back?"

"She won't live for more than a few days."

Dread snaked up her spine, and she pulled her white stone from her purse, rolling it between her fingers. "She'll die?"

"Yes. Put your charm away. I've got to refill you. You drained the rest of your remaining energy in your foolish attempt at fighting me."

She opened her mouth to protest, but she was too tired for an argument. "How do you refill me?"

He crossed to her, holding out his hand. She grasped it, and he pulled her up. As she stood, dizziness fogged her mind, and he slipped an arm around her back to steady her. "I will imbue you with Emerazel's fire."

She was suddenly acutely aware of his bare skin and the heat radiating from his body. She looked down at the slow rise and fall of his chest, drinking in his delicious, earthy smell. *Oh, God. I don't have the hots for this guy, do I?* "Will that be painful?"

"No." His gaze slid down to her shoulder. "I'm just going to put my hand on your scar. My heat will flow into you."

"Okay." She couldn't take her eyes off his stunning face. *No wonder he's full of himself.*

Kester pulled down the strap of her gown, then her pink bra strap. The cool cabin air tickled her skin. He pressed his palm flat against her shoulder. He closed his eyes, chanting in his strange language. A glorious, tingling heat pulsed from his fingertips over her skin, caressing her neck. The heat moved slowly, whispering around her throat, slipping lower over her breasts before pulsing down her abdomen. Was it her imagination, or was his thumb moving slowly up and down on her lower back, lazily stroking her skin through her silk dress? A hot, euphoric thrill seeped into her body, blazing through her core, and she fought the urge to press herself against his strong body. Molten power ignited her veins, and she felt a smile curl her lips. *I'm back.*

Kester opened his eyes, gazing down at her. "Better?" His thumb still languidly stroked her lower back, and she could feel herself arching into him.

Her eyes lingered on his perfect lips, and for just a moment, she considered kissing him—before she reminded herself that a) he was an entitled wanker most of the time, b) Zee's unconscious body lay just a few feet away, and c) his nickname was "the Headsman." *Probably not a good idea to kiss someone named for an executione*r.

She rolled her neck. "I feel amazing. I'm ready to find this incubus."

Chapter 27

$\mathcal{K}$ester crossed his room, pulling open a drawer in a small, wooden dresser. He took out a black sweater, slipped it over his chiseled torso. "There's a little problem with our plan."

"What?"

"I have no idea where to find Abrax. He's an ancient and powerful incubus. He dwells in Nyxobas's Manhattan lair, and I have no idea—"

"I know where he was going."

Pulling on a pair of grey trousers, he shot her a sharp look. "He told you?"

"He mentioned a place called Oberon's. Something about wanting to bring me there as a pet."

Kester curled back his lip in a snarl.

"Do you know what it is?"

"No, I was hoping you might."

"It's a private club for the fae. Unfortunately, they have a strict door policy, enforced by ancient and powerful magic even I can't manipulate. You can only get in if a fairy gives you explicit permission." He nodded at Zee. "And she's the only fae I know. Obviously, Abrax is connected."

Ursula shook her head, the guilt pressing on her chest like a rock. "If Abrax is as elusive as you say, I'm not letting this lead get away." It was her fault Zee's soul was missing. If she hadn't screwed up her first mission with her off-putting personality, none of this would have happened. And, of course, if F.U. hadn't carved the mark in the first place, Zee would be sipping a champagne cocktail in Club Lalique right now. "There must be someone you can bribe."

"The fae aren't interested in money."

"Are you serious? Have you ever been shopping with Zee?"

"She's an exception—she's a solitary fairy. Most of the fae in New York are part of Oberon's court, and have all the wealth they could possibly desire."

"Oberon's court. That's where we're going? Some sort of fairy realm?"

"Yes. And Oberon is their king." He slipped into a pair of shoes. "Maybe we can catch Abrax coming in or out. It's our best chance."

"But he had a huge head start." She closed her eyes, trying to think of all the times she and Katie had sneaked into clubs in London when they couldn't afford the entry fee. They'd usually asked a bartender or waiter they knew to add them to the list. "Are there staff there? A hostess you could charm?"

Kester paced across the floor like a caged animal. "We won't be able to talk to them until we get in. It's in another dimension. The only way in is through magic we can't control."

Another dimension? Bloody hell. "Well, how does Zee's hairstylist get in? Luis? She said something about how he's always there with redheads."

Kester stopped pacing, and his green eyes flicked to hers. "Tell me about him."

She rubbed her forehead. "I don't know much, except that he's slightly creepy and into gingers."

"How big is he?"

"Big. Muscular. About your size."

Kester rubbed a hand over his chin. "He might be fae."

"What would a fae be doing cutting hair, if they're infinitely wealthy?" She touched her lips. "Though you did say they're hedonists—and he was a little too fond of massaging my hair. He leaned down and sniffed it at one point. I did think that was odd."

"Exactly. Fae have their own particular earthly pleasures that excite them. For some it's food, for some it's sex. And for Luis, apparently, it's hair."

"I'll call him."

Kester nodded. "Good. Just don't tell him why we want to go. Oberon's is supposed to be used for pure pleasure only. If he invites any trouble inside, he'll be banned for life."

She bent down, snatching her purse from the floor. "Don't worry. I'll use my silky charm." She pulled out her mobile phone, and dialed Luis's number. He picked up on the third ring. In the background she could hear "Girl, You Got a Magic Body" playing.

"Hi, Luis. This is Ursula. You, um, cut my hair recently."

"Mmm. Ginger. You want a scalp massage?"

"Actually, I was wondering if you're going to Oberon's tonight? I heard you talking about it with Zee when you were doing that amazing thing to my scalp. And, well, I just wanted to try it out. I've heard it's the best place to enjoy yourself."

"I wasn't planning on going. But for you, I could change my plans."

"Ooh, that's wonderful." She let her voice drip with honey. "And Kester will be with me."

"Oh," he said flatly. "They won't want the Headsman inside."

"I'll let you touch my hair," she blurted. "It's important. I mean, it's important that I enjoy myself." *Lure him in, Ursula, like a master.* "And it's important that my hair... enjoys itself... with your fingers on it. You can smell it." *Bollocks.*

"Mmmm." She heard him take a long breath through his nose. "Yes. Let me get dressed. You'll be on the list under Kester's name. Peele. I'll tell them to make an exception for tonight, and the wards will be lifted for both of you. Your hair will get to enjoy itself with my hands all night." He hung up with a click.

She grimaced at what she'd just agreed to.

Kester was staring at her. "That was your silky charm?"

She scowled. "Hey. It worked. I'm getting us into Oberon's, which is more than you could do. Let's go." She was charged up with Emerazel's fire, and her body burned with power.

"Not so fast. We have some preparation to do first." He looked down at her blood-soaked dress. "Staring with getting you out of that gown."

She arched an eyebrow. If Zee's unconscious body weren't a few feet away putting a damper on things, that statement might have made her blush. "And what did you have in mind?"

"Fae fashion is extremely opulent." He walked around her, his gaze sliding down her body. "I think I know just the right look for you."

She crossed her arms. "You're going to dress me?"

Before she'd even got the words out, he was chanting in his magical language, and his magic caressed her skin. Her dress began to transform, the grey silk taking on a stunning grass-green hue. It floated around her legs as if on a vernal wind, the delicate fabric skimming over her thighs. Two long slits inched up the front while her neckline plunged. Gold vines snaked around her waist to just below her breasts, holding the stunning fabric in place. Silver bracelets appeared on her wrists, and a warm, white fur jacket appeared in his hands. With a graceful flourish he placed the jacket on her shoulders.

Staring at his creation, he ran a finger over his lower lip. "Now you look perfect."

She glanced down at her ensemble. "I didn't have you pegged as a clothing designer."

"There's very little I'm not good at."

She nearly pulled a muscle rolling her eyes.

Chapter 28

$\mathcal{H}$e turned to one of his bookcases and began retrieving magazines from a shelf and tossing them onto the floor. Each featured a boat on the cover, and had titles like *All Things Sailing* and *Anchors Away.*

She narrowed her eyes. "Is there some sort of nautical solution to Zee's missing soul?"

He leaned over, staring into the shelf. "I need to consult my grimoires. We need to conjure a protective ward to prevent the incubus from using his shadow magic on us."

"You know when a magical ward would have been helpful? When I was at the opera." She stepped closer, peering over his shoulder. The magazines had hidden a metal button, and Kester pushed it. Something clicked loudly, and a nearby bookcase swung forward on a hinge, creaking over the floor. On the back of the bookshelf was a small collection of swords and knives, but the real treasure seemed to be a hidden alcove in the wall, that glowed with that magical amber light. As she peered over his shoulder, she saw that the light protected a small collection of books, just like the ones in the Plaza apartment.

"I'm going to need your help in a minute."

That was something she'd never thought she'd hear him say. "What do I need to do?"

He glanced at her. "A ward spell derives its strength from the souls of the people who create it. Magic is always more powerful when there are multiple spell-casters. If we cast one together, it will be doubly strong."

"And we'll be reading from one of those books?"

"Yes." He held his hands over the amber light, closing his eyes. Slowly he intoned a single word, his deep voice a velvet caress over her skin: *Oriel*. As soon as he'd enunciated the final syllable, the glow on the bindings ebbed away.

The driving wind battered the boat, and Kester ran a finger along the spines of the volumes, muttering to himself. "The *Heptameron* is too celestial. The *Liber Juratus* should have it." He pulled it from the shelf and began flipping through the pages, skimming the text. "Ok, here it is. Honorius's Armor—this will repel almost any magic." He pointed to the looping lettering written on the page. "It's Angelic. Do you think you can read it?"

She stepped over to his side, looking down at the yellowed pages. She couldn't quite understand the words, but she knew how to sound them out—just as she had when she'd first summoned Emerazel. Obviously, F.U. had done something useful with her time. "Definitely."

Kester began to read and Ursula joined in. As soon as they began to speak she felt the magic rushing over her skin, like she'd just stepped into a warm bath. As they intoned the spell, her skin grew warmer and the sensation grew more sensual. The words almost seemed to draw her closer to Kester, like a magnetic pull. Underneath his cedar smell was something darker she couldn't identify, something that drew her in. The dull ache of loneliness that always seemed to gnaw at her heart began to soothe.

As they intoned the final stanza, she felt his arm brush against hers, sending a jolt of electricity through her body. But at the final utterance, the spell between them snapped away. Ursula gasped like she'd been dropped into the river outside. For a moment, her skin felt like it was encrusted with ice, then a dull fatigue took over again.

"What was that? I felt something..." She struggled to describe the sensation.

He closed the book, sliding it back onto the shelf. "That was a magical aura, a byproduct of casting a spell. It's strengthened my aura, giving me a sort of magical armor from fae weaponry. On top of that, any spell I cast will be more powerful now."

"Your aura? What about mine? You said the spell would protect *us*."

"It protects me, and I will protect you. There's a good chance we'll need to fight our way out of there."

She fumed. "My role is to be protected? I thought I was supposed to be a demon warrior now."

"Swords are great, but you don't know any magic." He crossed to Zee, scooping her up from the table. "Look, I'm going to tuck Zee into bed and get myself ready. We'll leave in five minutes." He disappeared into one of the rooms in the bow of the boat.

Alone in the main cabin, Ursula had time to look around. The fire crackled invitingly in the stove, while the spray from the river lashed the portholes.

With a groan, she stretched her arms over her head. Her whole body ached like she'd just gotten over the flu. Giving Kester part of her aura was apparently hard on the nervous system—not to mention the rest of the magical shitstorm she'd been through this evening.

She walked to one of the bookshelves. For some bizarre reason, learning that Kester was a voracious reader was the most shocking revelation of all tonight. She scanned the spines—a row of the classics: Shakespeare, Melville, Dante, Dumas.

Ursula pulled out a volume of Homer and flipped it open. The pages were stiff and smelled of fresh ink; he wasn't reading these books. The shelf below held more recent novels: Doyle, Verne, Burroughs, Christie, even Brontë. The spine of Jane Eyre was creased and faded. Flipping through, she noticed some underlined passages. *I am no bird; and no net ensnares me: I am a free human being with an independent will.*

Kester's heels clapped over the boards, and she nearly jumped out of her skin, suddenly overcome by the feeling that she was invading his privacy. She shoved the book back on the shelf before glancing at him.

He now wore a moss-green shirt, open to his stomach to expose his chiseled chest, and leather bands around his wrists. His trousers were midnight blue velvet, and fitted to his body, and boots were laced up to his knees.

Ursula gave a low whistle. "You look amazing."

He frowned. "I look like a knob. But this is how they dress." He picked up the white fur jacket he'd spelled into existence and passed it to her. "Joe will be here any minute. I'll instruct you in the car on the way over. Are you sure you're up for this?"

She shot him a sharp look. Ursula was gradually coming to understand that F.U. hadn't been a girl to be trifled with. "Don't underestimate me, Kester Peele. Let's go." She slipped into the jacket, and strode off his boat into the stormy winter air.

Chapter 29

The Bentley stopped on a deserted New York City block, the street lined with darkened brick buildings. Ursula stepped out of the car, tugging the fur coat tightly around her flowing green dress. A rusty steel door in a brick wall wasn't exactly what she'd expected for a portal to the faerie realm. There was nothing around it but a small buzzer set into the brick, and a camera discreetly positioned above the door. The air smelled of stale piss.

Wrinkling her nose, she clutched her wyrm-skin purse, her good luck charm tucked safely inside. "Are you sure this is the right place?" she asked.

"Yeah, this is it." His green eyes flashed a look that said *don't second guess me*. "Do you remember your instructions?"

"Of course." How could she forget them? He'd made her repeat them to him on the way over in the Bentley. "Don't speak to anyone. Don't eat or drink anything, but somehow manage to convey debauchery while not having any fun whatsoever."

"You'll have to maintain control. You've never been exposed to a legion of fae auras before. Even going in there might make you susceptible to hedonistic impulses."

"And you won't be susceptible to these impulses?"

"Males don't react to the fae aura in the same way. We're more likely to get possessive or territorial. All the more reason for you to stick near me, so I don't have to murder anyone who tries to take advantage of you."

"I feel like we're walking into some kind of caveman era."

"Their culture is different from yours. The women are submissive. They're only around to please the males."

She shuddered. *What did he mean by 'your culture'?* She made a mental note to ask him about that later. "What century are these people from?"

He shrugged. "The king is nearly a hundred thousand years old. So, yes, caveman era."

Her stomach tightened. "Are you serious?"

"I'll need to act as though I've claimed you. An unclaimed women can be taken by the king."

"What does *claiming* me mean?"

"It means it's a good thing you find me attractive."

Her mouth dropped open. "What are you talking about?" she sputtered.

"Don't think I didn't notice." He adjusted his leather wristbands. "Anyway, that's not important. Abrax will probably be swanning around Oberon. We need to get invited into the king's inner circle. You'll have to catch his eye, while making it clear you're with me, or he'll try to drag you away to mate with you. The fae are quite keen on redheads."

"Drag me away to mate? You've got to be kidding me."

"Just let me do the talking. I know you'll hate it, but in the fae world, these matters are only handled by men. They respect physical strength." The frigid wind rippled his dark hair.

"Can we just get this over with? It's no wonder Zee got the hell out of the fae world."

Kester pressed the buzzer. Nothing sounded, but after a few moments, the door cracked open. A young man with long, silver hair peered out, the room behind him obscured in shadows.

"Your names," he prompted. His fingernails were filed into points and painted white.

"We're on the list under Peele," said Kester, wrapping his arm around her waist. "Guests of Luis."

The man's eyes flicked to Ursula's red hair, and she tossed it over her shoulder for emphasis.

"Of course." He shut the door, and they waited. At least a minute passed as Ursula drummed her fingers against her thighs, trying to force images of Emerazel out of her mind. With Zee's soul missing, there hadn't been time to think about her own fate yet. But how long could Kester keep the fire goddess in the dark about her failure tonight?

Kester shot her a sharp look. "Relax. You look like you're on a suicide mission."

"We *are* on suicide mission," she snapped.

At last, the man reopened the door and beckoned them into a high-ceilinged hall, draped on one end with lush green curtains. The walls were bare, seemingly made of tree bark, and dimly lit with honeyed light. At first she thought the light came from candles, but when her eyes adjusted she saw miniature luminescent orbs hanging in the air above them.

The fae's eyes matched his silver hair; she hadn't once seen him blink. It was deeply unnerving. "Welcome to Oberon's." Halfheartedly, he held out a hand. "May I take your coat?"

Ursula pulled off her jacket and handed it over, but the fae simply yelled, "Mavelle!"

A raven-haired female in a transparent red gown hurried through the curtains, grabbing Ursula's fur jacket before disappearing again.

I guess that's the female submission thing. God, she was going to hate this place.

The male fae beckoned them toward the curtains. With a flick of his wrist, he pulled them aside, revealing an enormous pair of wooden doors, ornately carved with oak leaves. A large stag's antler was affixed to each door as a sort of handle. The doors were inscribed with gold letters that seemed to twist and move like living creatures—just like the walls in the locked room she'd broken into.

Without a word, the fae grasped the antlers, pulling open the doors.

Ursula sucked in a breath, gaping at the enormous hall. They walked forward onto a small balcony, and she peered down at a stairwell that curved to a dance floor below. Fae danced and drank over a floor carpeted with wildflowers and grass.

Still, her eye was drawn upward. Great columns of wood, as thick and sturdy as the trunks of redwood trees, supported a ceiling so far above them it disappeared into darkness. Glowing orbs lit the hall, some as small as insects, others as large as horses, swirling and dancing in the air above their heads like sea creatures buffeted by an unseen tide.

"How does this place exist?" Ursula breathed.

Kester slipped a hand around her waist. "Magic," he whispered.

She glanced down at the crowd, at the fae dressed in stunning styles she'd never seen before—flowing silks of sapphire, plum, and fern green; limbs ensconced in curling gold jewelry. One woman sported hair that pulsated blue and green like the lights of a deep-sea fish. Another, dressed only in gossamer film, spun in a circle, sparks of magic streaming from the tips of her fingers like summer fireworks. Around the edges of the hall, leather clad men sat in wooden chairs, watching beautiful women dance in nothing but a few strategically placed seashells and flowers. Deep, resonant music filled the air, vibrating through Ursula's body, and she inhaled the rich scent of moss and lilacs.

Flipping heck. She hadn't even drunk the alcohol, and she was already getting seduced by the atmosphere.

"Stay focused." Kester grabbed her hand, leading her down the stairs. "Abrax will be skulking somewhere near the king."

As she stepped onto the dance floor, fae brushed against her. They moved effortlessly, their bodies swaying in perfect rhythm to the beat that trembled over her skin. There was a charge—an energy—in the air; it intoxicated her, and she had to remind herself why she was here. *I'm here for Zee.*

Kester slid his fingers down her arm, leaving a trail of tingles, and grabbed her hand. "Scan the crowd, but he'll probably be in the king's inner circle. He doesn't trifle with commoners."

"What are you going to do when we find him?"

His jaw suddenly tightened, and a hint of violence glinted in his green eyes. "I'm going to try not to rip him limb from limb, but I make no promises." The terrifying look on his face was enough to shove the lingering waves of pleasure to the back of Ursula's skull, and she let him lead her between the dancers.

They threaded their way through the sea of writhing fae as she scanned for Abrax. They moved deeper into the hall, and the men's clothing changed, becoming more formal—stiff golden brocades and ruffled lace collars. The women, of course, still wore transparent gowns and scraps of lace. As Ursula watched the ladies dance, it was hard not to let her own hips sway, or feel a thrill at Kester's body brushing against hers.

She leaned into him, whispering. "What's with the Elizabethan ruffs?"

"These fae are part of King Oberon's court."

Just as she was going to ask what the king looked like, she glimpsed something between the dancers: surrounded by armed males dressed in golden armor, a tall fae sat enthroned on a low wooden dais. His pale hair shone in the light, his body radiating a shimmering golden glow.

Ursula gaped. "Is that the king?"

Kester stepped in front of her. "Don't look him in the eye yet."

"What's the matter?"

"You're new here. And you stand out. If we want to get into his inner circle, we want him to notice you, but not claim you." He slipped one arm around her back, touching her cheek with his other hand. "I need them to know you're here with me."

With Kester standing so close, it was hard not to breathe in his delicious loamy aroma, and she wanted to wrap her arms around him. The music trembled over her skin in rushes of pleasure. Part of her mind screamed that Kester had an arrogance problem, that she hated guys like him, that she needed to stay focused on... something. Only she couldn't remember what. Her gaze landed on a beautiful blond fae dressed in white lace lingerie, dancing for one of the fae males. *It would be so great if I could just let go...*

The slow, sensual beat reverberated through the hall, hypnotizing her, and her gaze flicked to Kester's stunning mouth. She glanced up at him, licking her lips. God, he was gorgeous, and the carnal glint in his eye was driving her crazy. Her pulse raced.

The music rippled over her body, sending thrills through her as the beat slowed down. With the rhythm pulsing, Ursula let her hips sway against him. She slipped her arms over his shoulders, pressing her body against his solid muscle. Delicious warmth radiated through his clothes.

Slowly, he leaned down, tracing his soft lips over her throat, his thumb lazily stroking her back.

"What are you doing?" she whispered, her pulse racing faster.

"Showing them you're taken," he murmured into her neck. He slid his fingers into her hair and gripped it tight, pulling back her head, then grazed his fangs along her throat. A hot thrill rushed through her belly, all rational thought leaving her mind. Was there some reason they'd come here?

High above them, magical orbs flashed like strobe lights and the bass reverberated through her very core.

"The king's watching," Kester whispered, his breath warming the shell of her ear. "I'll just make sure he understands he can't claim you."

Ursula ran her hand down his strong back, and his eyes took on a glazed look. He leaned closer, pressing his warm mouth against hers. The touch of his soft lips sent fire racing through her veins, and she arched into him, her lips parting. His tongue brushed hers, and she wanted to rip off his clothes and run her hands all over his golden skin. *This* was why they'd come here, right? Heat coursed through her; she wanted him to pull her into a corner and—

From behind, a hand gripped her shoulder, ripping her out of the kiss. With a tremendous effort, she pulled away from Kester, and turned to see two guards in golden armor, their blond hair and pale blue eyes exactly like Zee's. Ursula's stomach tightened, and she forced herself to move away from Kester as she surveyed the men. That kiss had completely knocked her off her feet, and she could hardly think straight. *Focus, Ursula. This is life or death.* The men's breastplates were finely-tooled, with silver stags around an oak leaf—but her gaze darted straight to the sheathed swords, encrusted with glittering pearls. *Always good to know where the weapons are.*

One of the guards spoke. "Oberon has requested an audience."

"We would be honored to speak to the king," said Kester.

The guards pivoted, flanking them. As they were escorted to the dais, the fae stopped dancing, and hundreds of eyes followed them. Ursula swallowed hard as the guards led them right up to the edge of the dais, where the king stood, flanked by soldiers.

Chapter 30

*U*p close, Oberon looked like four hundred pounds of pure muscle. His outfit was formal—regal, even: a yellow robe tied at his waist with a golden belt and a pair of silver pauldrons to protect his shoulders. He held a halberd with a copper-plated point in the shape of stag's antler, and he stared at them with a grim expression. A sword lay strapped across his back. It was a hall of pleasure, but he'd obviously come ready for a fight.

"What brings you to my hall with this beautiful female, *Headsman*?" His voice was melodious and soft, but he still managed to spit the last word like he'd been fed a piece of spoiled meat. When he spoke, long pointed teeth shone in the amber lights.

"We simply wanted to partake in the festivities." Kester's eyes scanned the room, probably looking for Abrax.

Were they getting close to that point where they'd have to fight their way out? Ursula eyed one of the guard's swords. She could draw it from its sheath with a quick yank, and slice through two of them. Unfortunately, she had no idea how to leave the hall, especially with all the guards that would descend upon her. Also, she had no idea what F.U. had been up to in her spare time, but New Ursula didn't quite feel like a murderer. Better to wait and see how things played out, before jumping right in with the stabbing.

"Here for pleasure?" Oberon's gaze raked her up and down, and she had the disconcerting feeling that he could see right through her gown. "She's a beauty. But she belongs to you?" His voice dripped with disappointment.

"She does."

The king sniffed the air, his lip curling. "One of Emerazel's," he hissed. "She must be hard to tame. I like that."

Gross. Ursula felt the fire rising in her chest.

"I'm still working on taming her." Kester gave a low bow, and she resisted elbowing him in the gut.

Oberon let out a snarl. "Since I can't have her, I would like to watch you mate with her."

Ursula's jaw dropped open. *What?*

Kester smiled nonchalantly, as if this were a completely reasonable suggestion. "Of course. But she's a bit shy. We must go somewhere with a smaller crowd."

Her heart raced. That wasn't what he meant by *claiming,* was it? Obviously, Kester was hot, but she wasn't about to put on a public show.

"Fine," said Oberon. "I'll take you to my exclusive suite."

Kester nodded. "She won't disappoint."

Ursula bit down a thousand angry retorts. *What. The. Fuck.* She tried not to scowl, reminding herself that they were here for Zee, and that surely Kester had some plan in mind that didn't involve shagging her in front of the king. Then again, it wasn't like Kester was open about his plans.

One of the guards beckoned them forward, and Kester led her onto the dais, pulling her close. Oberon stamped the butt of the halberd on the wood. With a slight jerk, the whole platform began to rise slowly into the air, until they were thirty feet off the ground.

Kester leaned into her, whispering, "Don't worry."

The dais continued to rise, until they were a hundred feet in the air, the crowd below growing smaller. She tried not to give in to the vertigo, or the disorientation of realizing that the columns were actually enormous tree roots. *Are we in a giant tree?* Dizzy, she stepped back from the edge.

"Magnificent, isn't it?" Oberon intoned from behind her. "I've ruled these fae since we first came from the heavens, and I never grow tired of the view."

She turned, surveying the king. His eyes were clear and his skin unlined. If she'd been asked, Ursula would have guessed he was no older than forty, though with his strange coloring and enormous size, he looked distinctly otherworldly. She wasn't supposed to speak, and this man was creepy enough that she was actually pleased with that particular demand. So she just widened her eyes, trying to look as innocent and stupid as possible.

He moved closer to her, bending over her neck and taking a long sniff. "Ahh. I never get tired of that, either. The scent of a female ready to mate."

Revulsion rose in Ursula's throat. *Get me out of here. I'll take Emerazel's hellfire over this guy.*

The king continued on his monologue. "I was born before the sundering, before the gods were exiled from the heavens, and yet I still thrill at the sight of a young beauty like you." He laced his fingers together. "Out of curiosity, has the Headsman told you how old *he* is?"

"Three hundred ninety-four," said Kester from her side.

Ursula turned, gaping at him. *He's three hundred and ninety-four years old?* That meant he'd been born in the 1620s, back when people thought diseases were caused by an imbalance of the humors, and went to public executions for fun. Did that mean *she* would have to reap souls for four hundred years to pay off her debt to Emerazel? A spark of anger ignited. Kester had been remarkably silent on that point—and what *was* his plan for this mating thing? It wasn't like she really trusted him.

She shuddered. Honestly, she wouldn't make it four hundred years. Not if she continued to fail at reaping souls.

Fire roiled in her blood, and she tried to push her panicked thoughts out of her mind. She needed to focus on getting Zee and Hugo's souls back, and then getting the fuck out.

The dais slowed, pulling up at a wooden balcony that jutted from a tree root.

"Welcome to my private apartment," said Oberon. "Some of my closest friends are here."

A lick of hope sparked. *Does that include Abrax?*

The platform slid neatly against the balcony, and the king's guards ushered them forward into another, smaller hall, its ceiling a network of flowering vines. In the center, vibrantly dressed guests stood around a banquet table, and others lingered around a bar carved from oak, sipping jewel-colored cocktails.

As Oberon led them into the hall, every one of the guests turned to stare at Ursula and Kester. Kester gave a cursory bow, but his eyes never stopped scanning, searching for Abrax.

The crowd parted for Oberon as he walked to the banquet table, laden with a suckling pig and fruit. With a low growl, the king pushed the food off the table. Rage burned in Ursula's chest. *Is he clearing space for us to mate? Am I supposed to replace the suckling pig?* She glanced around the room, searching desperately for Abrax, but she couldn't find the bastard.

Oberon turned, his lips curled back from his sharp teeth. His footsteps echoed through the room as he approached Ursula, and her stomach tightened. He stopped just inches from her, and warm light glinted off his rings as he reached up to touch her cheek.

Okay, this has gone on for long enough.

"Don't touch my mate," said Kester, his voice booming.

"I can see the fire in her eyes," the king snarled, touching her neck. "I want to tame—"

Dropping her wyrm-skin purse, Ursula snatched his hand, molten hellfire inflaming her veins. She was an ancient fury, come to bathe the world in fire. "I'm not fucking around anymore," she shouted. "Give me Abrax or I will burn this place to the ground."

The king's face contorted in agony; smoke curled from his hand. The guards drew their weapons, but Kester was already chanting in Angelic. As he spoke, his words froze the king and his guards. They grimaced with agony, the sound of crunching bones and sinews filled the room as fae bodies twisted, breaking. The king gagged, his eyes bulging.

So that's why he got the creepy nickname.

While Kester crippled Oberon with his magic, she let go of the king's arms, stealing a sword from one of the guards. It felt glorious in her hands, light and swift. "Where is Abrax?" she demanded—louder, so the whole crowd could hear.

Frantically, her eyes scanned the room for any signs of him by the back of the room, but it wasn't until she turned to look back at Kester that she saw the incubus.

Abrax stood right behind Kester, tendrils of inky midnight magic curling off him like smoke.

"Kester!" she shouted.

But it was too late. In a blur of shadowy motion, Abrax snapped Kester's neck. The crack of his spine echoed off the ceiling, and horror blared through Ursula's skull.

Chapter 31

As Kester's limp body crashed to the floor, Ursula lifted her sword. His spell no longer held the fae in thrall, and they snarled, eyes flashing at her. She gripped the sword, raw panic tearing her mind apart. *Kester. Kester is dead.* She tried to shove the horror deep into her mental vault. She couldn't let fear overcome her now, not when a pack of furious fae surrounded her, baying for her blood.

But as she stared into the vengeful face of the fae king, something else began to surge, coursing through each of her muscles: a sharp sense of sureness, as if she knew exactly how each of her joints needed to move. Primal wrath hit her like a wave, imbuing her body with a dark power. *I will avenge him.*

Oberon reached behind him and drew a wicked looking sword from the sheath on his back. His eyes locked on hers, his grin a thing of terror.

But hot battle fury overtook Ursula, and she grinned back, cutting her sword through the air in a display of her skill. She was no longer Ursula. She was Vengeance, ancient and primal. When Oberon lunged, she was ready for him. His blade struck hers, and the sound of clanging swords rang out. The king was fast—almost too fast for her—and his sword slashed above her head with a *whoosh.*

I will avenge him.

Wrath flooded her nerve endings. She began to circle Oberon, her movements fast and precise, and she saw a glint of fear in the king's eyes. In a lethal dance, they whirled and ducked, fast as the wind. The air rushed over her body, until the king began to falter. She scented his fear, wanted his blood.

As the king tired, his guards moved in, swords drawn, and she was no longer fighting one fae, but three. She spun, her sword clashing in a blur of steel, slicing into muscle and flesh. Arcs of red blood sprayed through the air, and she no longer knew who she was fighting; she only knew that she wanted to kill.

Another guard swung for her and she ducked, her sword slashing for his legs. But the fae leapt into the air, bringing the pommel of his sword down on the back of her head.

Pain exploded through her skull; she stumbled back, dropping her blade. Her vision darkened and rough hands grabbed her, pulling her to the floor.

When her vision cleared, the king and Abrax stood above her while six fae guards pinned her to the ground.

"You stupid bitch," Oberon spat. "Once I'm done using you for pleasure, I will flay you alive."

Rage stole her breath. *Kester is dead. And they're going to kill me. Bastards.*

Wild with fury, she struggled to free herself, but the grip of the fae's hands were too strong. Abrax bent low, narrowing his eyes. He touched her cheek, purring. "What kind of thing are you?" He ran his fingers over her skin, and bile rose in her throat.

"Strip her," said Oberon.

Fire. In her panic she'd forgotten to use Emerazel's fire. She let the volcanic rage blaze white-hot, and the fae released her.

Just as she was scrambling to her feet, a growl rumbled

through the hall. A dark beast crashed into the crowd of fae, green eyes blazing. The female fae screamed, running for the movable dais. As soon as they crowded on, it began to lower.

Kester? The hound circled her, snarling at the fae who surrounded her with swords drawn. He was protecting her.

Relief flooded her. How the hell was he alive?

It struck her like a bolt of lightning. *The spell.* Whatever spell they'd chanted before leaving had actually worked. Not only that, but it must have changed his hound form. He was ten feet tall at least.

She rose, snatching the fallen sword from the ground.

Kester's eyes blazed; blood dripped from his jaw. A guard swung for him, and he roared, picking up the fae in his teeth and flinging him across the room.

The king drew his sword again, his eyes locked on Ursula. "Filthy animals."

Kester snarled at the king, who now stood surrounded by a troop of fae guards.

"Get him to safety," one of them shouted. As they closed in around the king, their bodies shimmered away, leaving behind only a pale, iridescent glimmer. The temperature in the room chilled by ten degrees.

Ursula whirled, gripping her sword and scanning the room for Abrax. The incubus stood near the balcony, gripping the king's halberd. Blood dripped from his fingers—Kester must have bitten him before lunging into the crowd.

Kester's lip curled back from his teeth, and his deep growl resonated through her bones. Abrax swung the halberd in a tight figure eight, his eyes locked on the hound. The incubus's blade began to glow, charging with some kind of magic. When he slashed it, a bolt of blue light shot straight at the hound. But

Kester had already leapt away. Snarling, he charged the incubus. Abrax dodged, moving like a cloud of curling black smoke and reappearing a few feet away. Kester skidded to a stop, just missing him.

Just as Abrax swung the halberd's blade, Ursula heard footfalls behind her. Sword ready, she whirled to find one of the king's guards remaining, his platinum hair swirling around his head like a living thing. "The king will enjoy playing with you once I subdue you." His pale eyes flashed, and he slashed his blade, but the battle fury already burned through Ursula, and she parried.

That sense of precision filled her muscles, warming her like a desert wind. *They think I'm an animal.* He was fast, but she was faster. *They want to slaughter me like a pig.* Their swords clanged as she attacked and he parried. She backed him against the bar until he faltered. *Kill.* She drove her sword through his chest.

As she watched blood bubble from his mouth, horror hit her. She'd just *killed* someone. But there wasn't time to think about what she'd done—not with Kester's growl filling the hall. She spun to find his jaws locked on Abrax's arm, snapping the incubus's bones.

Her hands shaking, Ursula stared down at her crimson blade. *What kind of killer was F.U.?*

The incubus's roar called her attention back to the fight, and she watched as his halberd skittered across the floor. Her heart sped up—they were too close to the edge.

Kester leapt for the incubus's throat, but he curled away in a cloud of black smoke, appearing again at the platform's edge. Kester pounced, and Ursula's world tilted as she watched them both plummet over the edge.

"Kester!" she screamed, running to the ledge. Her blood roaring in her ears, she peered into the abyss. Desperately, she hoped to see Kester clinging by his fingertips to one of the tree roots, but there was no sign of him. Far below she could see the orbs swirling, and the music thumped in the distance. Panic stole her breath, and for just a moment, the steep drop into oblivion called to her, like a magnetic pull.

But oblivion did not await her at the other end of death. Eternal hellfire awaited her.

All the blood rushed from her head, and she fell to her knees. He'd survived the neck snapping, but surely even magic couldn't save a body from a fall like that. Her chest welled with an aching sadness, before pure terror overcame her. *There's no way out.* She was stuck in a fae's subterranean lair with an army of soldiers who wanted to rape and murder her. Even death wasn't an escape.

There was no air. *I can't breathe.*

Please let this be a terrible nightmare—there was no fight, no fae, no incubus. Kester didn't fall to his death. In a few moments she'd wake up in her East London flat, ready to drink tea on the couch while Katie regaled her with details of all the guys she'd kissed the night before.

Ursula closed her eyes, taking a deep breath. The floor of the hall was still a thousand feet below her, the abyss oddly inviting in her desperation.

She turned back to the balcony. Apart from the crumpled body of the guard she'd slaughtered, it was empty. Blood stained the wood, and the sweet, metallic smell was overwhelming. She scanned the floor for her wyrm-skin purse, but she couldn't see it anywhere. It must have gotten knocked off the ledge in the fight. Her heart hammered against her ribs. *My white stone.* She had nothing now.

She glanced down again at her bloodied hands. She'd killed someone tonight, with a great degree of skill. What the hell kind of monster had F.U. been? A trained killer? An assassin? And what had happened to Kester?

A hollow opened in the pit of her stomach. Kester's fall would have landed him right in a crowd of fae who wanted him dead. And what did that mean for *his* soul? He hadn't paid off his debt yet, even after four hundred years. Tears stung her eyes, but she clenched her jaw, marshaling her resolve. This was not the time to cry.

Distantly she could hear the beat of the music. *Thump. Thump.* She couldn't tell where her pounding heart ended and the music began.

The fae king wanted her dead, and at any moment he and his guards could return to finish the job. Even if she was some sort of master swordsman, she couldn't fend them off forever. But with the dais gone, there was no way out. *Thump. Thump.*

The sigil. If only she could find something flammable.

Her eyes darted to the bar in the back, and she rushed across the blood-slicked floor, stepping over the guard's corpse. Bottles lined the back shelves, and with a shaking hand she snatched a bottle of a dark-looking spirit. She popped the cork and gave the bottle a sniff, then grimaced. It had to be at least a hundred proof.

The bass deepened. *Thump. Thump. Thump.* Distantly, the crowd cheered, the party still raging. Maybe incubi and hellhounds falling to their deaths from the king's balcony was an everyday occurrence here. She wanted out of this awful place.

In the center of the room, she poured the whiskey in the shape of Emerazel's sigil.

Thump. Thump. The bass was so loud it rattled the floor. How could they continue to dance, with the two pulverized bodies in their midst?

The beat was almost deafening. Something was happening in the hall, but just as she started toward the edge, a gust of icy wind rushed over her skin. She stared in horror as enormous wings rose above the balcony. *Thump. Thump. Thump.* She stared into Abrax's cold, beautiful face.

He looked glorious and terrifying at the same time, like a medieval painting of the Angel of Darkness. His body had transformed, and claws and talons had grown from his hands and feet. All around him, black mist twisted and swirled like ink in water. His frigid gaze fixed on hers.

"Did you think I forgot about you?" Gracefully, he landed on the edge of the balcony and stalked closer.

Ice ran up her spine, and she stumbled back. *Where the fuck is that sword?* Her gaze landed on the king's halberd, discarded on the floor. She dove for it just as the incubus swooped in, his talons raking the wood. She slid across the floor, grasping for the weapon, but the incubus caught her leg with one of his talons, yanking her toward him, ripping through her flesh. As the pain pierced her, she unleashed an agonized scream.

Abrax flipped her over, yanking her under him and pinning her to the floor, claws piercing her wrists. He was going to tear all the flesh from her bones, and the agony blinded her. She arched her back, screaming.

"Really, Ursula. That blade wouldn't have stopped me," he growled, his leathery wings spread out above her, and pressed his claws further into her flesh. Pain screamed through her forearms.

Her pulse raced, the pain so intense she couldn't think straight. She wouldn't be able to fight him anymore, not with her muscles torn apart. "What do you want from me?" she managed.

He leaned closer, whispering, "I want to know who you are." His voice was soft, seductive.

She gritted her teeth, trying to think through the agony. "You and me both," she choked out. Fury flooded her, and she let Emerazel's fire blaze, burning like the sun's core, until it seared the incubus's hands, igniting his clothes. He leapt up, his wings beating the air. Embers sparked from his wings, and he swooped over the main hall, circling like a beast of prey. He wasn't finished with her.

Blood poured from her wrists, and flames licked at her body. Emerazel's fire had ignited the whiskey, and the sigil blazed brightly around her.

Her eyes flicked to Abrax, who was diving right for her, his face etched with cold wrath. She closed her eyes and chanted the sigil spell, just before the incubus's powerful body had the chance to slam into her.

Chapter 32

*U*rsula reconstituted on the floor of the sigil room. For once, she'd remembered to hold her breath, but the pain that tore through her arms and legs was far worse than the soot in her lungs. She glanced down at her ravaged forearms, and the gashes in her leg from Abrax's talons. They had ripped right into the muscle, and blood pumped from the wounds. Dizzy, she tried to stand, pain splintering her limbs, and only made it to her knees. Her body shook violently, and nausea overwhelmed her. An image flashed in her mind of the slumped fae corpse—the man she'd so casually killed.

She couldn't give in yet. What if Kester was still in the fae realm, still alive somehow and being tortured to death? Nauseated, she stayed on all fours, watching the blood pour from her wounds.

Kester could have saved his own skin at least once by giving her up to Emerazel after her failure. Was that why he'd been so reckless tonight—because he knew he'd probably die anyway? Her stomach heaved, and she vomited.

Suppressing a scream, she forced herself up, her legs shaking. *How long until Emerazel comes for me?* Her right leg had been shredded by the talons, and she only lasted a few seconds before she was on the floor again, crawling this time. Slowly, each movement torture, she dragged herself into the hall. There was an extra cellphone in her bedroom. It would be agonizing climbing the stairs, but she'd get there eventually. *As long as I don't bleed out first.*

Blood smeared the hall as she crawled. If anyone wanted to fight her now, she'd just roll over and give up. *Just get to the phone, Ursula.* As soon as she dialed 911, help would be on the way. They'd stitch her up in the ER, maybe sew her veins back together. The gashes went straight through to the bone, but it would give her some time.

She paused, gasping for breath. *I'm not going to make it that far...*

What other options did she have? Kester had used a healing spell after the fight with the moor fiend. A healing spell would get her, quite literally, on her feet.

Focus, Ursula. Could she recall the spell, like she had with the sigil spell in Club Lalique? Probably not. She'd been unconscious when he'd chanted it over. She closed her eyes, racking her brain. Maybe it was somewhere in that procedural memory of hers. But, she had nowhere to begin.

The pain drowned out nearly all rational thought. She leaned back against the wall, closing her eyes and taking deep breaths to manage the agony.

She could *read* Angelic, even if she couldn't produce a spell out of thin air. What she needed was a spell book. Her eyes snapped open. *The library.* Those books had to be Henry's collection of grimoires, and she'd seen Kester unlock the books on his shelf. All she had to do was recite the unlocking spell and skim through their pages.

With a shock of pain, she forced herself onto her hands and knees again and crawled down the hall to the library. The hallway had never seemed so long before—but she'd never felt like she had knives piercing her bones before.

Kester. He had some sort of history with Abrax, she was pretty sure. He'd had an intense reaction when she told him about the incubus. He'd already wanted to kill him. Whatever their history, she wanted to hunt down Abrax and finish the job for him. She shuffled forward, groaning as she reached the library.

Almost there.

She dragged her broken body to the locked books. They stood just as she remembered them, lined up on the bottom shelf with that familiar glow emanating from their bindings. Grimacing, she reached for one, but the force field pushed her hand away.

She grunted, trying to think clearly. *How did Kester do it?* He'd simply held his hands out and recited a spell.

Not a spell, she thought. *That word—like a woman's name.* Gasping, she rolled onto her side and held out her shaking hands. She closed her eyes, picturing Kester's mouth as he spoke the word, his deep voice caressing her skin, and she repeated after him. "*Oriel.*"

As soon as she finished, a magical aura whispered over her skin, just like it had when she'd chanted the spells with Kester. The glow around the books flickered for a moment but didn't disappear. *Bollocks.*

She slumped back to the floor, the pain in her legs pure agony. Her breath came in short gasps, and the blood continued to pump from her wounds, staining the rug. There wasn't much time left.

She closed her eyes. If Oriel was a name, then maybe each of these locking spells were personalized, like a password on a computer. And if this apartment had belonged to Henry... How the fuck was she supposed to guess Henry's password? She knew nothing about the man apart from the festive state of his organs after his death. Her heart thrummed. Had she seen anything in the apartment, any photographs...?

The painting. There was a painting in the living room of a beautiful woman named Louisa. And if Kester had named his spell after a woman...

She reached out her hands again, choking out the name. "*Louisa.*"

For a moment she thought she'd guessed wrong, but then the yellow glow faded. Relief washed over her. *Finally getting somewhere.*

Her eye raced along the titles on the books' spines. There were copies of the *Fasciculus Chemicus* and the *Theatrum Chemicum Britannicum*, an ancient-looking book simply called *DAEMONS*, and an Angelic book that translated to "Lenus's Healing Spells and Poultices." *Bingo.* She pulled it from the shelf with a thud, barely able to lift herself off the floor. She flipped through it, translating the Angelic spell names at the top. God, she was so tired. She needed to sleep...

But if she fell asleep, she'd wake again bathed in flames.

Fear pushing her on, she refocused her attention. Spells for curing rashes, tinctures for alleviating gout, and conjurations by Ashmole, Norton, and Starkey. She flipped through an entire section on bovine maladies and crop sickness, rapidly losing the will to live.

Her hands were beginning to shake uncontrollably, and she glanced back at the shelf. One book was different from the others—smaller and made of leather, with no name on the spine. It looked more like a journal than a spell book. *Henry's ledger.* She pulled it from the shelf and flipped through page after page of Henry's adventures as a hellhound—each soul he'd claimed, rendered in his spindly handwriting. Desperately, her eyes searched for anything about injuries or a healing spell, until at least she neared the end of the book.

"Collected a pact from Gloria Franklin. A beautiful woman, but Emerazel's fire made her quite the diva. She scratched me so deeply that I had to incant Starkey's Conjuration..."

She almost screamed with relief. *Starkey's Conjuration* it was. She'd seen that one. She flipped back through *Lenus's Healing Spells*. Her vision began to narrow, darkening at the edges.

Please, gods, work.

She focused her dimming sight on the page, and read through the Angelic words about healing waves of light. The words rolled of her tongue, and as she got to the final stanza, she nearly smiled—it was the part she'd heard Kester recite over her broken body after she'd fought the moor fiend—the part about healing waters and leaching away pain.

At the final words, the air charged with a crackling electricity that traveled over her body in a rush, washing through her flesh and muscle. When it reached her arms and legs, a tremendous shock ripped through her. Her tunnel vision narrowed all the way down to a point, until nothing remained but Ursula and the darkness.

Chapter 33

$\mathscr{U}$rsula opened her eyes, staring at the library ceiling, her head resting on *Lenus's Healing Spells*. Her gaze darted to the window—still dark outside. Wind rattled the pane.

I'm not burning in an inferno. I must be alive.

She sat up, examining her arms and legs. Not a single scar remained, and her muscles felt strong enough to run a mile. If it weren't for the bloodbath around her and the shredded gown, she might have been able to convince herself it had all been a terrible dream.

She rose, surveying the room. *Blood everywhere.* It looked like a crime scene, red spattering the rug and books. Stepping into the hall, she eyed the trail of gore that led back to the sigil room, overcome by a desperate desire to clean it all up. She didn't know what sort of killer F.U. had been, but the sight and smell of it turned her stomach. Worse, the trail of blood in the hallway sparked something in the darkest recesses of her memory, something she didn't want to remember...

Frantically, she rushed to the kitchen, yanking open the closet and grabbing a mop and bucket. Her hands still shaking, she filled the bucket with water from the sink, and a hefty dollop of soap. *I need to get rid of the blood.*

She nearly spilled the bucket in her rush to drag it back into the hall, where she manically pushed the mop over the boards, sopping up vomit and gore. *I need this gone.* She'd killed someone tonight, and she'd seen Kester die. She hadn't known him long and hadn't liked him most of that time, yet she had the strange feeling that she'd miss him terribly if he were truly gone. She could envision his perfect face, his lips as he'd kissed her. *Please, Kester, don't be dead.* Maybe he'd bust through the door unannounced at any minute.

What the hell had happened in the fae realm? She didn't even know what Abrax had been doing there in the first place. Kester had said the fae were unaligned—they had nothing to do with the god of night.

She scrubbed the crimson-stained floor, trying to push out the image in her mind—Kester falling over the ledge—but the horrible vision kept returning to her. Abrax had slaughtered him viciously, without waiting to hear what they'd needed. They hadn't come to the fae realm to hurt anyone, just to get Zee's soul back. And she'd failed—miserably. Again.

Something cold and primal chilled her heart. She wanted revenge.

She'd lost not one but two souls tonight. She glanced down the hall at the sigil room, hoping to see Kester's athletic frame suddenly appear by some magical stroke of luck. But she was an idiot for counting on things like luck to save her—things like her stupid white stone. Luck was for the desperate, not for those with any sense of control over their lives.

A harsh, gnawing emptiness welled in her chest, and she threw down the mop. She needed to get control for once in her life, before Emerazel showed up and dragged her to the underworld. Maybe she could still reclaim Zee's soul. She could at least try.

And maybe—with Zee's help—she could find out what happened to Kester. If she was the one missing, Kester wouldn't just sit around mopping floors and crying. He'd do something about it, for fuck's sake.

Adrenaline coursed through her blood. She would be different—a New Ursula, one who took the hand she was given and dealt with it.

First, she needed to get out of her tattered, stained gown. She raced upstairs to the bathroom, stripping off her dress and turning on the shower. She stepped in, letting the hot stream of water wash the blood into the drain. She was already feeling better. After just a minute, she turned it off and toweled dry before crossing to her bedroom.

She rifled through her drawers for some of the black clothes Kester had bought her. *If I'm going to be an assassin, might as well own it.* Kester had been right—she wasn't a "spring colors" girl anymore. She was a demonic killer, and it was time to get used to it. If nothing else, she wanted to hunt down Abrax and rip out his claws, one by one.

She slipped into a pair of black leather pants, her black boots, and a dark top before pulling on a jacket.

She needed to hunt down the incubus. She'd get Zee's soul back, and then she'd slaughter him for what he'd done to Kester. Or, at least, she'd die trying.

Except—hadn't Kester said he'd been searching for Abrax for years with no success, and that tonight had been their only chance? So where the hell was she supposed to start? She didn't know the first thing about demonic lairs.

She crossed through the hall, thundering down the stairs. Whatever the case, she needed to start by reclaiming Zee's unconscious body.

She hurried to the armory, grabbing Honjo from the rack. A sense of strength flooded her as soon as she picked him up.

In a drawer under the rack of weapons, she found the Kevlar sheath that allowed her to attach the sword to her back. As she armored up, she stole a glimpse of herself in the mirror. She looked like an angel of death. *Good.* That was what she was tonight.

On her way to the sigil room, she grabbed a bottle of whiskey from the kitchen, taking a long slug and grimacing as it burned her throat. This would do to light the sigil.

As she poured the whiskey into the furrows of Emerazel's sigil, she chanted the words she'd learned the first night she'd met Kester. At the last word, flames engulfed her, burning her body to cinders.

Moments later, she was hunched over on her hands and knees in Kester's boat, coughing. *Dammit, why can't I remember to hold my breath?*

Only moonlight lit the inside of the boat. The cold stove stood in the center of the room, its fire now dead. As the sigil flames cooled around her, she caught Kester's scent—his warm, cedar smell, and her heart ached.

Her jaw tightened. There was no time for sentiment now. She had a mission to accomplish. But before she could rise, she saw the blade of a sword coming right for her head.

Chapter 34

She leapt away, hitting the floor hard and rolling behind the bookshelf they'd moved earlier. Somewhere on the other side of the cabin, her attacker chanted in Angelic—a spell for light—and a luminescent orb appeared in the center of the room. *So much for hiding in shadows.*

Kester had told her not to enter a fight unless she had a good chance of winning, so she wanted to get an idea of exactly who she'd be fighting. From her position, peeking around the bookshelf's edge, she could see his outline glinting in the orb light. *Armor—fae armor.* She'd killed one fae tonight. She'd kill another if she had to.

The fae soldier's heels clacked over the boards, and she reached over her shoulder to unsheathe Honjo, stepping out from behind the bookshelf.

The man had long, honeyed hair, and his handsome face split into a wide grin. His suit of armor was ornate complete with silver vambraces to protect his forearms. "Looking for a fight, little girl?"

"Yes, unless you want to take this opportunity to piss off, which I strongly suggest. For your own benefit," she added, for emphasis. She was going to have to work on her sword fighting smack-talk.

Laughter danced in his eyes, but in the next moment, his face hardened, telegraphing an imminent strike.

Ursula parried gracefully, knocking his sword into one of the wooden bookcases. "I don't want to hurt you. But I already killed one of your brothers tonight. What's one more?"

The guard ignored her, yanking his sword free with a growl.

His movement left an opening, and with a flick of her wrist, she slid her blade between his hand and the vambrace, slicing his skin. He grimaced, and she pulled away her blood-stained sword. "I did warn you."

"My orders are to bring you to Oberon. Dead or alive."

This time, he didn't telegraph his strike, and she had to dodge behind the stove. He stalked after her, armor creaking, backing her into a corner. She sliced Honjo, but the fae parried, sparks showering from their swords. He rounded the edge of the stove, swinging for her face. She ducked, and his blade whistled through the air only inches above her head. She had to do something offensive, but she didn't know how to penetrate that fae armor without room to wind up in the cramped corner.

The image of Kester's falling body blazed through her mind again, and fury flooded her. She lowered her shoulder and charged.

The force felt like tackling a steel beam, but she'd gotten the leverage right. The guard toppled back, hitting the floor with a crash that sent his sword skittering across the room.

Ursula stood over him, pointing Honjo at his throat, piercing the skin just enough to draw a small drop of red blood. "I did warn you."

Fear shone in his eyes, his grin gone. "Have mercy."

"A coup de grâce then?"

"Please don't kill me..."

"What happened to Kester?"

"I don't know..." he stammered.

"Don't lie to me." Her voice came out in a cold roar, almost foreign to her.

"He died," the fae yelled. "He fell to the ground and died. His body was mangled. He's with his beloved fire goddess now, which I'm sure is what the filthy dog always want—"

Ursula stabbed downward, but not into his throat. Instead she drove Honjo into the gap between breast plate and pauldron, her blade tugging on the sinews of his shoulder until it *thunked* against the wooden boards. He screamed piteously, but dark fury filled her. "I didn't like where that sentence was going."

The guard moaned.

"Don't worry. You'll live." She wasn't sure where this cold, icy Ursula had come from.

She crossed to the other end of the boat, pushing open the door to Kester's room. She cast one last glance at the moaning fae. "If I hear any spells or incantations, I'll be back to reap your soul."

Dim light from two portholes illuminated Kester's bedroom. Tucked into his bed, Zee slept, her chest rising and falling slowly.

Ursula scanned the room, her throat tightening. The walls were steel blue and the bed was covered in a grey duvet. The room was tidy, and a small bookshelf hung on the wall above his bed, lined with more old novels. This was Kester's home. He'd been alive for four hundred years, and she'd led him to his death tonight.

Apart from the bed, the room was sparsely furnished with a small reading chair and a dresser. Something glittered on the top of the dresser—Kester's reaping pen. Ursula stuffed it in her pocket before turning to pull the covers off Zee, who still wore her bloodstained opera gown. Ursula slid her hands under the fae girl's petite shoulders, lifting her from the bed. She was lighter than Ursula expected, and she carried Zee back into the the main room, cautiously eyeing the soldier. He was just where she'd left him, pinned to the floor like an enormous entomologist's specimen. "What do you want with that whore?" he spat.

"She's a friend of mine."

"You know she's tainted? King Oberon never lets a fae leave his troop unless they're unclean."

"King Oberon is unclean," she shot back. She didn't know what that meant exactly, but clearly the old fae king was a filthy bugger. She hoisted Zee over her shoulder like a sack of potatoes, and gripped Honjo's hilt. "I'm going to free you now, but only because I want my sword back."

She ripped the blade from the fae's shoulder. He screamed, hands gripping the wound.

She trained the point of the dripping blade at him, backing away. "If you get up, I'll stab you through the other shoulder."

She stopped when she reached Emerazel's sigil. Holding Zee tight, she whispered in Angelic. At the last words, she and Zee disintegrated in a burst of flame.

Ursula was gasping for breath by the time she reached the gothic bedroom in the Plaza apartment. It wasn't every day that she carried a limp body up a flight of stairs.

She dropped Zee on the black canopy bed, ignoring the animal skulls that lined the walls. She tucked Zee under the blankets and slipped out the door, her body aching.

A tear slid down her cheek, and she wiped it on the back of her hand. She'd retrieved Zee's body, only to learn that Kester had died in the fall—died trying to clean up her mess, in fact. She'd only just been getting to know him, still hadn't gotten the chance to learn his secrets. Who had Oriel been, and what had she meant to him?

No use wondering about it now. She still needed to figure out exactly how to hunt down an incubus lair. Kester would have known what to do. The man had been an experienced hellhound with an encyclopedic knowledge of spells and arcane magic.

Of course, she *did* have a literal encyclopedia of arcane magic in the library below. A lick of hope ignited, and she rose.

Chapter 35

The library was just as she'd left it, with blood drying on the rug. She collected the grimoires, organizing them on the table. In one pile, she stacked the volumes that were way off-topic—the farming spells, and curses.

She flipped through the *Picatrix,* but it was a jumble of arcana, astrological facts, and descriptions of heavenly deities. Into the discards it went.

That left only one book: *DAEMONS.* As if its title wasn't forbidding enough, the heavy volume was bound in a black leather that reminded her of Abrax's wings. Dread whispered over her skin as she cracked it open. Someone had rendered a long-toothed demon in excruciating detail, his head capped with a blood-soaked conical cap, a pile of bones laying at his feet. Along the top of the picture were two words: *Red Cap.*

She flipped the page. Amongst a pile of gold and jewels sat a monstrous man with bull horns protruding from his temples. Above his head his name read: *Raum.*

With a shiver, she reminded herself that these were her people now.

At least this book was going in the right direction. It didn't include any words—only pictures—but it appeared to be some sort of demonic guide.

She flipped through from the beginning: *Aamon, Apollyon, Abezethibou, Abrax, Abyzou...* She stopped. Flipped back one page. Even without the name *Abrax* emblazoned on the top, she'd have recognized him: black wings, talons sharp as knives, and the face of an angel. The incubus had his own page, and someone had written in the margin—Henry's spindly scrawl, by the look of it.

Try as I might I haven't been able to learn much about Abrax. He appears to have led the assault on Mount Acidale, but after the battle he disappeared.

Ursula shut the book. To say that he'd reappeared would be a major understatement. *Bloody hell.* The fact that he had his own page suggested she was up against one of Nyxobas's most powerful demons. She gritted her teeth. She still didn't know where to find him.

She glanced at the clock—two a.m. Her body burned with a mixture of adrenaline and exhaustion, and she scanned the shelves again, searching for Henry's ledger again. She'd scanned through it quickly before, but maybe there was something in there about Abrax, considering Henry had been researching him.

She pored through the ledger, filled with page after page of conquests, starting in the 1830s.

Near the end, where he'd written about Starkey's Conjuration, he'd written the name *BAEL*. Below, he'd scrawled:

"I have imprisoned him in my study. Despite my attempts at persuasion, he refuses to reveal the location of the New York lair. When my interrogations rendered him mute, I used Perrault's Enchantment to put him to sleep."

Bael. That was the beautiful man upstairs.

Her heart raced as she reopened *DAEMONS*. With a trembling hand, she thumbed through to the letter *B*. The sleeper's perfect, wrathful face glared at her from the page, his features etched with sublime fury, lip curled back from his teeth. An enormous pair of golden wings jutted from his back. At the bottom of the page, written in Angelic, were the words *Sword of Nyxobas*.

She dropped the book, and the bang of the cover hitting the table shattered the silence.

She'd been calling herself an angel of death tonight, but the real deal lay on a bed just one floor above her.

Ursula stood in front of the iron-studded door, the reaping pen in one hand, and a contract in the other. She wasn't going in there without a plan, and for extra security she'd strapped a kaiken dagger to her belt.

After spending the last three quarters of an hour arguing with herself, she kept returning to the same conclusion: her only option was to wake Bael.

She'd read Henry's journal entries from the beginning, starting from the time he first contacted Bael to the moment he captured him. He was a little sparse on the details, but she'd learned Bael was some sort of high-value prisoner. Henry had planned to use him as leverage in negotiations with the night god.

Even with this sketchy information, it was clear that all roads to Abrax ran through Bael, and the sleeping demon was her only connection to the incubus.

She just had to wake an ancient demon and convince him to tell her where to find the incubus.

Fear slithered over her skin. It wasn't just that she had to wake Bael that turned her stomach—it was *how* she had to wake him.

Her grip tightened on the dagger, and she chanted the word *Louisa*. After the glow around the door dissipated, she pulled it open and stepped inside.

The interior was just as she remembered. Gold astrological symbols glittered against midnight blue wallpaper. Dusty alchemical glassware stood solemnly on the shelves. Yet this time the air held a strange tension, like the room was holding its breath.

She moved toward the bed, gripping the reaping pen. She had a plan to get a little leverage of her own, but the idea of it sent fear racing through her body.

Tendrils of inky magic curled off Bael's body like smoke, and the air around him crackled with a dark power. Her gaze flicked to the crimson gore staining the sheets. She recoiled, bile rising in her throat. He'd had wings in the picture—beautiful, golden wings. Had Henry cut them off during his interrogations?

Her eyes roamed his chiseled features, his face perfect in repose. His arms, even after months asleep, still rippled with muscle. Despite his otherworldly beauty, the sight of him terrified her. Even unconscious and bound in iron chains, he exuded raw, dark power.

Clenching her jaw, she touched his hand, already feeling his dark magic flowing through her like waves of electricity. She slid the reaping pen into his enormous fingers, folding them around the pen until they loosely gripped it. She held the contract up to the pen's nib, and in a haphazard scrawl, she scratched the letters B A E L. *Bingo.*

She had no idea if that counted as a legitimate signature, but it was at least worth a shot. He was immortal, so he shouldn't care too much, but if he was pledged to Nyxobas, he'd surely want to reclaim his soul for his shadow god. And that meant he'd need to do what she wanted if he wanted to retrieve it.

Taking a steadying breath, she folded up the contract and shoved it into her pocket before drawing the kaiken dagger. Dread inched up her spine.

What she had to do next was even more horrifying than touching his hand.

According to the books, there was only one way to wake someone from Perrault's Enchantment.

Tonight, Ursula would have to kiss the Sword of Nyxobas.

She clutched the dagger, her entire body rigid with tension, before exhaling slowly. *I've got this.* Surely demons like him were bestial creatures, and the scent of fear would only stoke his predatory instincts.

She leaned over him, somehow repelled and attracted at the same time to the shadowy tendrils of power coiling off his muscled body.

"Relax," she reassured herself. "He's bound in chains, and I've got his soul." Still, she placed the tip of the dagger against the soft flesh between his ribs. If he attacked, it would take only one thrust to puncture his heart.

She leaned closer. He smelled of sandalwood, a scent both ancient and exotic. His eyelashes twitched. She almost jumped across the room, but then she realized it was her own nervous breath that had made them flutter. She eyed his lips. For a man made of pure muscle, they seemed oddly sensual.

Marshaling her resolve, she closed her eyes, leaning closer. Her heart threatened to gallop out of her chest as she pressed her lips against his warm, soft mouth.

Chapter 36

$\mathcal{F}$or a moment, nothing happened, then a powerful thrill rippled over her skin, and she jumped away from him.

Bael's eyelids snapped open, and he surveyed her with glacial, pale eyes that sent raw fear snaking in her gut. Her pulse racing, Ursula's grip tightened on the dagger.

His eyes flashed with ancient wrath; his voice rumbled through the room like thunder. "What did you do to me?"

She tried to stop herself from shaking. She couldn't show him her fear or he'd find a way to rip through the chains and pulverize her. "We'll get to that."

"Who are you, little girl?" he barked. "Where is the other hound?"

"I'm Ursula. Henry is indisposed." Probably best not to mention *he's been eviscerated* just yet.

He narrowed his icy eyes, studying her. "Do you know with whom you speak?"

"Bael. Sword of Nyxobas." *Shit. Maybe he hates that name.*

"Good. Now release me," he growled.

"Sure. I can release you."

When she didn't move toward him he added, "Now."

"I'll release you *after* you tell me where I can find Nyxobas's lair."

The tendrils of dark magic swirled around him. "No."

She raised the kaiken. "Abrax stole my friend's soul, and I want it back. And he has another soul that belongs to me."

His smile was a thing of terror. "Do you mean to threaten him with your little dagger, hound?"

"I have a sword."

"Abrax is the Lord of Alnath, the eldest son of the Nyxobas. A little hound like you cannot stand against him."

Holy hell. She'd felt pretty good with the sword tonight, but she was clearly way out of her depth. Still—she had no choice. Finding Abrax was the answer to every one of her problems.

"Henry was able to bind you pretty well." She looked pointedly at the iron chains that wrapped round the demon. "For a mere mortal, he put you in quite the predicament."

Bael yanked on his chains. "Fetch him for me."

"That won't be possible." Her heart still thudded hard, but Bael at least seemed well contained by the chains. "He's dead."

"How?" Bael didn't so much say the word as growl it.

"He was murdered."

He closed his eyes, and took a long breath. For a moment, she almost thought he'd fallen back asleep—until he unleashed a roar that shook the entire building. It was a terrifying, bestial sound that threatened to tear her apart. She fought every instinct screaming at her to flee into the hall and down the elevator. When he glanced at her again, his eyes were black as night. "He was *mine* to kill. Who killed him?"

"I don't know."

"I will find the one who did it and rip his heart from his chest."

Nerves of steel, Ursula. Nerves of steel. "I don't doubt that, but from your current position that may take some time."

Bael studied her, his eyes seeming to peer into her very soul. For a moment she thought he might roar again, but then he gathered himself. "Tell me how he was killed."

"He was found in Central Park. Apparently, his intestines were strung from the trees like Christmas tree ornaments."

Bael strained against the iron shackles, his muscles taut. "Let me out of here," he roared.

"Will you help me find Abrax?"

"I'm going to find Abrax and tear his ribs through his back. Henry stole something from me, and Abrax was the one who murdered him. That means Abrax has my possession. So let me free if you want to find him, little hound, because you don't stand a chance on your own."

She shifted uncomfortably, her pulse racing. She was going to have to tell him about the soul thing. If he didn't know about her leverage, he'd just eviscerate *her*.

"I was a little worried you might be opposed to working with me," she began, "since you're a shadow demon."

"It's true. I feast on Emerazel's creatures."

Her mouth went dry. "Right. So, as leverage, I got your signature." She pulled the contract from her pocket, unfurling it so he could see, and focused on trying to keep her voice steady. "I put the pen in your hand and made you sign. Now, if you want your soul back, you have to do what I say."

For a moment, a deathly silence filled the room, and Ursula could hear only her own heartbeat. Then, Bael's face shifted—eyes darkening and horns growing from his brow. Cold fury glinted from his black eyes, and Ursula stumbled back, hands trembling. Bael threw back his head and roared again, the sound shaking the entire building, rattling the chandeliers and floorboards. Dark magic swirled wildly around him, snaking through her body. Every instinct in her body told her to run.

When his roar quieted, he closed his eyes, his body shaking with fury, and after a moment, his face returned to normal. He glanced at her, eyes a pale, icy grey again. "Unchain me."

Suddenly, she no longer wanted to release him. He was going to slaughter her. She swallowed hard. "I'm not sure you won't kill me."

"I can't kill you, as you so cleverly ensured. You have stolen my soul and given it to that great monstrous whore, Emerazel. You have your leverage. Unchain me, so I can murder Abrax and get my soul back."

Ursula crossed her arms to hide their shaking. She didn't want to anger him, but she had the upper hand now, and she was going to find out what she could. "What did Henry take from you?"

Bael's furious gaze never left her eyes. "Do you see these bloodstains beneath me? He cut off my wings."

"Why would he do that? Part of your interrogation?"

"And because they're incredibly valuable." He studied her carefully. "What sort of a hound are you?

Apparently, she'd asked a stupid question. "I'm new. How did you know I was a hellhound?"

"You smell of Emerazel's fire." There was a hint of distaste in his voice.

She glanced at the stains again. "Why does the blood look fresh?"

"The wounds aren't healed. If they heal, it won't be possible to reattach my wings. Until I find them, I must remain mutilated. Do you have any more questions, girl?"

"Doesn't it hurt?"

Bael glared at her, the *yes* left unsaid.

Ursula paused, considering what to say next. Which, in hindsight, she should probably had been doing all along. "What makes your wings so valuable?"

"They allow me to fly," he snarled. He didn't say *obviously*, but his tone clearly implied it.

She shook her head. "Abrax already has wings, and I saw him fly."

"You saw him in his true form?" Bael interrupted, surprise flickering across his face. "And you survived?"

She wanted to shout *obviously*, but instead she shrugged like it was no big deal. Bael didn't have to know that she'd almost bled to death in the library. "You didn't answer my question about why he'd want the wings."

He clenched his jaw. "They were a gift from Nyxobas himself. I will be condemned for eternity if I don't find them."

"How do you know he hasn't given them to Nyxobas already?"

"Because if he had, I'd be withering in the shadow void, not trapped in a room with one of Emerazel's dogs."

"Why wouldn't he have—"

"Do you always ask so many questions, little girl? I can't give you these answers. Only Abrax knows. If you free me, I will take you to him."

Ursula gazed into his pale eyes. If she could ignore the fact that he was terrifying, he had a certain sublime beauty, his grey eyes such a stark contrast with his golden skin—warm and cold coming together, like storm clouds tinged by a rising sun. He looked like a god himself—hell, he practically *was* one as far as she could tell.

She wasn't convinced he wouldn't murder her when she removed the chains, but what choice did she have? If she didn't get to Abrax, both she and Zee would lose their souls. "I'll release you. If you help me find Abrax without killing me, I'll give you your soul back." She had no idea how to give a soul back, but she wasn't about to mention that now. Anyway, he was immortal, and he'd never need to know.

"If you fail on your promise to return my soul, your fate will be worse than Henry's."

"I don't doubt it."

"Now unchain me," he roared.

She took a deep breath, eyeing the chains. The links were dull grey. Compared to the glowing wards that had guarded the bookcases and the door to Bael's room, the chains appeared positively mundane.

"How do these chains hold you anyway? They don't look magical."

"Henry forged them with magic. You can't see it," said Bael with an audible sigh.

"So is there a lock somewhere?"

"Melt the links with your fire."

She winced. She was liable to set his whole body on fire, and then she had no doubt he'd tear her limb from limb. "I don't, um, exactly have very good control of my fire."

"Of course. I almost forgot that you don't know what you're doing."

Ursula picked up a link of chain, testing the metal with her fingers.

"I only just learned I was a hellhound a few days ago. I have no memory. Kester just showed up in my kitchen—"

"Kester? The Headsman? He *lives?*"

Grief flooded her, and she forced back the tears. "Not anymore. Not since a few hours ago."

Bael growled. "You lie. I killed him at the great battle of Mount Acidale."

"What? No. I've been with him the whole time. Abrax just murdered him."

Bael's eyes blackened again, the horns once again appearing. He thrashed on the bed, the chains around his body smoking. He screamed in frustration, but his face had returned to its beautiful, human form. Against his skin, the iron links sizzled and hissed. The room filled with the smell of burning flesh. Through gritted teeth he spoke. "Release me. Now."

"I'm trying to, but you need to stay still."

The chains were white hot. Whatever spell Henry had worked into the iron, it was fighting back, burning the demon. She paused, her hand inches from the smoking metal.

"It won't burn you. Hellhounds are immune to fire," said Bael. The only clue that he was in agony were a few clipped vowels.

Ursula closed her eyes. She needed to channel her fire. Draw just enough to melt the chain. Her stomach clenched a little. This time, if she lost herself to the flames, Kester wasn't standing by with a fire extinguisher.

She thought of Rufus's smug face—her old standby for calling up the hellfire—and heat began to kindle in her fingers. *It's working.* Her fingers glowed, and a thrill of excitement raced through her.

On the bed, Bael lay perfectly still, probably enduring intense agony as she gathered her flames. He hadn't taken a breath for a minute or two. Was he alive? She glanced at him, at his beautiful face that stared at her with anticipation. It was like she was trying to solve a math problem with the teacher standing just over her shoulder—an exceptionally handsome teacher. The fire in her veins sputtered and died.

"Bollocks." She unsheathed the kaiken dagger. This, at least, she was good at.

"You know you can't kill me with that."

"I'm not going to kill you. I do hope you'll return the favor." She flipped the knife in her hand. With all her strength she stabbed downward, thrusting the tip of the dagger into the gap in one of the links. Then, with a twist, she snapped the chain in two.

Chapter 37

For the briefest of moments Bael stared at her. Was that incredulity she saw in his eyes? Red welts were seared into his arms where the chains had burned his skin. Then, like smoke caught in a breeze, he slipped free. In an instant, he gripped her shoulders, his face taught with fury, and he slammed her into the wall with the speed of a gale-force wind. His strength was terrifying. He slipped a hand around her throat and snarled, "You gave my soul to the fire goddess. You deserve to die a painful death."

Ursula's heart hammered against her ribs. *This is it. I'm going to die.* "You can't kill me," she stammered. "I have your soul."

"You're lucky I'm not at my full power, or I'd compel you to do as I pleased," he growled. He relaxed his grip on her, but his eyes continued to bore into her. "Of course one of Emerazel's dogs would act dishonorably." He stepped away, glaring at her with disgust. "Stay here."

Ursula raised her dagger in a shaking hand. "You need to take me to—"

But he was already gone. Just a rush of air and dark magic, and the sound of the door slamming. She started after him, and something heavy crashed outside the door. He'd locked her in. *The fucker.*

She tested the door anyway, but it wouldn't budge. Muffled noises echoed through the wood—doors opening and shutting and unidentified banging, a demonic rampage through her apartment. As she was deciding whether to try her luck on the ledge, she heard a scraping sound by the door. She whirled, just in time to see the door ripped from its hinges.

Bael stood in silhouette, shadowy magic curling from his enormous body in dark tendrils. Backlit by the crystal chandelier, he filled the doorframe. The man was a mountain of muscle. In one hand he clutched one of the Zhanmadao swords. The blade was close to five feet long, but looked smaller in his grip. In his other hand, he held Honjo.

"The wings aren't here."

Ursula had to fight every instinct to run for the window and throw herself off the ledge. "You said Abrax has them."

"I had to be sure you weren't lying about Henry—that you weren't secretly working for him. I had to be sure that my wings weren't hidden here."

"And now you're *sure* that I'm not working for Henry?"

"Yes. I can hardly smell Henry's stench anymore. He hasn't been in this apartment in months. Kester has been here, though."

Ursula's eyes locked on the sword in Bael's hand. Why had he brought it? She was defenseless with the stupid dagger. He could hack her to pieces in an instant. *Don't antagonize him.* That's what Kester would have told her. *And don't let him see your fear.* "I admire your taste in weaponry."

"I feel more comfortable with a blade in my hand." He tossed Honjo to her, and it spun through the air. She caught the hilt nimbly, and relief flooded her. He wasn't going to murder her. Shockingly, her plan was working for once.

"I smelled you on that one. Please understand that you can't use it against me, or you will die." He spoke matter-of-factly.

"That is fairly obvious." As she followed him out the door, her eyes flicked to her overturned dresser. Apparently, he'd used it to barricade her in.

As they walked through the hall, the sword hanging loosely in his grasp, his eyes followed her every move. She had the distinct impression he was calculating and recalculating how quickly he could decapitate her if Honjo so much as twitched in her grip.

Up close, he was downright terrifying. Where Abrax was all lethal grace, Bael was pure, shadowy power. His arms were massive, knotted with muscle. She was certain he could tear her limb from limb without breaking a sweat. He'd certainly rearranged her entire apartment in only a few minutes.

"How do you move so quickly?"

"Emerazel gives you access to her infernal flame, Nyxobas lets me draw upon his shadows." It wasn't much of an answer, but his expression told her that she wasn't going to get any more than that. He cast her another disgusted look. "Your natural smell is polluted by Emerazel. It sickens me."

"You know, in the human world, it's kind of weird to comment on how people smell."

"You're not human."

As they walked down the stairs, Bael continued to glare at her, but didn't speak. God, he was unnerving.

She cleared her throat, watching as he pushed the elevator button. "How are we getting to this lair?"

"We drive."

Drive? "We're not using some kind of magic method?"

"I can't fly, and without my wings..." As they stepped into the elevator, he studied her carefully, a look of uncertainty on his face. "I don't have all the magic we need, since one of your brethren mutilated me."

"I guess it's a good thing we've got Joe."

His pale eyes slid to her, as if he was staring right through to her soul. "I must warn you that you're in way over your head."

She nodded grimly. That much was clear.

Ursula and Bael stood on a crumbling pier, completely alone. A row of industrial tanks roughly the size of two story buildings towered over them. The black waters of the East River flowed nearby.

Chilled by the winter winds, she hugged herself. "So this is the lair?"

Bael growled. He hadn't said much in the car, beyond giving basic instructions to the driver—"right," "left," and "next exit" being the entirety of his dialog. Not that Ursula had been in the mood for talking. While the streets had flickered by, cold and desolate in the early morning darkness, she'd rested her head against the window and shut her eyes. She desperately needed sleep at this point.

Now she stamped her feet to stay warm in the cold. Out of habit, she took a mental inventory of the weapons she carried. One, Honjo strapped to her back. Two, Kester's reaping pen stuffed in her pocket. Three, a kaiken dagger hidden in her boot.

Lastly, zipped into her jacket were a flask of scotch and a plastic lighter.

Scanning the buildings, Bael gripped the great Chinese Zhanmadao sword. She suspected he had a bunch of other weapons hidden beneath his coat, pilfered from the armory during his rampage.

"Down here," he said at last, nodding to a stairwell that led to the river.

She followed him down a flight of rickety steps to a rusty old pier. The air bit her skin, and she wished she'd brought a warmer coat.

Bael muttered the spell for light, and a small orb bloomed into existence above his head. He peered around, looking for something, then bent and pulled on a rope that dangled into the water. From the shadows under the pier, the hull of a small rowboat glided into view.

"We're going onto the river in that?"

Bael nodded, then turned the boat over to dump out the water.

Ursula shivered as her toes slowly lost feeling.

"Get in," Bael said at last.

She sat in the front, while the demon took the middle seat, his weight creaking the boat's old wood. He pulled a pair of oars from under the seats. Dipping them into the water, he pushed off, maneuvering them onto the river. As she sat in the bow, her back to the river, she could see the whole of New York City lit up before her. With each stroke of the oars, the gleaming lights seemed to get a little smaller. Had it been only a few days since Kester first brought her here? Her whole world had changed in the blink of an eye.

Bael rowed silently, his oars gliding effortlessly in the water, the river rippling behind them.

Ursula twisted around to see where they were headed. In the gloom, a dark shape loomed. She strained her eyes, just making out the form of a small island.

"Are we going to that island?"

"Yes."

"That's were Nyxobas's New York lair is?"

"In a manner of speaking."

Man of few words. She peered at the island again as they rapidly drew closer. Trees covered the land, but no lights glinted from the forested depths.

They pulled up on a gravelly beach and Bael hopped out into knee-deep water, dragging the boat onto the rocky shore.

Ursula stepped onto the rocks. Ice slicked the stones, but the tread on her boots gripped them tightly. She glanced at Bael, who already stood at the tree line, his pale eyes watching her impatiently as she hurried up the beach.

"You could have waited," she grumbled when she reached him.

"We were exposed on the beach."

Before she could ask where they were headed, he started into the dark forest.

It was slow going as her boots crunched between frozen kudzu vines. She had to shield her eyes from branches that clawed at her face. After a few minutes they broke clear of the underbrush onto a narrow animal track. Bael paused, sniffing the air. A thin dusting of virgin snow covered the ground. No one had been here.

"It looks like we're alone," she said, more to break the tension than anything else.

"That may not be true. Most of Nyxobas's brethren are nocturnal, and most can fly."

In her mind's eye, an image flashed: Abrax standing over her, his great leathery wings beating the air. She reflexively reached to touch Honjo's hilt from where it protruded from the sheath on her back.

With Bael in the lead they moved along the path, deeper into the island, until the dense underbrush cleared. This would have allowed Ursula to see more of the interior, had the canopy not simultaneously thickened.

On her left, a dark form towered above them, but Bael hardly paused as they neared it. Up close, she could see more clearly in the pale moonlight—an abandoned building, completely overgrown with kudzu, as if the vines were trying to suffocate it. The path wound on between more abandoned buildings, totally desolate in the cold light. Ursula had a distinct feeling of déjà vu, like she was again walking between the towering blue stones on her way to her trial with the moor fiend.

At last, the path opened into a clearing. Bael held up a hand, and Ursula stopped behind him.

"What is it?" she whispered.

"We've reached the lair."

Chapter 38

*A*n enormous Victorian building towered over the other side of the clearing, its dark windows staring vacantly like empty eyes. A dark wrought-iron gate covered its door, giving the appearance of a row of black teeth. Her mouth went dry. She knew it was stupid, but right about now, she really wanted her lucky stone—her anchor. She had to wonder if all of this would have been an ordinary day in the life of F.U.

She shivered, staring at the building. "What *is* this place?"

"It was once a hospital. The brethren of Nyxobas live here now."

"This is his headquarters?"

"Were you expecting something more grand? You'll find that Nyxobas is less concerned with aesthetics than your monstrous goddess." He sniffed, his back stiffening. Drawing his sword, he stepped into the center of the clearing. Ursula unsheathed Honjo, gripping it like her life depended on it. *Which, come to think of it, it probably does.*

"I am Bael. I wish to speak to Abrax." His voice boomed through the forest, rustling the leaves and sending shivers over her skin. Ursula scanned the building, but saw nothing move.

A voice hissed from the darkness of the ruin, "We were wondering when you would finally deign to visit us." A dark form materialized in the shell of a window on the second floor, face hidden in shadow.

"I seek Abrax," Bael roared.

"Abrax sends his regards, and offers his apologies that he couldn't be here to see you die in person." The silhouette disappeared into the depths of the decaying structure.

Bael spoke softly. "Get ready to fight, Ursula."

Her pulse raced, adrenaline igniting her nerve endings. This did not seem like a good situation, even with the Sword of Nyxobas on her side.

He leaned closer, whispering, "The only way to kill a—"

There was a movement in front of Bael, a blur of shadow so fast she couldn't make it out. Bael's sword flashed in the moonlight, and something thumped on the ground. A severed head rolled before her feet, its mouth lolling open. Ursula suppressed the urge to vomit as the head shriveled and blackened before crumbling into ash. The crunching of bone cut the silence, and she turned to see Bael holding a dripping heart in his hand. "The only way to kill a vampire is to cut off its head and rip out its heart."

She swallowed. "Right."

Footfalls sounded to Ursula's right, and she swung Honjo reflexively, the blade slicing into something soft—a young woman's stomach. Bile rose in her throat as the girl shrieked.

Ursula froze. This was different than the fae—she didn't even know who this woman was yet, or if the woman had meant to kill her. And moreover, her opponent looked like an innocent teenager, her blond hair cascading over a pink, floral dress. Sobbing, the girl at the end of Ursula's sword tried to pull the blade from her gut, and Ursula's stomach turned.

"I'm so sorry—" she stammered.

"Don't apologize," barked Bael. "Cut off her head,"

Ursula yanked out her sword, and the girl lunged at her, fangs bared. She ducked, slicing upward, and Honjo's razor-sharp edge ripped through the girl's jaw. Through her remaining teeth, the girl growled, ready to attack again. The little blonde no longer seemed quite so human.

"The whole head, Ursula," Bael shouted from somewhere in front of her.

"I'm working on it." *Don't you have someone to fight?*

Slowly, the girl circled her, the wound in her gut apparently forgotten.

More footfalls crunched over the snow, moving in a blur of motion to her left. A dark-haired man appeared by her side, fangs bared. They were trying to flank her. Shifting her weight, she slashed toward the man. In one fluid motion, Honjo ripped through his spinal column like a freshly sharpened butcher knife. She arced her sword right, slicing through the neck of the jawless girl. Two heads thumped to the ground.

"Good," said Bael now at her side. He leaned down, punching through the man's chest cavity to rip out his heart. Almost instantly, the body turned to ash, and he moved on the girl. Then he disappeared in a swirl of shadows.

Gripping Honjo, Ursula scanned her surroundings for movement, attuning her ears for footfalls. A clash of steel turned her head, and her gaze landed on Bael, locked into combat with a trio of men before the hospital's gates.

His movements were swift as a storm wind, his sword gleaming like quicksilver. The fighting sped up, so fast she couldn't track their movements. Blades flashed. A head thumped to the ground. Then, with a spinning slash, Bael separated two more heads from their necks.

As the bodies of the men crumbled, Ursula stared at Bael in disbelief. Even without his wings, he moved like a god. What would he be like *with* them?

After ripping out three more hearts, Bael turned to the derelict hospital, and Ursula gaped at the empty windows, trying not to think about what other demonic nightmares might make their homes within the decaying hospital.

"Don't provoke my wrath, Fiore. Your little vamps are outmatched. Besides, I have no quarrel with you. I'm here for Abrax."

"Who's Fiore?" Ursula whispered.

"The leader of this pack of vampires."

The dark form appeared at the window again.

"Abrax has promised me a place in Nyxobas's inner council if I bring him your head." Fiore's voice was faintly accented and cold as tundra.

"You and I both know that's not going to happen," said Bael.

"He showed me your wings. Without them, you're just as mortal as that mongrel you brought with you."

He's mortal? No wonder he was so desperate for his wings back.

Bael growled. "I will get them back. Why don't you come down here and fight me, Fiore? If you win, your reward is the soul of a hellhound."

"What?" Ursula raised her sword.

"He won't win," said Bael simply.

She glared at him. *Pretty confident for a mutilated demon.*

Fiore's silhouette disappeared from the window. A moment later he reappeared by the entrance. Unlike the vampires they'd decapitated, he was a mass of pure muscle—only slightly smaller than Bael. A pair of katanas gleamed in his hands. A smaller vampire with cherubic blond curls stood by his side.

Bael squared his shoulders. "Do you accept my challenge?"

"It really is sad how far you've fallen," said Fiore. "If you'd like me to put you out of your misery, I accept. Emerazel's cur will be your second?"

Bael nodded. "To the death then."

Bloody hell. Ursula's palms sweated on Honjo's hilt.

Bael backed into the clearing, raising his blade—nearly five feet of lethal steel.

Fiore circled, his katanas poised like the fangs of a serpent. There was a flash, followed by a great clash of metal, as they struck in unison.

Through a blur of shadow and steel, Bael spoke. "I will give you a clean death if you tell me where to find Abrax."

"The only death you'll be getting is your own." Fiore's voice gave no hint of exertion.

As their swords engaged, Ursula's eyes began to adjust to the intense speed, tracking their strikes. Fiore slashed; Bael parried. Before Bael could recenter his blade, Fiore's second sword drove at his chest. It was a brutal strike, but Bael managed to leap out of range, rolling across the snowy clearing to rest on his back.

While Bael lay on the snow, Fiore closed on him like a shark sensing blood. The Sword of Nyxobas didn't move. Ursula reached for her sword, but then Bael lashed out with his foot, his toe connecting with the back of Fiore's knee.

The vampire's leg buckled, and he fell to his knees. In a whirl of shadow, Bael sprung up and kicked the katanas out of reach. He lowered his own sword to the vampire's neck, just piercing the skin. "Tell me where to find Abrax."

Fiore's lips pressed together in a thin line. The two demons glared at one another.

"Any last words?" asked Bael.

Fiore's eyes flicked to where the blond vampire stood. From under his coat, the blond vamp drew a small crossbow.

Ursula lifted her sword, but it was too late. The bolt flew through the air, piercing Bael's mortal chest. Ursula's entire body went cold as she watched Bael topple back into the snow.

Fiore scrambled to his feet, snatching up one of his swords to deliver the final death blow. Power flooded Ursula as the night wind rushed over her skin, and she charged across the snow, Honjo ready in her grasp. A bolt whistled by her head, just as she swung for Fiore's blade. She knocked Fiore's strike off course, his blade driving into the dirt only inches from Bael's neck.

Fiore's dark eyes widened as he pulled his sword from the frozen earth. "What *are* you?"

Before he could strike again, she kicked him hard in the groin. He grunted, hunching over, swords falling to the snow.

Ursula pressed Honjo against his throat. Just as she'd seen Bael do, she kicked Fiore's swords out of reach. She scanned the building, looking for Fiore's second, but the smaller vamp had disappeared. She called into the darkness, "If you shoot me, I swear my last act will be to slice Fiore's head from his shoulders."

No one responded, but neither did an arrow come winging at her heart.

She glanced at Fiore, whose face had gone white. "Help me move Bael."

He grunted.

"Do it, or I will cut off your head." Ursula pushed Honjo against his throat. A thin line of blood wetted the edge of the blade.

"Okay." Fiore held up his hands, and she eased up on the blade, giving him room to bend over.

Fiore gripped Bael's jacket, and she heard the high demon groan.

Thank God he's not dead. "Drag him into the trees," Ursula commanded, imbuing her voice with as much authority as possible.

Fiore dragged Bael by his shirt, pulling him into the trees, and Ursula followed, her blade never more than an inch from his neck. When he'd pulled Bael out of the clearing, he rose, and Ursula pushed her blade against his throat again. "Where is Abrax?"

Fiore's eyes narrowed, his mouth pressing into a thin line again.

"No one is going to save you this time," said Ursula. "Blondie ran away."

Fiore closed his eyes. "I will die and deliver my soul to Nyxobas."

"Who said your soul was going to Nyxobas?" Still holding Honjo to his throat, Ursula pulled the reaping pen from her pocket. It glinted in the moonlight. "I'm sure my goddess will happily provide you a warm place to live."

His eyes snapped open. "No."

"Then tell me where to find Abrax."

"I don't know where he is." For the first time, his eyes betrayed real fear. "He didn't tell me."

"What *do* you know?"

"He spends all his time at Oberon's. They're working together on something. I don't know what."

"Good. Now you get what Bael promised you."

"What?"

"Your clean death." Ursula swung Honjo, severing his skull from his spine.

Chapter 39

The vampire's body crumpled to the ground. *Bloody hell, do I really need to cut out his heart?* Maybe F.U. had been a trained killer, but New Ursula didn't feel like a full-blown psychopath. Just a few days ago, she'd been painting wildflowers on a wall and clothes shopping like a normal person, and now she stood over a vampire's headless body, trying to decide if she should mutilate it further.

So F.U. had been some sort of master swordsman, but organ carving took her into serial-killer territory. How exactly would a vampire's head return to his body, anyway? Surely it would take some effort. Maybe a vampire doctor. Perhaps she didn't really need to *kill* him; maybe it was enough just to keep him out of her way. She ran to grab one of his katanas from the clearing, before running back to stab it hard through his shoulder blade, pinning him to the ground like she'd done with the fae.

She turned to Bael, kneeling by his side. The demon's enormous chest rose and fell slowly, his head resting against the root of a fir. His dark eyelashes lay closed, just as when she'd first seen him in the Plaza Hotel. Around the base of the bolt, his blood bloomed in a crimson circle.

She knelt next to him. "Bael," she whispered. He didn't move. *Dammit, you need to wake up.* If she was going to return to Oberon's, she'd need his help. And more than that, she didn't want to be responsible for sending his soul to Emerazel. *Shit.* Why had she forced him to give up his soul?

"Bael." She said it louder this time, pushing his shoulder. His pale eyes opened, locking on her.

"Get it out of me," he whispered, eyes closing again.

She looked at the bolt. The wood's grain was twisted and coiled. Was it enchanted? Hesitantly, she touched it, but no flash of pain shot up her arm.

Setting down Honjo, she drew the dagger from her boot. Carefully, she cut away Bael's shirt, revealing his muscled chest. Every inch was inscribed with tattoos, astrological and alchemical symbols intermixed with Angelic script. Her eyes flicked to the wound. Blood bubbled from where the bolt had impaled him, just under his collar bone. A few inches to the left, and it would have punctured his heart.

What was her plan? It wasn't like she could call an ambulance. She'd need to heal him with Starkey's Conjuration spell. She just needed to rip this thing out first.

Ursula gripped the blood-soaked bolt. This wasn't going to come out easily. She slid her leg over him, straddling his chest, and closed her eyes. *I'm only pulling a piece of wood from a man's chest. It's not as bad as cutting out someone's heart.* With a jerk, she yanked it free, then tossed it into the woods.

Bael howled, thrashing. Smoke rose from his wound. He arched his back, and she pressed her palms against his shoulders, trying to calm him. "Bael, you need to lie still, so I can heal you."

The demon's eyes had gone black, glinting with primal violence, but his body went still.

She leaned over him, touching his skin lightly with her fingertips. "Relax. I pulled out the bolt." *Like you asked me to.*

At the touch of her fingers, he sat up with a start. He gripped her shoulders so hard she thought they might break, pulling her to him. "You tried to kill me." He spoke quietly, but quiet rage laced his voice.

"I'm trying to help you."

"Abrax, you bastard. You tried to kill me."

Bollocks. He's lost it. "I'm Ursula. Abrax isn't here."

His eyes remained as dark as night, and he growled. "You will never possess the house of Albelda. As the Sword of Nyxobas, I will slay you."

"Bael, relax. I'm going to heal you."

He rose, throwing Ursula off him. "The god of night granted me immortality. I was chosen by him—" He swayed, then fell forward, the ground trembling at the impact. His body twitched, and she looked closer at his back.

She gaped in horror. Through his ripped shirt, she could see that fresh blood covered his back. Between sodden bandages, blood poured from the two huge wounds where his wings had been. The fight with Fiore must have re-injured them. Nauseated, Ursula looked away.

What had Bael told her about the wings? He couldn't be healed, or he'd lose his chance to reattach them. That meant Starkey's Conjuration was out. Still, she needed to do something to staunch the bleeding. It wasn't like she'd ever taken a first aid course, but maybe she could just jam up the wound somehow, stop them from leaking blood everywhere. Whatever he'd done back at the Plaza wasn't working anymore. She took off her jacket. The high-tech fabric didn't look very absorbent, but her shirt was all cotton. She pulled it over her head, as an icy wind whipped at her bare skin.

Drawing the kaiken dagger from her boot, she began cutting the fabric into strips.

As she stuffed the strips of fabric into his wounds, Bael groaned. Ideally, she would have boiled these first to prevent infection, but she didn't exactly have that option right now. The strips were staunching the blood flow, but they wouldn't stay in place on their own. With a bit of effort, she pulled off his belt, and threaded it under him. Then she buckled it into place across his chest.

She sat back, surveying her work. The blood wasn't pouring from the wounds any more. He could still die, but she'd bought them some time. How exactly could she get his soul back to him? She still wasn't clear on that point, but she didn't want him bleeding out before she got the chance.

She glanced up. The rising sun was beginning to stain the sky a dusky rose, chinks of pale light dappling the snow. *Morning already*. She shivered in the brittle air, tugging her jacket tighter around her bare skin. This would be a good time to use Emerazel's fire to heat herself, but she was far too exhausted for any sort of anger. An icy wind rustled the oak leaves above her. They needed to get out of here before they either froze to death or fell victim to a vampire slaughter.

She dug out the flask of scotch, pushing back the tears. This had been the worst night of her life. *Or at least, I think it was. It's not like I know for sure*. She took a swig, the whiskey burning her throat. Then she stood and began to pour it in the shape of Emerazel's sigil.

Ursula stood in the shower's hot water, letting it thaw the tips of her toes and pound against the tired muscles in her shoulders.

She squeezed some shampoo into her hand and began to lather her hair. The scent of eucalyptus mixed with the hot steam.

Bael still slept on the floor of the sigil room. She hadn't been able to move his enormous frame.

She rinsed her hair. Her entire body ached like it had been pummeled with tiny fists. After she got out of the shower, she wanted to sleep, just for a few hours, so she didn't completely lose her mind.

She turned off the water, stepping into the bathroom. Her black clothes made a sorry-looking pile on the floor. Of course, she was never putting them on again—they were soaked in Bael's blood. She wrapped herself in a towel and padded back to her room, where she slipped into a cotton t-shirt and knickers.

Too tired to dress further, she crawled under the covers, her entire body burning with fatigue. Pink morning light filtered in through the blinds, warming the room.

When was the last time she'd eaten? She had no idea at this point. She stared at the wildflowers she'd painted on the wall, but they didn't feel like home anymore. How could anything feel like home when you had no idea who you were in the first place? She let her eyes drift closed, feeling a wave of sleep wash over her, soothing her body. Her mind filled with images of fields of aster, bathed in moonlight—

A pair of strong hands gripped her shoulders, and her eyes snapped open.

Bael kneeled over her, the strap of his belt tight across his chest. His cold gaze bored right through her. "Where's Fiore?"

Ursula's heart raced, and she blinked away the sleep. "Fiore?"

His enormous hands tightened on her shoulders. "Why are we here? Why aren't we at the lair?"

She pushed his hands away and sat up, having forgotten what she was wearing—or rather, *not* wearing. For a moment, Bael's eyes flicked down her body before he averted his gaze. She pulled the sheets up around her. "I used Emerazel's fire to bring us here. You were bleeding to death."

Bael looked at the window, unwilling to make eye contact. "Fiore cannot hide from me. I will rip his sinews from his bones until he talks."

"I'm not sure he'll be talking any time soon. I pinned his body to the ground with his own sword before I cut off his head."

Bael head swiveled back to look at her, and his eyes darkened. "You did what? I needed information from him."

"I only cut off his head after he told me me where to find Abrax."

A hint of surprise flickered in Bael's eyes. "Where is the usurper hiding?"

"I'm not sure I entirely trust you yet. You did offer up my soul to Fiore, if I recall."

"That was a tactical decision. Fiore wouldn't have agreed to a duel if there weren't something in it for him."

"What if you'd lost?" She looked him straight in the eyes. "Oh, wait you *did* lose." Bael let out a low growl, but Ursula held his gaze. "If I tell you where Abrax is, you must promise never to sell me out again. One of those promises on the honor of Nyxobas or whatever you said before."

The demon's jaw tightened, but he nodded. Ursula suspected that the nod might have been a tactical decision as well—not nearly as binding as a verbal pledge.

"Fiore said Abrax went back to Oberon's," said Ursula. "Probably should have gone back there to begin with, since that was the last place I saw him."

"What's he doing with the fae?"

"No one seems to know, except that they've formed some sort of alliance."

"The fae don't form alliances with earthly gods."

"Things have changed, I guess. You have no clue what they'd be doing together?"

Bael looked at the window again, considering the question. "If Abrax and the fae were united, they could make a play for Nyxobas's shadow kingdom." He coughed, wincing in pain.

"Are you ok?"

"I'll manage."

She eyed the belt binding his enormous chest. "I'm not sure if it helped, but I bound your wounds."

"Of course you did." His pale eyes threatened to pierce her soul. "You won't stand a chance against Abrax without me."

"I did pretty well against your vampire friend."

Bael's fists clenched so tightly his knuckles whitened. "Fiore was a dead man as soon as his second became involved," he said through clenched teeth.

Obviously, this was a tender subject. She glanced at his shoulder, which seemed to be clotting. "I got out the bolt that they shot you with, but I couldn't do anything for the wound."

"You mean the quarrel?" Bael's fists unclenched a little. "It was carved from a hawthorn tree. Hawthorn wood is an anathema to creatures of the night, especially if it's forged with iron."

Ursula winced inwardly, thinking of how the wound had smoked when she'd pulled the bolt from his chest. "You're better now?"

"Good as new."

She crossed her arms in front of the sheet. "There's one little problem. We can't get into Oberon's without the invitation of a fae."

"Ursula. I am the Sword of Nyxobas. I go where I choose."

"You take that name quite seriously, don't you?"

His eyes lingered over her bare legs for a moment before his jaw tightened. He turned, walking out of the room. "Seven hells, woman. Put on some clothes."

Chapter 40

They stood in front of the unassuming grey door—the portal to the fae realm. Bael had ransacked the apartment for a shirt large enough to fit him, though the fabric still strained over his chest, threatening to tear.

"Are you sure this is the place?" he asked, nodding at the rusted door. "It doesn't look fae."

"I guess the fae are less concerned with aesthetics than Nyxobas."

"Nyxobas eschews frivolity. It is a sign of weakness. The fae are the opposite." Bael's eyes narrowed, inspecting the stone. "I imagine they simply have this place glamoured."

Ursula reached to press the buzzer, but he grabbed her hand. "Don't alert your enemy of your presence before you attack." He stepped back from the door and studied it for a moment. Then, in a blur of black wind, he slammed his foot into the door. It splintered with a crack of shearing steel.

She gaped. "That won't alert them?"

"Not as much as a bell," he grumbled. While Ursula pondered this logic, the demon unsheathed his sword and stepped inside. "Come."

"Right."

Ursula followed, gripping Honjo. Bael muttered his orb spell, illuminating the interior with amber light. This time, no doorman waited to collect their jackets.

The enormous wooden doors blocked their path, and their golden Angelic inscriptions glittered ominously in the half light. Ursula's hands sweated on Honjo's hilt, as an uneasy feeling settled over her.

"Last time, we walked through those doors and they took us to Oberon's hall," said Ursula. "I think they're some sort of portal. But we can't get through those doors just by kicking through them. There's some sort of impenetrable fae magic—"

Bael closed his eyes, chanting in Angelic. Dark magic swirled around his body, whispering past her skin in thrilling tendrils of power. He opened his pale eyes again and pulled the handles. Slowly, the doors creaked open. With a final glance behind them, they walked through.

A cold breeze nipped at her ears, and she stiffened as they stepped into a thick fog. Instead of illuminating a wooden balcony, the glow of Bael's orb was quickly swallowed up by a swirling mist. The air smelled of wet wood and fresh pine needles.

"This isn't Oberon's hall. Do you know where we are?" she whispered.

"No," he replied, his tone suggesting he was entirely unconcerned by this turn of events.

Oberon's voice pierced the mist. "I'm so glad you could join us at my high court."

Bael turned, sniffing the air, and the mist swirled faster. "Reveal yourself, Oberon," Bael's voice boomed. "We simply want to parley."

"Will you swear that on the soul of Nyxobas?"

"I will."

The mist thinned, revealing the golden glint of fae armor in silvery moonlight. It was night here—maybe it was always night in the fae realm.

Slowly, the forms of at least a hundred fae soldiers came into view. A chill snaked up Ursula's spine. Each soldier held a pike, aimed at them. They weren't in the hall; they were outside somewhere, on some sort of wooden platform.

She started to raise her sword, but Bael grabbed her wrist, pushing it down. This was not a fight they were going to win.

The mist continued to dissipate. Beyond the soldiers, tips of trees became visible in the clearing air. Where *were* they? Ursula glanced down and her knees almost buckled as a wave of vertigo hit her. Apparently they were standing on a platform of branches woven together like the nest of a giant bird. Through the branches, she could make out the dark form of an enormous tree trunk—and beyond that, nothing. Just darkness. Ursula had a suspicion that Oberon's hall was buried somewhere far, far below them.

The king's voice came from behind them. "What was it you desired to ask me?"

Ursula spun around, her gaze landing on Oberon, who sat on a wooden throne carved into the form of a kneeling stag, its antlers forming his seat. He wore a silver robe, and a small circlet of gold in his pale hair. A golden satchel lay at his feet.

"Is it true that you've struck a deal with a whelp of Nyxobas?" Bael demanded, as if he was in a position to demand things.

"I am a hundred thousand years old, as old as the earthly gods," said Oberon. "I should have the power of a god." He flicked his fingers and the guards moved to flank them, keeping their pikes trained on Bael.

"And you think Abrax will grant you that?" His voice dripped with disdain.

"He's pledged his loyalty to me. We will lead his brethren out of the darkness and into the light. Abrax and I will rule the mortal realm together."

On cue, Abrax stepped from between a pair of soldiers to stand by Oberon's side. Ursula's breath caught, as an icy chill constricted her chest. She remembered how Abrax's claws had carved chunks of flesh from her legs. He'd tried to murder her—twice.

"Give me my wings," Bael roared, and the platform beneath them trembled. Ursula clamped her hands to her ears, the sound sending a rush of pure fear through her bones. God, he was terrifying.

In front of them the pikes of the fae soldiers quivered and shook like reeds in a storm.

"You can scream all you want, but your wings are mine," said Oberon, his eyes sliding to the golden satchel. From within, he drew two pieces of skin.

Ursula grimaced. *What the fuck is wrong with these people?* Blood dripped from between Oberon's fingers. She strained her eyes, just making out a tattooed design on the strips of skin: golden wings. *Those* were Bael's wings? Yuck.

"If you damage my wings, I will tear your spine through your throat." Bael didn't scream this time, but pure venom laced his voice, and somehow, it was worse than his roar.

Oberon ignored Bael, holding the skin higher. "These wings are a direct conduit to the magic of Nyxobas." The soldiers cheered again. "With their power, we will no longer need to conceal ourselves in this realm. With their power, we will rule the mortals."

Abrax stepped forward. "Are you ready to receive them?"

"I am."

"Good. I want Bael to watch."

Ursula wasn't sure what was happening, but her stomach turned.

Oberon let his robe drape off his back, exposing his skin in the moonlight. From behind him, Abrax drew a thin dagger from his jacket. The king bowed his head.

"Get away from my wings." Bael boomed, the timbre of his voice shaking her.

Oberon turned his head to address his soldiers. "If the fallen demon speaks again, incinerate him." The soldiers began to weave the ends of their pikes through the air, magic hissing and sizzling at their tips. Ursula's heart raced. This had not turned out well.

Next to her Bael stood, his entire body rigid with tension. She could tell that it took every ounce of his willpower not to charge forward.

Abrax held the dagger over Oberon's back. "Prepare yourself to join the kingdom of Nyxobas," he solemnly intoned.

"I am ready for the power of the night god."

Abrax's dagger glinted in the moonlight. Then, like a silver meteor, it plunged into the center of Oberon's back.

Chapter 41

O beron threw back his head, screaming in agony. As the king slumped, Abrax grabbed him in his arms. Ursula felt an icy chill ripple through the air as the incubus drained Oberon's soul.

For a moment, the fae soldiers stood transfixed, as if they weren't sure if this was all part of the process, until Oberon's limp body tumbled to the ground.

"Get down," said Bael, pulling Ursula to the floor and shielding her with his arms. Above their heads, the pikes unleashed their magic like a thousand lightning bolts.

For few moments it was eerily silent, until a voice cried out, "The king is dead!"

Ursula lifted her head. Abrax stood by the throne, Bael's "wings" clutched in a bloody hand, the body of the king at his feet. Fae soldiers circled him, their pikes ready.

"Your king was weak. It is better that his soul join Nyxobas in his kingdom of eternal night."

"Avenge the king!" the soldiers shouted, shooting another round of magic. It didn't seem to touch Abrax, who glided closer to the throne. He chanted in Angelic, moving fluidly in a swirl of black tendrils.

Bael rose, pulling Ursula to her feet with an iron grip. "Get your sword ready."

Dark mist rose around them again, churning and twisting like a maelstrom. In the center of the vortex, a small figure appeared. With child-like proportions and an innocent face, it could have been a cherub—a theory that was immediately invalidated when it leapt onto a nearby soldier and began tearing the flesh of his face with sharpened teeth. The vortex whirled faster, and more and more of the horrific cherubs appeared, attacking the soldiers with inhuman speed.

Bael pulled her close, shielding her again. "First we kill the Oneiroi. You must move quickly to defeat them. Then, we get my wings." He released her, and with a bone-trembling battle cry, he charged at Abrax.

Ursula gripped Honjo, her gaze darting around as she tried to figure out what to do. A few feet from her, a soldier writhed on the ground, one of the Oneiroi attached to his head like a leech. Honjo effortlessly sliced the creature from the fae's scalp.

A blur of movement at the edge of her vision warned her that an Oneiroi was coming her way. She ducked, and as the demon passed over her head she cut her sword upward. Hot ichor splashed in her face. It smelled terrible, like sour milk. Gagging, she wiped it from her eyes.

Hopping to her feet, she spied Bael fighting through a group of the demons. She ran to him, cutting through the necks of two more Oneiroi. This time, she managed to avoid drenching herself in their juices.

Bael carved through them with the stunning grace of a seasoned warrior, his sword swirling effortlessly through the dark mist. Each one of his movements was precise, calculated, no energy wasted—and with each stroke he dispatched another Oneiroi, until the last of their bodies lay on the platform. He'd hardly even needed her help. He turned to Ursula, pale eyes focusing over her shoulder. "Duck."

She crouched, glancing up just in time to watch Bael decapitate another Oneiroi above her head. The little demons were fast, but predictable. They went straight for the throat.

She straightened, and Bael lowered his sword. "That's all of them."

She turned to see the once-orderly platform strewn with Oneiroi corpses, and her heart clenched. She knew they were monsters, but dead, they looked like *children*. Among them lay the bodies of dead and injured fae warriors. Other fae scrambled around, shouting confused orders to search for the incubus. Blood soaked the woven branches, giving the platform the appearance of the nest of a bird of prey.

"Where is Abrax?" she asked.

Bael inclined his head, leading her to the throne, and he pointed to the floor. The wood before the throne opened into a stairwell that led down into the tree's trunk. Carved from wood, it was narrow, big enough for only one man at a time. This passage must have been Oberon's private entrance to his high court.

Bael started in and Ursula followed. He had to crouch, his broad shoulders brushing the walls. Ursula had a bit more room, but not enough to hold Honjo unsheathed. With Bael in the lead, she was probably safe, but she kept a hand on her dagger's hilt.

They passed a few corridors that led off into darkness, Bael sniffing at each before continuing downward. Her thighs burning, Ursula lost track of how many flights they descended. As the adrenaline from the fight wore off, the tension returned to her shoulders. They were going straight to Abrax. She'd seen what the incubus could do. Hopefully, Bael had some sort of plan, though she wasn't getting the impression he was particularly cautious.

"This way," he said suddenly, turning into a dark passage. She could just barely make out the shapes of doorways in the dark wood hall. Bael stopped, and Ursula bumped into his back.

"Don't make any noise," he whispered.

"I wasn't—"

Bael's hand covered her mouth, another strong arm wrapped around her stomach. Somehow, he'd slipped behind her in the darkness. That shadowy movement thing he did was *extremely* unnerving.

"He's in there," he whispered into her ear, giving absolutely no indication which door he'd meant. He released her.

Before she could ask him which room he meant, he was in front of her again ripping open the door with a splintering crack. Apparently, his whole plan was to charge in. She followed, drawing Honjo from her sheath.

Chapter 42

$\mathcal{A}$ brax stood in a tall stone hall, resting against an oak table, arms folded. Starlight glittered through arched windows. Wisteria and honeysuckle climbed the stones, their sweet scents filling the air, and grass carpeted the ground. It was a beautiful, idyllic scene—a stark contrast to the slaughter that was probably about to unfold.

Abrax looked at his nails, seemingly bored. "I don't have time for this."

Bael pointed his sword at Abrax, his rage almost palpable. "Where are my wings?"

"Someplace safe."

"Return them to me."

"Mortal," Abrax spat, "you and Nyxobas have no dominion over me. Not anymore."

Bael lunged, his sword on a lethal trajectory. But the incubus slipped away, and the blade cut through the air. Like a toreador dodging a charging bull, Abrax directed Bael's momentum into the table. Bael was an astounding fighter, but weakened without his wings. Ursula's mouth went dry. *We might not make it out of this.*

Bael spun, his sword slashing ferociously, but the incubus slipped away again in a blur of black smoke. He emerged in solid form, hands clamped around Bael's throat. Ursula's heart skipped a beat. *This is it.*

Black smoke swirled off Abrax. "I never understood your allegiance to Nyxobas. The things he's done to you. To me. He's not a god—he's a tyrant." Something crunched as he squeezed Bael's neck. "A tyrant that understands only strength and power, and depends on you to enforce it. This is why I will bring him your wings." Bones crunched in Bael's neck, and Ursula's stomach swooped. "And your head." Shadows gathered around him, midnight tendrils reaching hungrily around Bael.

Time to get involved. Ursula readied Honjo, but as she stepped forward, Abrax casually flicked a finger at her. Dark filaments raced across the room, tightening around her chest. They squeezed the breath from her lungs. Agony gripped her chest, her body shaking. *Air. I need air.*

Abrax's grey eyes flashed. "I will create a new realm of the night without you."

Air. Please, let me breathe.

Bael clutched Abrax's arm, straining to break the grip, but his eyes were locked on Ursula, almost pleading as the light in them faded. His eyelids closed.

Air before I die... Ursula thrashed against the magical bonds, desperate for release. *I can't die yet, not before I've done something.* Something simmered within her, and the fire began to simmer, her veins blazing. The air around her crackled with infernal magic.

Abrax dropped Bael, spinning to face her. "Don't even think—"

Her scream cut him short, as the fire poured from her like an exploding star, burning through the filaments.

Right now, only one thought screamed in her mind: *kill Abrax.* He'd torn her legs to shreds, stolen Zee's soul. He'd thrown Kester to his death—and right now, it looked like he'd killed Bael.

Ursula lifted her sword, the blade glowing. She pointed it at Abrax. Flames licked along the steel, and she pressed forward. "I don't believe you've met Honjo," she said. She slashed—a short, controlled swing, carving an eight-inch gash across Abrax's chest. The smell of burning flesh filled the air.

The demon bared his teeth. "You honestly think you can defeat me?"

"No," she snarled. "But I can hurt you before I die."

Abrax backed away as she advanced, her blade sparking with heat. She knew it was futile; she'd seen his power. At any moment he'd transform and rip her limb from limb. Still—this time, at least, she'd make him work for it.

Flames twisted and writhed along her blade, and its heat warmed her face. She slashed at him again, but he dodged, and Honjo only cut through wisps of smoke where he'd been standing. He tended to dodge to the right; she could use that.

"Come and get me then," he said, a lascivious grin on his lips. "A little pain just whets my appetite."

She feinted and stabbed to the right, where she knew he'd dodge. Honjo sizzled, the sword's burning tip plunging through his gut.

The smile disappeared from his lips. He started to speak, but she twisted the blade, wrenching it up towards his heart.

Abrax unleashed a chilling scream.

"Got you," she said.

But before she could finish the job, he dissipated again, leaving Honjo stabbing only vapor.

She heard a voice behind her—speaking Angelic—and she whirled. Horror wrapped its cold fingers around her heart as she stared at Abrax in his true form. Black wings beat the air, and the temperature dropped ten degrees. His talons clattered on the floor; the wounds on his chest and stomach were gone, replaced by rippling muscle.

Abrax roared, and the sound sent a chill racing up her spine. He slashed at her with a talon, but she dove under the table. When she rolled to her feet, he was gone. Heart thrumming, she searched the starlit room. *Where was he?*

Agony seared her shoulder as a claw pierced clean through her. With a jerk she was lifted off her feet, skewered like a piece of meat at a slaughterhouse. One of Abrax's arms slipped around her waist, and he breathed into her ear. "Now, *I've* got you."

The pain stole her breath. She needed to call on her fire—to burn him off her, but she couldn't think straight. *My sword... where is my sword?* She glanced down at Honjo on the floor. In the shock of the pain, she'd dropped him.

Abrax tore at her shoulder again, and she let out an agonized scream.

"I have someone you need to meet," he said in his honeyed voice. The talon had punched out under her collar bone, and agony burned through her mind, her vision blurring.

"You've disrupted my plans," he said.

She closed her eyes, trying to manage the pain. She heard Abrax open a door, and then he ripped his talon from her shoulder. When her body hit the floor, her vision went dark for a few moments. When it cleared again, she found herself staring at bare stone walls.

Gasping, she tried to take a deep breath, but her chest ached. Blood bubbled from under her shirt. Abrax must have punctured a lung. At least she knew Starkey's Conjuration spell now.

As she whispered the spell, a soothing magic washed over her, healing her injured shoulder. She gasped with relief, all the pain ebbing from her body. *I will never again take the absence of pain for granted.*

Standing shakily, she surveyed the gloomy cell. Iron bars blocked the windows, and iron plates lined the walls. The door behind her was solid metal. There was even an iron cot in the corner. She looked closer, her blood chilling. A body lay on it.

"Hello?"

No response. Ursula dug out the dagger from her boot. *It's probably a corpse, but better safe than sorry.*

A dirty blanket covered the figure—a man by the shape of him, his head turned to the wall.

"Hello?" She said it louder this time.

Holding the dagger ready, she rolled him onto his back and stifled a scream.

Kester.

Chapter 43

The hellhound gaped at her vacantly—the same glazed look she'd seen on Zee's face. Abrax had drunk his soul.

A lump rose in her throat, and her hands trembled. "I thought you were dead." Even if he couldn't feel it, she slipped her arms around his neck, feeling the warmth of his body against hers. She'd *grieved* for him. And, now there was a chance—a very small chance, but one all the same—that she could save them both.

Apart from the fact that I don't stand a chance against the incubus.

She pinched Kester's arm, but his eyes remained shut. He wasn't waking up. The silence of the room was oppressive, broken only by an uneven drip of water.

Sitting on the end of the cot, she ran through her options. She still had the dagger, the reaping pen in her pocket, and a half-consumed flask of scotch. A lesser woman would finish off the rest of the scotch right now. She could get them out of here with Emerazel's sigil, but that would leave Bael behind, and she still wouldn't have anyone's soul. Her friend would die, and Emerazel would send her to the inferno. *Not a great outcome.*

Could she kill Abrax? Maybe stab him with the pen when he returned? Unlikely.

Bollocks. What other options did she have? Abrax wouldn't leave her in the cell forever. He'd be back to suck her soul or slowly torture her to death.

She'd need to stab him with the reaping pen. That was the best bet. If she stood by the door with her back flat against the wall, she might have a chance. She'd slash with the dagger and jam the pen into his chest.

Before she could move to the door, she heard a shuffling on the other side of it, then the iron ripped open with a bang. *There goes my element of surprise.*

The dark silhouette of a man stood in the doorway. Not Abrax. Not Bael. Yet she knew instantly he was one of *them.* Another powerful shadow demon. Darkness emanated from him, and fear slid through her bones. The lights dimmed, and around her, the room seemed to fall away. She now stood on the edge of a precipice, black and bottomless—a void. Her entire body went cold, and for a moment the chasm called to her, beckoning her into its bottomless depths.

The room refocused as the demon studied her, his eyes shining like starlight. Ursula lifted her dagger.

The demon stepped closer. His skin was pale as milk, a stark contrast to his raven-black hair. He wore a black cloak that swirled around him like smoke on the wind. His stunning features looked a lot like Abrax's. "Put the dagger away," he cautioned, his cold voice sliding over her skin.

Ursula clutched the dagger in front of her. As she recognized his face, terror ripped her mind apart. He had the icy eyes of the man in her dreams. "Who are you?" she stammered.

"Most know me as Nyxobas."

A sharp tendril of dread pierced her.

Looking past her at Kester's limp form, the god continued, "Kester and I have met previously. You, however, are new to me." Yet, the way he said it, she could tell he wasn't convinced. "Who are you?"

"Ursula," she stammered.

"Ursula." He closed his eyes, savoring the word like it was a delicious morsel. "Like the constellation?"

"I guess." Why had Abrax wanted her to meet the god of night? "Why are you here?

"Abrax summoned me. It seems that Bael has gotten into some trouble."

"He's alive?"

"What do you care if a demon lives or dies?" Nyxobas's eyes narrowed.

"He helped me."

Nyxobas studied her with a keen intelligence. "Interesting." turned, beckoning her to follow. She didn't know where he was taking her, but questioning a god seemed like a bad idea. Ursula stuffed the dagger into her belt and followed Nyxobas into the starlit stone hall.

Bael and Abrax stood a few feet from each other, and Abrax glared.

Nyxobas stalked in front of the incubus, his cloak swirling around him. "Abrax, my oldest son. Why have you carved The Sword's wings from his shoulders?"

Abrax's eyes burned with cold rage. "Bael is weak. The edge of Nyxobas's Sword has grown dull—so dull that he allowed one of Emerazel's hounds to imprison him and torture him. It was that cur who carved the wings from his back. I merely tried to retrieve them for you."

Nyxobas turned to Bael. "Is this true?" The rage in his voice was unmistakable.

"It is." A line of blood dripped from the corner of Bael's mouth, but he didn't wipe it away.

Bloody hell, this isn't going well. She needed to intervene. "Did your son mention that he murdered the fae king?" said Ursula.

The god's eyes bored into her and the edge of his lip twitched. "The fae are worthless, godless creatures."

At his words, she thought she saw a flicker of fury cross Abrax's face.

Nyxobas turned to Bael, his voice steely. "You know the punishment for losing your wings?"

"Yes." His eyes flicked to Ursula's again, but she couldn't read his meaning. He dropped to his knees. The blood roared in Ursula's ears as Nyxobas gripped his sword.

An execution. That was the unspoken punishment. Bael would be sent to the inferno. *I need to do something.*

But what the hell was she supposed to do? Nyxobas was a god. She didn't stand a chance against him.

Nyxobas raised the sword. In moments Bael's head would be rolling to her feet, and his soul—

"Stop!" Ursula shouted. "If you kill him his soul goes to Emerazel."

Nyxobas's eyes flashed to hers. Pure malevolence bored into her, but he stayed his sword. "What?"

"I took his soul for the fire goddess. When he lay asleep, I forced him to sign."

"Is that true?" Nyxobas's voice was pure wrath.

"I felt the change in my soul. It has been tainted," said Bael, and the agonized tone of his voice suggested he'd have preferred death to this admission.

Nyxobas threw the sword to the ground, unleashing a primal roar.

Chapter 44

$\mathcal{T}$he whole room seemed to vibrate, and Ursula hoped the roar wouldn't fell the entire tree. Shadows whirled, and Nyxobas appeared in front of her, his eyes black and bottomless. Icy darkness washed over her, then she was standing at the edge of the void again, staring into its depths. A few glimmers of memory whispered past her eyes—the fields of wildflowers in the moonlight, someone teaching her to fight—a woman, her hair like fire. But then the images disappeared, drifting away like a smoke in the wind.

She stared once again into the darkness, ice gripping her chest.

Nothing.

This was what death looked like: cold and solitary. Everyone died alone, left only with their own thoughts and memories, stripped of everything but identity. But she had no identity, hardly had any memories, and there was nothing but the void.

Her fingers itched to touch her smooth, round rock, but it was lost. She had nothing but the gnawing emptiness, drawing her deeper. Soul-crushing grief pressed on her chest, so cold and harsh she could hardly breathe.

"Release his soul at once." Nyxobas's voice rang into the void.

The desolation was so sharp and oppressive she could barely speak, until at last she choked out the word "No," her body trembling.

"Then I will kill you."

Nyxobas was terrifying, but she had nothing left to lose. As she looked up at him, her vision refocused. She concentrated on her feet, planted firmly on the floor. "Kill me, then. I'm going to die anyway. Abrax stole a soul I was supposed to collect. When Emerazel finds out she'll send me straight to her inferno." Ursula felt the fire begin to burn within her. "So you can kill me now or you can wait for Emerazel to do it for you, but I'm not going to give you Bael's soul." Not to mention, she didn't even know *how* to return a soul.

Nyxobas's eyes darkened. Before she could stop him, he grabbed her arm in an iron grip. She could feel his power race through her, cold and lethal.

The god reached into her jacket, yanking her flask from her pocket. Pushing her away, he began to pour it on the floor. It took her a moment to recognize Emerazel's sigil. He chanted—some sort of spell for fire—and as the flames flickered, he summoned Emerazel.

At his final words, the goddess appeared with a burst of flame. Immediately, the room felt unbearably hot, like Ursula had been shoved in an oven. Across from her, Abrax and Bael writhed in agony.

This time, Ursula knew not to stare her into the goddess's eyes.

"You summoned me, Nyxobas?" the goddess hissed.

"Your cur tricked one of my demons into signing a pact with her against his will."

Ursula could feel her body burn; Emerazel's burning gaze must have turned to her. "Oh *really*?"

"So I tricked him," shouted Ursula. "Since when are demons supposed to play fair?"

"Let me see the paper," said Emerazel, her voice simmering with rage.

Shaking, Ursula dug in her pockets, but they were empty. "I can't find it. It must be back at the Plaza," she sputtered, like an idiot student who'd forgotten her homework.

"I saw the contract," said Bael, eyes burning with fury. "I felt it. The fire whore has my soul."

Nyxobas's lips peeled back from his teeth. He looked like he might roar again.

"Well, that settles it, then," said Emerazel. "There are no rules about how a pact is signed. His soul will hold a place of honor in my inferno. He *is* a gorgeous specimen of man, and I'm sure I can make use of his body."

"Perhaps we can make a deal," said Nyxobas, his voice icy.

Ursula's gaze raised just high enough to catch Emerazel's ashy smile. "Oh, I think not. I can tell Bael has a powerful soul."

Nyxobas's cold gaze flicked to his son. "Get the Headsman." Without a word Abrax disappeared into the hall. A few moments later, he returned, dragging Kester's body over the floor.

"What have you done to Kester?" said Emerazel. The room grew hotter, like the inside of a volcano.

Please make it stop.

"I took his soul," said Abrax. "He wasn't very careful."

Heat rolled off Emerazel in waves. Even Nyxobas seemed to be affected, wiping a line of sweat from his brow.

"Fine. A soul for a soul," said Emerazel at last.

Abrax lowered Kester to the ground. For a moment the incubus looked at Ursula, his expression burning with pure hatred, then he knelt. With an unnatural jerk, his back arched and a golden light unspooled from his mouth, curling into Kester's. As the last of Kester's soul passed from between Abrax's lips, the incubus fixed his eyes on her. They were black as pitch, his expression almost feral. There was no doubt in her mind that he desperately wanted to kill her.

Even from where she stood, Ursula could see the color begin to return to Kester's face. His eyelids twitched, and he moaned softly.

She cleared her throat. "What about Zee and Hugo's souls?"

Abrax stared at her, disbelieving. "Those were fairly acquired."

"Hugo agreed to give me his soul." Emerazel's voice sizzled through the room like water on hot iron.

"What will you give me in exchange?" asked Nyxobas.

"What do you want?"

The god of darkness looked at Ursula, a small smile on his lips. Dread tightened Ursula's chest.

"Her?"

"Yes."

Emerazel frowned, considering. Ursula wanted to scream. This couldn't be happening. Just one peek at the void of shadows had been terrifying. Now she might be sent there permanently.

Nyxobas, sensing Emerazel's reluctance, added, "I don't need her entirely. Just a portion of her soul would suffice."

"I'll share Ursula with you. You'll get her skills for half of each year."

Nyxobas grinned. "This is acceptable to me."

"Wait," Ursula sputtered. Emerazel's eyes blazed, and Ursula could feel the goddess begin to control her. There would be no arguing her fate, but maybe she could save another.

"Are you returning Zee's soul too?"

The night god's smile widened. "Whatever you want, my little hound."

Ursula wasn't sure if she wanted to drop to her knees with relief or run screaming through the halls, but at least everyone was going to live.

On the floor, Kester moaned again, and Ursula rushed to him, putting her hand on his chest. His green eyes fluttered open.

"Ursula?" he whispered.

She cupped his cheek. God, she was glad to see him. "Yes, Kester. It's me."

He smiled weakly. Then his body spasmed, eyes rolling back into his head. He'd passed out. Apparently regaining your soul wasn't easy on the nervous system.

The room suddenly went cold, and Ursula looked up. They were alone. Emerazel, Nyxobas, Abrax, and Bael had all disappeared. She gotten everything she'd wanted, but an uneasy feeling still whispered over her skin. *Why* had Emerazel agreed to that deal? Why give up a perfectly good hellhound for half the year, just to get the soul of a pop-star and to save a fae girl she could not care less about? It didn't make any sense.

A rhythmic sound vibrated through the walls—the drumming of hundreds of feet. The fae soldiers must be looking for them. Whatever Emerazel's motives, Ursula didn't have time to unravel them now.

Straining her thigh muscles, she dragged Kester into the center of the sigil Nyxobas had lit on the floor. She held Kester's limp body, intoning the sigil spell, and with a scorching heat they burned into ash.

Chapter 45

$\mathcal{U}$rsula hugged her coat around her, stalking over the icy pier to Kester's tugboat. Cold wind nipped at her face as she rapped on his door.

Kester pulled it open and smiled, his cheek dimpling. "Ursula. Did you miss me?"

"Terribly. It's been at least eight hours since I dragged your body from the fae realm."

He arched an eyebrow. "And you've come back for more of my body? In that case, come inside."

She rolled her eyes, stepping onto the boat. Her eyes flicked to the floor, where blood had soaked into the wood. "Sorry about the blood stains on the floor."

"Was that your work? I didn't know you had such a vicious side."

"I *did* let him live, which was more than he was going to do for me." Pulling off her coat, she plopped onto his green sofa. Tonight, she was back in her spring colors—sky blue and amber. She needed a night off from being a lethal, blood-soaked assassin.

Kester collected a bottle of whiskey from one of his bookshelves, and began pouring it into two glasses. "You impress me. Did you come by to celebrate your first victory?"

"I wanted to see how you were doing. Zee has been in my apartment all day pounding champagne and ranting about shadow demons. She seems a little on edge."

He joined her on the sofa, handing her a tumbler. "That's just how she is."

"And I don't understand the deal that Emerazel made with Nyxobas. Why would Emerazel want to give up a hellhound for half the year?"

Kester sighed. "The gods have been warring for a hundred thousand years. They always will. If they strike a deal, it's because they think they can get some advantage over the other. My guess is that they both think they can use you in some way. I imagine Emerazel hopes you're going to spy for her."

"Lovely. So no matter what happens, I'm going to enrage at least one of them, and probably both."

"You'll need to be very careful. You'll need my guidance, of course."

She took a sip of her whiskey, rolling the peaty taste around her tongue. Her muscles still burned, and she still hadn't managed to sleep more than an hour at a time. Every time she'd closed her eyes in her bedroom, a vision of the void had haunted her. Was that where Bael was now? Her chest tightened. Maybe Nyxobas had chosen to spare him. Bael was terrifying, but she didn't want to be responsible for his fiery afterlife.

Her gaze slid to Kester, his skin a beautiful gold in the warm lantern light. "Why would Emerazel want me to be her spy? I don't even know what I'm doing. Isn't that obvious?"

He held her gaze. "You're not a normal hellhound."

"There are normal hellhounds?"

He smiled. "More normal than you. Hellhounds who don't burn when they encounter their goddess. Hellhounds who don't repel incubi, and who have a basic grasp of their own history."

Cold dread prickled over her skin. "I'd seen Nyxobas before. I saw his eyes in my dreams."

Kester eyed her over the rim of his drink. "You've certainly earned your nickname."

"And you yours." The whiskey leant her boldness. She had to know about Kester's past. She took another sip, and it burned her throat as she swallowed. "Who was Oriel?"

Surprise flickered across his features, and he studied her face for a moment, as if deciding whether or not to tell her. At last, he spoke. "My sister."

"Were you close to her?" She must have died centuries ago.

"I was." His eyes glistened with pain. "Until Abrax stole her soul, sent her to the shadow void."

A lump rose in Ursula's throat. "Because you were a hellhound?"

"That's *why* I became a hellhound. I needed power to avenge her. And I still haven't succeeded. Abrax is Nyxobas's son. He's not an easy man to kill. But Emerazel made me a promise: once I'd filled my ledger, she would find a way to reclaim Oriel's soul. I just needed to do everything she told me, to please her in every way. Every soul I reaped, every person I killed—it all had a purpose. It was all in the name of getting Oriel out of hell. Only I've started to wonder if Emerazel has any intention of sticking to her bargain. As I've come close to filling my ledger, she's only added more pages. And yet I keep going, because if I fail, all of it was for nothing."

Ursula swallowed hard, almost wanting to look away from the raw pain etched on his face.

"When my soul was stolen in the fae realm," he continued. "I experienced just a brief glimmer of Oriel's torment. Pure, crushing isolation. Complete abandonment in the void. That is what Oriel has felt for centuries. And it hit me like an arrow to my heart: there is no Oriel anymore. After all that pain, her mind would be completely shattered, lost in the rush of Nyxobas's night winds."

Sorrow tightened Ursula's chest. "I'm so sorry, Kester."

He lifted his glass, his eyes suddenly clearing. "But you got me back from that. I owe you my sad, sorry life."

She touched his arm. "We got through the impossible last night. We reclaimed your soul, and Zee's. And I'm spared from Emerazel's punishment. Maybe we can free ourselves from our debts to the gods."

He shook his head. "You can't fight the gods, Ursula, even if you fought Abrax. And didn't I tell you not to take on fights you couldn't win?"

"It worked last night, didn't it? We got everything we needed."

"But you lost your lucky rock." Mischief glinted in his eyes again.

"I'm not ready to joke about that yet." She scowled, then arched an eyebrow. "Wait. How did you know I lost that? I never told you that."

He reached into the pocket of his grey trousers, pulling out her smooth, white stone.

Her heart sped up. "How did you *get* that?"

"After my body reconstituted on the dance floor, I grabbed this out of your wyrm-skin purse. I would have returned it sooner, but Abrax interrupted me." He folded his fingers around it, curling it to his chest. "And now, I'm afraid I'd become quite attached to it. It's brought me such good luck, you see. You'll have to find your own."

She lunged forward, spilling her whiskey as he held it above his head, out of her reach. She climbed onto his lap, prying it from his fingers.

As she slid the stone into her pocket, he gazed up at her, his face a picture of innocence. "Any excuse to get your hands on me."

She opened her mouth to protest, before closing it again. His hand slid around her back. God, he was beautiful. And right now, she could kiss him, feel his soft lips against hers again. But even with the thrilling sensation of his hand on her back, his thumb moving slowly up and down—something stopped her.

She couldn't unsee the sadness in his eyes. Her own brush with the shadow void had chilled her to the bone, and she couldn't shake her mind of that soul-crushing emptiness. She slipped off Kester's lap, hugging herself. Maybe Bael was in that shadow void now, tormented by complete and utter abandonment.

"Are you all right?" he asked, studying her closely.

She nodded. "My brush with Nyxobas left me a little unnerved."

"The lord of the shadow hell has that effect on people."

She touched his cheek. "I'm glad to have you back. Even if you kidnapped me the first time I met you."

"Sorry about that."

She rose, pulling on her coat. "I'll see you tomorrow. Just remember to knock, like I did."

"I wouldn't dream of barging in."

Smiling, she pulled her coat tight as she stepped out into the icy winter air. She slipped her hand into her pocket, pulling out her white stone to roll between her fingers, its smooth surface comforting her as soon as she touched it.

She had to admit, some things weren't looking good. Emerazel planned to use her as a double agent, Nyxobas had his own devious agenda, and Bael remained a prisoner, possibly dead.

The cold wind rushed off the East River, biting her skin through her coat as she walked to the Bentley. But at least she was alive, and so was Kester. That was certainly a better outcome than she'd expected last night. And maybe it *wasn't* so impossible to fight the gods.

Moreover, with every day she spent among the demons, she was one step closer to learning the truth about herself, to learning the story behind her memories of the flame-haired woman, and the person who'd taught her to fight.

Sometimes, the utterly improbable did happen. After all, if Kester could find a tiny white stone in a sea of angry fae warriors at a dance party—maybe there was a chance to free the hellhounds.

She pulled open the back door of the Bentley, stepping into its warmth. As Joe turned on the engine, she let her eyes drift shut, soothed by the car's soft hum. Before she took on the ancient gods of wrath and death, she'd need at least a few hours of sleep.

Thanks for Reading

We hope you enjoyed **Infernal Magic**. Book 2 doesn't come out until Fall 2016, but in the meantime we think you might enjoy our novel **Magic Hunter** which takes place in the same magical universe.

Yours,
Nick & Christine

Also by

C. N. CRAWFORD

The Vampire's Mage Series
Book 1: *Magic Hunter*
Book 1.1: *Shadow Mage*
Book 2*: Witch Hunter*
(Summer 2016)

Demons of Fire and Night
Book 1: *Infernal Magic*
Book 2: *Nocturnal Magic*
(Fall 2016)

The Memento Mori Trilogy
Book 1: *The Witching Elm*
Book 2: *A Witch's Feast*
Book 2.1: *The Abysmal Sea*
Book 3: *Witches of the Deep*
(June 2016)